THE
DEAD
CAME
CALLING

A VISCOUNT WARE MYSTERY #3

J. L. BUCK

CAMEL
PRESS
KENMORE, WA

CAMEL
PRESS

A Camel Press book published by Epicenter Press

Epicenter Press
6524 NE 181st St.
Suite 2
Kenmore, WA 98028

For more information go to:
www.Camelpress.com
www.Coffeetownpress.com
www.Epicenterpress.com

Author's website: janetlbuck.com

The Dead Came Calling
2023 © J. L. Buck

Library of Congress Control Number: 2022946226

ISBN: 9781684920891 (trade paper)
ISBN: 9781684920907 (ebook)

Printed in the United States of America

Acknowledgments

Many thanks to my family, both children and grandchildren, who are so incredibly supportive of my writing.

Chapter One

Sussex, England, 11 October 1812

Rain pounded on the roof of the carriage. A lightning strike split the sky, releasing a pungent odor that seeped inside the stylish conveyance. Thunder boomed like the cannons of war, and one of the high bred horses gave a frightened whinny. Hitting a deep rut, the coach lurched precariously before righting itself.

Lucien Grey, Viscount Ware, took little note of the storm, other than to place a hand on the seat to steady himself. His hooded gaze rested on nothing in particular, his mood attuned with the unsettled weather.

Salcott Hall loomed minutes ahead. Even though he was the heir, Lucien had not set foot in the earl's seat in Sussex for three years, and that last visit had ended in a row before dinner was over. No one would bar the door to him, not even at this late hour approaching one in the morning, but his actual welcome was tenuous, the situation likely to be awkward at best. He expected to find the house dark, indicating his father and upper staff had gone to bed. If fortune was with him, any conversation with the earl—best faced when well-rested—would be delayed until morning.

The years of estrangement from his father had eased during the past ten months, yet the estate held too many unhappy memories for Lucien to view the visit with equanimity. He had little desire to relive the past when a grieving father had turned his back on a small boy. If his grandmother's lady's maid had not written apprising him of her mistress's ill health, Lucien would still be in the city. Irascible and out-spoken the dowager countess might be, but he was exceedingly fond of her.

His lips tightened. Why the devil had his father not told him of her frailty? Salcott could be obtuse at times, but if the abigail had the right of it, how could the earl have missed the dowager's rapid decline in the three months since she had returned from her London visit?

Shaking his head in an attempt to dispel his moodiness, he found the very thought of last summer in London had brought to mind the other source of his discontent, the image of an intriguing lady with fair curls and laughing blue eyes. Not that she was in the city any longer, that was the essence of the problem. London was flat without her.

Ironically, his budding interest in Lady Anne Ashburn, the Earl of Chadley's only daughter—a lively combination of wits, stubbornness, and an elusive dimple—had been cut short in August by illness in her own family. She had rushed to her invalid mother's bedside in Warwickshire, and two weeks later, Lucien had received a brief note, advising him her mother's health was such that Lady Anne would not be returning to London in the foreseeable future.

So why was she still fixed in his head? He'd known many beautiful women—his friend and former mistress Sophy, the incomparable Widow Stine, for one. What was so special about Lady Anne? Their acquaintance was less than a year—thrown together twice by perilous events beyond their control, not the most ideal circumstances for building a lasting relationship. Surely the kisses they'd shared had been no more than the inevitable consequence of those highly charged experiences…ultimately meaningless.

He gave an annoyed huff. *No excuses, Lucien. You kissed her because you wanted to.* And it was most improper…despite her sweet response. Many young ladies of the ton would have insisted he declare himself. Not Anne—she had laughed it off, saying that beyond their two adventures, a handful of social calls, and dances at balls, they barely knew each other. Another unusual attitude—others might have called that kind of attention a courtship. Nonetheless, he and Lady Anne had agreed it was far too early for serious commitment, and yet…

Perhaps he should write and inquire about her mother's health again.

Lucien's woolgathering ended abruptly as the coach hit another deep rut in the road, briefly lifting him off the seat. He shifted toward the window, wiped off the wet film, and peered at the countryside, drawing a heavy breath when he spotted the familiar church spire of Salcott village. *Not long now.*

The carriage rounded a curve, began the climb to the manor, and wound through well-kept tenant cottages. His father was a good steward, a trait Lucien strove to emulate during his recent visit to his own small estate in Waring. As they passed Dower House, he noted the lights were out at his grandmother's residence. He would not have stopped, even if the hour were not so advanced, for he refused to add to village gossip beyond what his rare visit would already engender. Proper respect toward the earl required him to present himself at Salcott Hall first and to lodge there. Despite some evidence to the contrary, Lucien's past behavior that had added to the father-son rift had risen from expediency, not a desire to flout tradition or discomfit Salcott.

He took a last look outside and noted the rain had stopped, at least for the moment. He straightened his cravat and smoothed back his dark hair as the carriage drew to a halt before the imposing grandeur of Salcott Hall. Lucien stepped down from the coach and paused to take in the full breadth of the sixteenth century stone edifice. He moved forward and tapped his fashionable cane on the massive oak doors.

After a brief wait, the double doors swung open, and a footman, probably the only one up at this hour, looked out, holding a candle in one hand. Curiosity, then recognition and surprise, flashed through his eyes.

"Master Luc! My lord…um, Viscount Ware." He stuttered to a stop.

Chapter Two

London, 12 October 1812

Andrew Sherbourne, second son of Baron Sherbourne and friend to Lucien Grey, woke on Monday morning to a knock on his bedchamber door in his family's London residence. He rolled over and stared at the overcast day outside the window. "What the deuce?" His head was a bit foggy after a late night of Faro at White's Club.

The door opened quietly, and his manservant Archibald slipped inside. "Sorry for waking you, sir, but a lady is downstairs insisting she must see you."

"What lady?" he mumbled, and then sat up with a jerk. "Who is she?"

Archibald gave a reproving twist of his lips. "She would not say, sir, only that she is an old acquaintance."

Sherry frowned, not liking the sound of that. "What's she look like?"

The slender manservant took a thoughtful pose. "Gently bred, I would say, sir. Dark hair, well-dressed, although not in the first stare of fashion. Rather ill at ease, I thought."

Egad. Sherry ran a hand through his auburn hair and reviewed the evening in his head. He found no memory of a liaison with such a female last night—just long hours of cards and an excellent port—nor did the description bring any particular acquaintance to mind. "What time is it, Archie?"

"Nigh on nine o'clock."

Ungodly early hour for a visitor. No wonder his head was fuzzy. He frowned as he fully absorbed Archie's words. Surely a proper

4

lady would not present herself to what was currently a bachelor's residence...at any hour. "Is she alone?"

"Well, no...."

Ah, that was better. The lady was escorted, but it still didn't tell him why she was there. Then he noticed Archie's hesitation.

"What is it, my good man? Out with it."

The manservant stiffened. "She has a *child* with her."

"Only a child? No gentleman escort?"

"I am afraid you have the right of it, sir. A small, rather active female child. The hallway vase has already succumbed to her, um, liveliness."

Sherry pictured the large green vase that had stood in the hall of the Sherbourne town residence as long as he could remember. *Ugly thing.* A smile tugged at the corner of his lips. *Well done, small child.* He shifted to sit on the edge of the bed. "I am intrigued and shall join our visitors shortly. Hopefully before the chit destroys something I care about. Where did you put them?"

"I thought the library best under the circumstances."

"Excellent. Books are far more durable."

"Just so, sir."

"Order a tea tray for us. Coffee for me. I shall need it this morning."

Sherry made a hasty job of it and was downstairs twenty minutes later. He paused in the doorway to survey his guests. A woman of small height and slim figure stood near the fireplace, her back to him; the child fidgeted on a leather-cushioned library chair, dwarfed by its size–a tiny child, no more than two or three years old by his guess, with dark ringlets and lively black eyes. Yes, he could see the mischief there. She jumped down as he entered the room and smiled, revealing dimpled cheeks.

"I'm Fanny" she said, bobbing a curtsey, nearly losing her footing. "Who are you?"

"Fanny," her mother chided as she turned around. "You should wait to be introduced."

That voice—Good lord. Sherry's gaze shot to the woman's face. "Maria!"

She flinched at the sharpness in the single word.

Devil take her. He could never mistake that pretty, deceitful face. He took an angry step forward but stopped as a serving maid entered the room with a tea tray and set it on the library table. "Thank you, Alice. We shall serve ourselves," he said tersely.

"Yes, m'lord." The maid shot him a curious look at his unusual brusqueness, curtseyed, and left.

Sherry waited until the door closed. "How dare you come to my home?"

The woman he had known in Paris as Maria Pembroke visibly stiffened her spine and took a deep breath. She appeared outwardly composed but a nervous hand gave her away in a familiar gesture as she reached up to twist a long dark curl.

"You look well, Andrew."

"Never mind the polite talk," he said curtly. "If you have something to say, do so, and leave."

"Mama?" the small child said, her eyes round and uncertain. "Is he angry?"

Sherry startled. He had forgotten the child.

Maria took the child's hand. "It's all right, Fanny. He is just surprised to see us." Maria gave Sherry a reproving look. "You are frightening her, sir."

Sherry bit back further recriminations, cooling his temper, while Maria lifted the child, set her back on the chair, and gave her a biscuit from the tea tray.

"Sit quietly, my darling, while I speak with Lord Sherbourne."

Silently chiding himself for being so gauche, Sherry pulled the cord for the maid. "We can do better than a simple biscuit," he said, producing a smile for the child's sake. "I am not accustomed to having such a young visitor, but I wager you would prefer sweet cakes and something other than tea."

Fanny returned his smile as the maid entered in response to his call.

"Alice, please take Miss Fanny to visit the cook and find her some sweet cakes and hot chocolate. Or whatever she wishes."

"Yes, sir." The maid held out her hand and spoke gently to the child. "Maybe we can also find a piece of fruit or cheese?"

When the door closed this time, Sherry had himself better in hand. "Well, madam, when I saw you last, nearly three years ago, Lucien and I were scrambling out a window at dawn while French soldiers with pistols and rifles were coming through the front door."

"It was not my doing, Andrew. Truly. How could you think I would betray you?"

He gave a bark of laughter. "Because I saw you. You were pointing us out to the soldiers."

"As though they could not see you for themselves," she said with asperity. "My gesture cost you nothing and was intended to secure a few moments of time for my own escape. And it did, just barely."

He frowned, studying her face. In light of what he had learned this summer—that Jeanne, the abigail of Maria's friend Lisette, had been a French agent—Maria's words gave him pause. Jeanne claimed Lisette had not been a party to their betrayal, but Sherry had not believed her, and nothing had been said to absolve Maria. But now...was it possible she had not played them false?

During four years of spying for England in the ballrooms and courts of France as part of the war effort, Sherry and his partner Lucien had befriended two young women—Lisette who was French, and Maria, an English woman—who claimed to be members of the French Resistance and were posing as ladies of the aristocracy to gather information. The four worked closely together and eventually became intimate friends. Sherry had thought he was falling in love with Maria...and then he and Lucien were betrayed to the authorities as English spies and forced to flee from certain death at the guillotine.

Sherry cleared his throat. "For weeks afterward, I told myself I had to be mistaken. We reached out for news, and hearing none, we feared you and Lisette were dead or under arrest, awaiting execution, and we hoped against hope that we still had time to rescue you. Then we heard of Lisette's marriage—to a French officer. And it all became clear, particularly when I recalled how you pointed us out to them." He narrowed his eyes. "Now you stand before me—alive and free, proof of your own complicity, for why else would the French have let you go? You should not have come here, Maria. Did you honestly think I could forgive you?"

"There is nothing to forgive." She lifted a hand to her throat. "I-I cared for you, Andrew. Very much. I thought we were in love."

What an actress she was. "Nonsense. Do not gammon me, dear lady. Love was never part of our relationship, but I own...I felt we had something—" He cleared his throat. "Precisely who, or should I say what, are you, madam? Not a patriot, I think. An adventuress? Taking advantage wherever you can?"

Her faced paled.

Sherry frowned, swallowing his venom and wishing he had not spoken quite so harshly. After all, it had been war time. They'd all done things they wished they had not. But why the devil was she here? Bringing all this up again?

He sighed and gestured for her to seat herself where Fanny had been. "Perhaps we should take tea before it grows cold." When she was seated, he poured a cup of tea and placed it in her hands before filling his own cup with coffee. "I do not mean to be cruel, Maria, but surely you admit the facts are damning."

She sipped the hot liquid. "To your way of thinking, maybe. But that is not how it was."

Sherry took the chair across from her, rested one boot on the opposite knee, and took a swallow of the bitter coffee. Ah, just what he needed. "Go on then. Tell me where I am wrong."

"Lisette's maid informed on you. I'm sure of it."

"Oh? Why so certain?" he asked, although he knew it was true. He wanted to hear what she and Lisette had known of Jeanne's betrayal.

Maria reached up to twist that curl again. "I knew she was working for both sides. Just wait," she pleaded when he made an angry snort. "Hear me out. Long before I met you, I stole a roll of bank notes from a French officer. Jeanne saw me and kept quiet. I thought it was because she supported the Resistance. But later, she threatened to expose me unless I, um, told her things from time to time."

Sherry's lips curled. "You mean you spied on us all those months?"

"No, not you, just small things I heard at balls and other social gatherings. Mostly rumors, gossip. Never anything big, I swear. When I first met you, I didn't realize you and Simon, uh, Lord Ware, I mean, were British agents until Jeanne told me."

"Not Lisette? She knew because my partner told her in confidence," Sherry said. "Why would she have shared the information with her abigail and not you?"

"Lisette didn't tell anyone. Jeanne told the two of us together. If Lisette already knew, she never said so, and she was not aware of what I was doing. She was always loyal to the Resistance."

"What about her hasty marriage? Explain that."

"I cannot, because I do not know. I fled to England the following night and have not heard from her since." Maria met his gaze for the first time. "She felt deeply for your friend. But a certain French officer had been in love with Lisette since childhood. Perhaps they married to save her life and prove her loyalty to France."

Sherry scowled, not sure what to think. Parts of her story rang true, but a good spy could make anything sound believable. Perhaps he would never know the truth...and did it really matter now? He waved a dismissive hand. "Enough. None of that explains why you are here. Surely you did not come just to plead your innocence."

She eyed him with a derisive snort. "I see it would have been wasted effort, but you are correct—a more pressing matter forced me to come. While escaping France, I killed a French agent. The details are unimportant, but recently, his brother arrived in England, looking for me. He seeks revenge and has come close to catching me...twice." She set down her tea and leaned forward, her gaze locked on his face. "I have come to you for protection, Andrew. Not for me but for our daughter."

"What? *Our* child?" Sherry rose to his feet, his heart racing. He had almost expected it. His thoughts had nearly ferreted out her purpose, but not quite. "Why should I believe you? Why wait three years to tell me?"

"I didn't know I was carrying a child when I returned home, and how was I to tell you? I didn't know where you were, and the only name I had was Andrew Rayburn."

"You managed to find me now."

"Yes, well, it did not matter back then. I desired nothing from you until I recently realized Fanny and I were in danger. In truth, it was not hard to discover Mr. Simon Grey was Lucien Simon Grey, Lord Ware, and that led me to his close friend, Andrew Sherbourne."

"It was never intended to be a deep cover," he murmured. "What is it you expect of me? Money? You have no proof this child is mine." Sherry paced the room shaking his head. *What a lot of poppycock.*

"I told you—protection is all. Would you truly deny your child?" Maria cried. "If you don't believe me. Go look at her again. She has your eyes, your chin."

Needing time to think this out, he latched onto her suggestion. "A fine proposal. Stay and have more tea. I shall see her and return post haste. This conversation is not over."

Sherry strode from the room and rapidly descended the back stairs, his thoughts swirling. *Good lord. Could it be true?* Was the child his?

He opened the kitchen door to the delectable smell of venison stew rising from a pot on the massive iron stove. Fanny sat on the floor at the cook's feet playing with one of the kitchen cats. Her mouth was smeared with red jam.

"How is our young guest doing?" he asked with a smile, his gaze already assessing Fanny's looks. A pretty child, dark hair, dark eyes. Frankly, she looked more like her mother than anyone else. Was there a faint resemblance to the Sherbourne family around the eyes? Maybe. Nothing as definitive as Maria had implied.

"We've been doing just fine, sir," Mrs. Cooper said, giving Fanny a warmhearted look. "I s'pose her mother is missing her already.

We better wipe that face before you go." She put down the long spoon she'd been using to stir the pot and reached for a kitchen rag. Fanny obediently stood and presented her up-turned face for washing.

Sherry chuckled. She was a charming waif.

He frowned at the sudden thump, thump of hurrying feet descending the servant stairs.

"Sir? Sir, where are you?" Archibald called. A moment later, he stuck his head in the kitchen door and grew wide-eyed at sight of the child. "Sir, may I speak with you in private?"

"Of course." Archibald's red face and heavy breathing filled Sherry with alarm, and he stepped into the hallway. "What is it, Archie?"

"The woman…she left, sir." Archie held up a heavy bag. "I found this in the front entry and went to ask if it was hers, but she was not in the library. I have looked everywhere. She is gone."

"That cannot be." Mindful of Fanny and other listeners on the other side of the door, Sherry kept his voice down. "She would not have left without her daughter."

"I am sorry, sir, but it appears that is precisely what she has done. I even looked on the street. No woman, no carriage."

Sherry sucked in a breath. "I see." Getting the household in an uproar would not help. "Well, no need to panic. We shall find her. She will most likely return shortly. Perhaps she remembered an urgent appointment."

Archibald looked at him askance. Neither of them believed that.

What had Maria done? Was she looking to rid herself of the child? Hard to believe—the chit appeared healthy and well-loved. He sighed, shaking his head. Maria would have much to explain upon her return. Meanwhile, he had a child on his hands. If only his own mother was in town. She would know exactly what to do.

"Take the footmen and start a wider search, Archie. See if you can locate the coachman who brought her or took her away. I shall take care of the rest." He straightened his shoulders and stepped back into the kitchen. Fanny was playing with the gray and white cat again, and Sherry crouched beside her. "Would you like to stay with Cook and the kitty a bit longer? Your mother had to leave for a while."

Fanny looked up at him, her eyes untroubled. "Yes. I know."

"How do you know? Did your mother tell you she would be leaving?"

She patted the cat and nodded.

"Did she say anything else?"

Fanny raised her small shoulders in a shrug, then laid one palm against her face and thought about it. "Be good."

By Jove. Maria had planned to leave her. But it was not the child's fault, and he gave her a quick smile. "I'm sure you shall be."

Mrs. Cooper's look was sympathetic, whether intended for him or Fanny, Sherry wasn't certain, but she appeared to have sized up the situation pretty quickly.

"Alice and I can watch her for a while, sir. I have a niece who is good with children if you think you'll need someone longer. She has taken care of her younger siblings before and has wished for a position as nanny."

Sherry stood and clasped the cook's hand in both of his. "You are truly a blessing, Mrs. Cooper. Let us see what your niece can do. Could you send for her right away?"

"I will, sir. Don't you worry about nothing. We'll take good care of the poor mite. And if Fanny tires of the cat before Jane arrives, Alice can take her up to the nursery. I believe there is still a box of toys in the playroom."

"I don't believe I pay you enough," he said with a relieved half laugh.

Her eyes twinkled. "No, sir, you don't."

"Count on me to remedy that next quarter." Sherry's grin faded as he dashed up the stairs. Thank god for loyal servants. What did a bachelor like him know about infants or a chit like Fanny?

With things under control for the moment, he grabbed his hat and called out to Archie. "Where are you? Any news yet?"

Alice appeared. "He went out several minutes ago, my lord."

"Yes, of course he did." Egad, was he losing it? After four years living on the edge in France, how could he be rattled so easily? Sherry hurried down the front steps, glanced up and down the street, then chose to go to the right. What the bloody hell was Maria doing? He had to find her and sort out the truth of her claims… good lord, could be truly be a father?

Chapter Three

As Lucien completed his breakfast the morning following his late-night appearance and entered the massive hall at the bottom of the stairs, the earl's long-time butler greeted him.

"Good morning, my lord. I was delighted to hear of your arrival."

"Thank you, Jeffers. Is my father about?"

"He is in his study, my lord. He has been apprised of your presence and is waiting to see you. May I say, it is splendid to see you."

Lucien flashed a smile. "Thank you, Jeffers. I shall find my way."

"As you wish, my lord."

The sound of Lucien's booted footsteps echoed on the marble floors. Contrary to what one might assume from his long absences from Sussex, he admired the Salcott family seat. Generations of earls whose distinguished portraits hung in the gallery had managed the estate and their fortune well, and it showed—gleaming woodwork, priceless tapestry, fashionable furnishings, all done with impeccable taste. The vases of fall flowers added a light and pleasing fragrance, thanks to an attentive and efficient household staff.

As it had been for two decades now, the hall was uncommonly quiet, devoid of the unruly noises made by children. His father, Arthur Grey, the Seventh Earl of Salcott, had remained unwed after burying his second bride when Lucien was nine. With James, Lucien's older brother, dying without issue, the house now waited in silence for a new generation...a responsibility Lucien was expected to fulfill.

Salcott strode from his study. "Lucien, my boy, I would have been awake to receive you last night if I had known you were coming." He gestured toward the study behind him. "Will you join me in sitting by the fire? The rain has left a damp nip in the air. Do you prefer tea or something stronger?"

"I fear I have developed a city preference for coffee, and I know from the breakfast room that you have it available."

"I too enjoy a cup now and then." Salcott rang for a servant and ordered a tray. "Did you rest well? It is a tiring journey from London."

"Yes, sir, thank you. A dreary trip, to be sure—wet and chilly." Lucien chose a seat by the fire. "I did not write of my intended journey, as I thought I would arrive before the letter, but you cannot wonder why I have come. I called for the coach as soon as word reached me of Grandmama's ill health."

Salcott scowled but waited as a maid entered with the requested tray and set it on a table by the hearth. "Ill health?" he asked the moment she departed. "I would not describe it that way. True, she has been not quite herself, but if she is ill, I was not made aware of it. Who told you this?"

"Her abigail, Hester. She wrote of her mistress's frailty and suggested I should make haste."

"You don't say." Salcott shook his head as he poured two cups of coffee and passed one to Lucien. He looked perplexed by the conversation. "I would have told you if I had serious concerns." He rose abruptly and rang for the butler.

Jeffers responded so quickly that Lucien suspected he had lingered in the hall hoping to overhear the cause of the heir's unexpected arrival.

"Your lordship?"

"Have you heard that the dowager is unwell?" Salcott asked with a frown.

"No, sir. Her ladyship's footman was here on an errand earlier this morning, and he said nothing of it." Concern flashed across Jeffers' face. "Do you wish me to inquire?"

Lucien looked at his father. "That should not be necessary. I am going to the Dower House in a few minutes and shall report back."

"Very good. Thank you, Jeffers. That is all for now," Salcott said, absently dismissing his servant. He raised a brow at Lucien. "What is that old woman up to now?"

"Are you speaking of Grandmama or Hester?"

His father's shot him a wry look. "Either. Both." Salcott picked up his own coffee and settled into a chair opposite Lucien. "Hester has been with her so long they have become an inseparable and formidable pair. Trust me, there is a plot in the works."

Lucien was too relieved by his father's report to be annoyed that he might have journeyed to Sussex for nothing, and his lips twitched with humor at Salcott's remark. Hester was indeed an institution, having been with the family since her own childhood. By rights she should be known as Miller as suited her present position of lady's maid, but everyone was far too used to calling her Hester, and she had chosen to remain so.

The earl sighed. "As it does not appear to be an urgent matter, before you take off to discover why they went to such lengths to lure you here—for which I cannot fault them, I might add—do tell me the latest news of London."

The following conversation was such a comfortable give and take that nearly an hour had gone by before Lucien reluctantly rose and excused himself.

"It is getting late," he said. "I wish to see Grandmama before she takes off to visit friends or attend one of her community events."

"Now that you mention it, I do not think she has been out and about so much lately," Salcott said thoughtfully as he walked him to the study door. "I would accompany you, however Mother is more likely to be honest if you go alone." His brow wrinkled into a worried frown. "Surely this will amount to nothing."

• • •

As Lucien was shown into the dowager's parlor, he was taken aback at the unguarded glimpse of her in the moment before she was aware of his presence. His father had somewhat allayed his fears, and he had not expected to find her paler than he remembered, shoulders drooping. She stared at the fire in the hearth, the open book in her lap forgotten—not the lively woman he knew. As soon as his name was announced, she straightened, her expression lightening, her brows arching in obvious surprise.

Well, that look was telling. She had not expected him. If a scheme was afoot, his grandmother might not be a party to it.

"Lucien! My dear boy, what a delight. I am pleased that finally you have come to Salcott Hall. It has been what? Five years or more." She raised her cheek for him to kiss, and Lucien obliged.

"Three years," he said, "but indeed, it has been too long."

"Well, you are here now." She gave him a speculative look. "Although I cannot but wonder why. What brings you to us?"

"How could I stay away from my favorite lady?"

"You have managed it for the last few years," she said, a short laugh belying the reprimand. "Which makes your arrival all the more intriguing. Do sit down, dear boy." She peered up at him. "Dare I believe you and my son have finally resolved your differences?"

Lucien saw the hope reflected on her face and chose his words carefully while he settled in a high-backed chair. "Not precisely resolved, but I come to you after spending a very congenial hour with him."

"Well." She folded her hands in her lap with obvious satisfaction. "That is progress, is it not?"

"Perhaps. Now tell me about yourself." Since she was already questioning the reason for his visit, Lucien knew a subtle approach was out of the question. "I hear you are not feeling quite up to snuff these days."

The dowager bristled. "Fustian. Who told you that? I may not be as spry as I once was, but I am not ready to be fitted for a coffin just yet."

Lucien could not hold back a smile at her bluntness. "No one would dare to suggest that, Grandmama. I am relieved to hear you are well, although you do look tired."

"A little perhaps." Her eyes searched his face. "Is this what brought you to Sussex? I am flattered…and quite touched." Her eyes moistened, and she dabbed at them with her handkerchief.

"What is it, my dear?" Lucien leaned forward, rather alarmed at this uncharacteristic display of emotion.

"Oh, pay me no mind." She sniffed and cleared her throat. "I suppose I have been a trifle out of sorts. The doldrums, only. I confess the country is a bit insipid after London."

"That is easily fixed," Lucien said, not believing for a moment she was missing the hustle and bustle of town. She'd stayed away for years and had hurried home this summer as soon as her town business was completed. He called her bluff. "Come back to London with me. You can stay at Hays Mews as long as you like. Or if you object to a bachelor's residence, I am convinced Father would open Salcott House for you."

"Good heavens, no. It was only a passing fancy. Shall I ring for tea?" Without waiting for his response, she pulled the bell beside her, ordered a tray when a servant appeared, and launched into another topic. "While you are here, we should call on Miss Eleanor, Lucy Drayton's great-aunt. I have not seen her in a while, and I know she would be delighted to speak with you. She was so grateful for your help this summer."

"She need feel no debt to me. Many helped, you know—Lady Anne Ashburn and Miss Barnett, for instance—and it was a sad outcome. I wish it had been in my power to bring her niece safely home. Nonetheless, I am entirely at your service. As my stay at Salcott Hall will be brief, shall we say after your luncheon, half two, perhaps?"

"Yes, that will be splendid. However, I am devastated to hear you plan to leave so soon. I give you fair warning, I shall attempt to entice you into a proper stay."

Lucien lifted a brow. "I hate to ask what you consider proper."

"A month, six weeks," the dowager said blithely.

He threw back his head and laughed. "Out of the question, I fear. You know I have responsibilities in London. Now, let us not talk of leaving when I have just arrived."

"But you will stay a few days?"

"Perhaps," he conceded with a smile. Lucien studied his grandmother. She had made light of any health concerns, but he was not entirely convinced. The dark, puffy circles under her eyes bespoke sleepless nights, and he would wager she had lost a bit of flesh since midsummer. Surely Hester could explain when he had the opportunity to question her regarding her mysterious letter.

They chatted several more minutes, mainly about the people she knew in London or the Sussex neighbors he remembered. Gradually he realized she had not been getting out in the community as was her custom. This was a worrisome change for a woman who had always been active in making visitations and lending her support to various local events. If truth be told, she was somewhat of a gossip and enjoyed every bit of it. Was her recent preference for home due to an infirmity she was concealing?

He finally stood, not wanting to keep her from her repast, and bowed over her hand. "I shall take my leave for now, Grandmama, and see you at half two. Are you certain we will find Miss Eleanor at home?"

"I shall send word, but we do not gadabout as much in the country, you know. I shall be ready, dear boy. Oh, and Lucien, try to maintain such a promising start with your father."

Lucien chuckled. "Yes, ma'am. I shall mind my words and avoid controversial topics."

Upon leaving the parlor, Lucien sought out Barnes, the aging manservant, and asked him to locate Hester.

"I am sorry, my lord, but she is not within the manor. She went to the village to visit a friend and has not yet returned. Do you wish me to send the footman to get her?"

"No, not necessary. I shall speak with her when I return to pick up the dowager after her luncheon." He chafed at the delay, but he would come early for the visit and get to the bottom of his grandmother's malady.

• • •

Lucien returned to Dower House at two, allowing time to speak with Hester. To his surprise and frustration, Barnes advised him Hester was once again unavailable—she was away on an errand.

"What, again?" It crossed Lucien's mind that she was avoiding him, and he was not best pleased. He would have pursued his suspicions, but Barnes reported the dowager had been in a flutter the last hour in her eagerness to visit Miss Eleanor.

"She has talked of nothing else, my lord."

Lucien nodded thoughtfully. "I shall not keep her waiting. When Hester returns, instruct her to remain in the house until we have spoken."

"Yes, my lord. I shall make sure she does."

"Thank you."

As Barnes had said, Lucien found his grandmother impatient to be on their way. She appeared strong and animated, but as he escorted her to his carriage and helped her in, he noted that she leaned heavily on his arm and did so again when they arrived at the neighboring Drayton estate.

Miss Eleanor, their elderly hostess, was so embarrassingly grateful for Lucien's efforts last summer in solving the mystery of her missing niece that he became uncomfortable and increasingly desirous of leaving. The Dowager Countess Augusta felt no such compulsion, and she and her friend gradually settled into a lively chat, so caught up in village affairs that they took no notice of Lucien's lack of participation.

Satisfied to see his grandmother enjoying herself, he allowed his attention to stray. Had Sherbourne gotten away on his intended trip to his family's country home? He suspected the primary reason for his friend's visit was that Miss Emily Selkirk lived only a few miles from Sherbourne manor, and he wondered how soon Sherry would be announcing his engagement.

Inevitably, thoughts of country life brought to mind Lady Anne's return to Warwickshire—why was it everything reminded him of her these days? He shied away from dwelling on that question and instead indulged in speculation of what she might be doing at her country home. Was her time spent sitting at her mother's bedside or was she out and about in the community, renewing old friendships, slipping back into the rhythm of village life and putting thoughts of London behind her?

Lucien let out an impatient breath. He must stop this uncharacteristic brooding on Lady Anne. In all likelihood, their paths would not cross again. He straightened with a sigh, returning his thoughts to the ladies' conversation just in time. His grandmother was saying her goodbyes.

On the way to the carriage, she caught her toe, and he laughingly took her up in his arms, lifting her into the coach. "Careful, my love. I cannot have anything happening to my best girl."

The dowager passed the incident off with a playful swat on the shoulder, but Lucien was worried at the fright he'd seen on her face. When he had escorted her safely to the parlor where she proposed to work on her correspondence, he set out to locate the elusive lady's maid.

He came upon Barnes in the main hallway, and the manservant pointed toward the servants' stairs. "She is talking with Cook, I believe. Shall I ask her to meet you in the study or perhaps the library?"

"No, thank you. I shall find her myself." Having noted how frail Barnes was looking, Lucien had no wish to risk the man falling on the narrow steps.

"But, sir—"

"No need to disturb yourself, Barnes. I would not have her escape me again." With a grin, Lucien hurried down the well-worn stairs, giving the butler no further chance to object.

Hester was sitting with the cook at the kitchen table—perhaps hiding in the kitchen was more accurate, considering the trapped look on her face when the women jumped to their feet upon his arrival. They both dropped quick curtseys.

"At last," he said, eyeing the tall, thin abigail. "I do believe you have been avoiding me, Hester."

"Your lordship, I am ever so sorry. It was impertinent to write to you in such a manner, but I did not know what else to do." She looked at Cook, and the slightly plump woman well-past her youth nodded in response. "Something had to be done."

"So, you are in this together," Lucien said, eyeing both women. "You conspired to bring me here under false pretenses." He kept his tone mild for he was not angry, just perplexed they had resorted to such unusual measures.

"Yes…and no," Hester said.

"She means, not exactly," Cook helpfully clarified.

"I see," he said, but of course he did not. They had yet to tell him anything. "Perhaps one of you could explain more fully."

"We more, uh…exaggerated, I'd say," Hester began. "The mistress has not been herself for several weeks."

"Not since *the fall*."

Cook's heavy words did not go unnoticed. Finally, he was getting somewhere.

"What fall? Was she injured? No one has mentioned a fall."

"Not truly harmed. A bump on her elbow was all," Hester said. "Mostly her pride, I'd say."

"And confidence," Cook added.

Hester nodded. "Yes, m'lord. I would say that is the truth of it."

Lucien curbed his impatience. "I value your opinions, of course, but if you would be so kind as to tell me what occurred, the facts please, beginning with the fall."

Hester sighed and dropped the dithering. "Yes, m'lord. More than a month past, her ladyship took a tumble in the rose garden. No one saw it, but the gardener heard her cry out and came promptly to help her. We looked her over and only found that single bruise, but she was shaken, Master Luc, and hasn't gotten over it." Seemingly unaware of calling him by his childhood name, she went on. "I cannot say just why she fell, but even with her cane, she is not as steady as she once was. Quite natural at her age, mind you, and we do try to keep an eye on her, but she doesn't always call for us when she should."

The cook sighed heavily. "That is the way of it, m'lord, and she has changed—not for the good, I might add. Never goes out, sits alone."

"Did you report the fall to Lord Salcott?"

"She forbade it. Said it was too trivial to mention. We knew better but couldn't go against her strong wishes."

Lucien understood their dilemma. If they disobeyed her, Grandmama would never trust them again. "What is holding her back? Is she fearful of another fall?"

"We think so," Hester said. "It's a worry for the rest of us. Cook and I can't be with her every moment, and Mr. Barnes is…well, he is getting on too."

As is the entire staff, Lucien thought, as he looked at the two women before him. They weren't more than a decade, if that, behind his grandmother's seventy years.

Hester fiddled with a button on her sleeve. "To be honest, sir, we have talked amongst ourselves, and we think her ladyship will not admit to her frailty, even to herself, and so she is hiding it. She has shut herself away and grown blue-devilled—if you don't mind me speaking so plainly, m'lord."

"No, no. I am thankful you told me." Hard to think of his strong-willed grandmother failing to face the truth, but Hester's story explained the hunched shoulders and shadowed eyes he had observed for himself. "Perhaps a companion is needed, a sturdy, younger woman," he said, thinking aloud.

Cook twitched her nose. "If she would allow one."

"Which you doubt."

"Don't you, m'lord?"

He reluctantly nodded. Salcott could always order it, force her to accept a companion, but Lucien would hate to see her pride so abused. "Have you another solution?"

Hester moistened her dry lips and glanced at the cook again. "Well, no, m'lord. That's why we sent for you."

Chapter Four

Lucien entered his father's study, still mulling over the situation at Dower House. The more he thought about it, a companion was the perfect solution, a woman who could provide good company, a helping arm when needed, and would see that the dowager got out to visit her friends. How could he convince his grandmother to accept one? Any argument he could think of that included her aging abilities or her sagging spirits was defeated from the start. It would be ideal if the proposal came from her, but his conversation with Hester and the cook had convinced him that was not going to happen. So...he needed a believable excuse to add a younger woman to Grandmama's household.

Salcott looked up from the ledgers on his desk. "Ah, Lucien. Have you come to save me from the estate accounts?"

"Just so," Lucien said absently.

Salcott frowned. "You seem pensive—a weighty problem? Not bad news from Dower House, I hope."

"Nothing alarming, but it is Grandmother," he said. Lucien shook his head and sank into a chair. "I spoke with Hester—and the cook who conspired with her to write to me—and I am bothered by what they said and by what I observed."

Salcott brows shot up. "Good lord, is something truly wrong with her?"

"She had a fall last month. She was not injured," Lucien hastened to add. "No more than a bump."

Salcott scowled. "I was not told of this."

"You know Grandmama. She ordered them not to tell you. Hence, the letter *to me*."

"Stubborn old woman." Salcott rose and came around the desk

24

to sit in a high back chair next to Lucien. "Tell me everything." As he listened to Lucien's account of the situation, Salcott's scowl deepened. At the end, he muttered, "Fond as I am of my mother, she can be most provoking."

Lucien chuckled. "She prides herself in being so, I believe."

"Yes, you *would* understand," his father said with a ghost of a smile.

"Are you implying her stubborn independence skipped a generation? Oddly enough," Lucien cocked his head, keeping a straight face, "I have been told by your fellow members of Parliament how much you and I are alike."

Salcott made a sound in his throat that sounded suspiciously like a snort, before he lapsed into thought. "We cannot allow her to fade away into the doldrums. I could force the issue by hiring a nurse."

"You could, and Grandmama would send her away...and the next one, if you persisted. You must agree she has the right to manage her own servants."

"Not when it is to her detriment." Salcott huffed. "I cannot like the thought of a row with her, but someone must be with her who can ensure her safety. Any thoughts?" He raised a hand. "Do not suggest I pension off Barnes and replace him with a younger butler. I broached the subject a year ago, and he made it plain he is not ready. Demme, Lucien, but he has been with us too devilish long to push him out."

"I agree we cannot sacrifice one for the other, but something must be done."

"Yes. Perhaps an under-butler," Salcott suggested. "Although... that would not provide assistance when Mother is in her private rooms. It really must be a female."

Lucien nodded, and silence reigned for several minutes as both men contemplated possible solutions. Lucien finally said, "I believe you must economize, sir...in light of your recent terrible losses on the market."

"Eh? I have had no losses. Where did you get that absurd notion?" Salcott stared at him.

Lucien struggled with a smile. "Are two houses for two people not an excessive drain on the estate? You have been rattling around in Salcott Hall for years, and Grandmother is doing the same at Dower House. You could combine the households."

Salcott's brows rose. "Do I understand you want me to live with my mother again?"

Lucien failed to hide his grin this time. "Why not? With several entire suites of rooms, surely the Hall has enough space for both. You might not see her for days or weeks, if you so desire. Even months while you are in London on Parliament business for the lengthy terms. Your household and her own staff—who would accompany her in any move to the Hall, except for one or two to maintain Dower House—could provide the support she needs."

"Ah, yes, I understand now—my so-called terrible losses have made this *economy* advisable." Salcott slowly rubbed his chin. "It might work. I very much enjoy Mother's company from time to time, and you are correct, Salcott Hall is more than sufficiently large. I could even open another wing. So much for true economy." He gave Lucien a wry look. "But how does this provide her with safety in her own quarters?"

"An inoffensive female relation might be found who is living in modest or less-than-ideal circumstances and would welcome residing in the greater luxury of Salcott Hall—not as a companion to Grandmama, heaven forbid—but as an act of compassion toward an impoverished relative."

The earl chortled. "What a devious plan. Mother will see through it, but I believe you have left her no grounds to object without seeming uncharitable."

Lucien wasn't certain his grandmother could be circumvented so easily, but they had a plan that just might work if handled with delicacy.

Chapter Five

London, evening, 12 October 1812

Pacing the floor of the elegant drawing room in the Sherbourne family townhouse, Sherry paused frequently at the front bay window to watch the street outside, anxious for the sound of a coach stopping or a knock at the door. The search of the neighborhood had yielded nothing. Maria had vanished as though she had never been…except for the child upstairs.

Hours had passed, and the street lamps were lit. Inside the house, the scent of wax and tallow permeated the rooms as sconces and candelabras pushed back the night, and still he waited. When Archie announced dinner, Sherry picked at his food for Mrs. Cooper's sake, but his appetite was gone. His chest tightened with each tick of the clock. Finally, over a stiff brandy in the study, he acknowledged Maria wasn't returning—at least not that night.

He let out a pent-up breath, shaking his head. The dratted woman had clearly come to his home for the sole purpose of saddling him with her child. Possibly *his* child, he amended. While she did what? Ran from this alleged Frenchman? Resumed her life—whatever it was—without the burden of a child? Or did she just need a little time to make other arrangements? No, he mustn't indulge in wishful thinking. If time was what she needed, she would have told him.

So, what did he do now?

Of course, the child came first. A temporary nanny would do for a few days, but long term…? Mother would help, if he asked. She would not turn any child away and would be delighted, loving the little girl unconditionally, regardless of her irregular birth…

if Fanny was his. And there lay the problem. He could not expose his mother to potential disappointment and heartbreak. She must know nothing of Fanny until he exhausted every possibility of locating Maria and learning the truth.

Finding himself suddenly worried by the child's silence, he climbed the stairs, bypassed the floor with the regular bedchambers, and arrived at the nursery. He opened the door and peered inside. Fanny was asleep, her dark hair spread around her face. She looked angelic and so very small. He would do right by her whether she was his or not.

Easing the door closed with a sigh of relief that all was well, he returned to the study to pen several notes of inquiry. It had occurred to him that he didn't know who Maria Pembroke truly was. During the war, those involved in clandestine work often chose other names. He'd never heard her mention another name, but that didn't mean she was who she said she was. In order to find her family, determining her proper surname was imperative. Reaching out to former associates in the spy world and reviewing the secret files in Lord Rothe's office would be the places to start.

He paused after writing the last letter and considered writing to apprise Lucien of the situation. Eventually, he decided against it and laid the quill pen down. His friend had rushed to Sussex owing to his grandmother's illness. Between her poor health and his thorny relationship with the earl, Lucien would have his hands full. No reason to disturb him—not yet anywise—and with luck, Sherry would have the matter resolved without needing his help.

Sealing the notes, he gave them to Archie to be dispatched by mail or courier. His manservant would know the fastest method, and Sherry was in desperate need of information as swiftly as he could get it. Although Fanny was a fetching infant, Sherry was in no position to raise her on his own. He needed to find Maria within the next few days, or he'd be forced to seek help from someone.

Leaning back in his desk chair, he marveled again at the quiet that had descended once he had bid the child goodnight. The day had been a revelation of pattering footsteps on the stairs and distant peals of childish laughter. He had often found himself smiling, well aware having Nanny Jane to keep the child occupied was a godsend.

Why had he not told her so? A nanny held a unique position in the household, under the supervision of neither housekeeper nor butler and with no one other than the parent to praise or correct her.

He let out a sharp sigh. It might take time to learn everything a father should do, but, if need be, he'd get the hang of it, for Fanny's sake. As he rang the bell for the nanny, it occurred to him he should have looked through the child's bag to see if there was anything that might indicate where she had been living or who her relations were.

Nanny Jane promptly presented herself. Despite the long day with her young charge, she appeared unruffled, her brown hair neatly pinned in place.

"You wished to see me, sir?"

"Jane, is it not?"

"Yes, sir."

"When you unpacked Miss Fanny's bag did you find anything other than clothes?"

"A few things, I believe." She rolled her eyes upward, thinking hard. "A doll, a child's cup, and a snuffbox wrapped in paper."

"Snuffbox? Strange that such an object would be packed with a child's belongings…unless by mistake. In any event, please bring those three items to me, Jane. I wish to examine them."

While she hurried to do his bidding, Sherry returned to pacing the floor. A snuffbox—not just strange, but right curious, it was. Had Maria put it in the bag by accident or design? Could the paper it was wrapped in be a note from Maria or a hint to where she had gone?

Jane returned carrying a basket with the items placed inside and set it on his desk. Sherry quickly unwrapped the snuffbox, set it aside, and smoothed out the paper to find nothing but a date: 5 October 1812, a week ago. Was it significant or simply an idle note Maria had made for herself and discarded, using the paper to protect the snuffbox? He laid it on the desk and picked up the ornate box—silver and somewhat tarnished. Turning it over, he found the engraved letters LSM and the year 1771, forty-one years ago. Perhaps a gift received on a birthday or other special occasion, but who was LSM? The child's father? A relation of Maria? If the latter, the M might mean Pembroke was *not* Maria's family name.

He looked in the basket at the two remaining items, a porcelain infant cup with angels painted on the sides and a hand-sewn doll with button eyes. He took out the cup and set it beside the snuffbox. These things might be all they had to locate Fanny's family.

He handed the doll and basket back to the nanny. He could describe the doll, if need be, and it would be better used to make Fanny feel at home. "You may return the doll, Jane. but first, tell me how today went." He gave her a smile. "I trust Miss Fanny did not wear you out."

Jane grinned. "Oh, no, sir. She is lively—but a sweet thing. I enjoy being here with her very much."

"Has she talked about where she lives, mentioned names, anything that would help us locate other members of her family?"

"She is so young—"

"How young?" he interrupted.

"I'm sure I couldn't say, sir. But she talks a lot, like my youngest brother, so three or four maybe."

Which might mean she was born before they left Paris. Was that even likely? How would Maria have hidden her pregnancy and the infant after its birth? Perhaps Fanny was just precocious—Jane was only guessing her age. "Sorry I interrupted. You were saying…"

Jane tilted her head in thought. "Besides her mum, she talked about Grandpapa and Uncle Percy. Oh, and Chary, but I think Chary is a dog." She shrugged her shoulders. "Sorry, my lord. I'm afraid that is all."

"You have been very helpful and are doing a splendid job, Jane. Thank you for coming to us so quickly." She bobbed her head shyly. "If Fanny says anything else about her life or family, please tell me right away. The smallest fact might help us to get her to her proper home." He dismissed Jane and went back to brooding, staring at the engraved snuffbox. He finally put it and the infant cup in a desk drawer and went upstairs to bed.

• • •

By Tuesday morning, Sherry could not sit and wait longer. Before setting out for Whitehall to access the information they had on Maria, he gave Archibald instructions to send word immediately if she returned or sent a message.

Arriving at the Marquess of Rothe's office, he found the head of Prinny's secret spy unit—and thus the man to whom Sherbourne and Lucien reported—had gone to the palace.

Mr. Sloane, Rothe's personal secretary, greeted him in his usual reserved manner. "Good morning, sir. You have saved me the effort of locating and dispatching a courier to you. Lord Rothe received your note and tasked me with providing you certain confidential information. I assume that is why you are here."

"I am. Pardon the rush, Sloane, but I rather urgently need to locate Maria Pembroke or some member of her family."

Sloane pushed his wire-rimmed glasses back in place on his nose and eyed him. "I have gathered what we have, sir, but I am afraid it is nothing more than we had three years ago when you were in France. Miss Pembroke was a member of the French Resistance, which does not preclude her from also working for the French government as your note implied, but the Resistance had nothing on her beyond her name. She was recruited and vouched for by Lisette Armand."

Sherry sighed. *Lisette.* "Good grief, Sloane. I had forgotten that."

"As for English families named Pembroke, it is not a unique name, but a large, well-established family originated in the south part of Oxfordshire."

"Is there by chance a Percy or Percival Pembroke?"

"Allow me to look." Sloane opened a large ledger, ran his finger down the columns, then went to a cabinet and pulled out a paper with a list of names. "There is a Henry Percival Pembroke, age forty-three, resides on a small estate in Oxfordshire. Could be who you're looking for or at least a relation."

"It's a place to start."

Sloane, who didn't often indulge in curiosity, gave Sherry a questioning look. "May I tell Lord Rothe whether your interest in this woman is private or of concern to our office?"

Sherry grinned. "Elegantly put, Sloane. You may tell him it is both. Maria contacted me two days ago claiming she was being pursued by a Frenchman, the brother of one of Boney's agents she killed three years ago. That is when she also divulged she had spied for both sides. Shortly after this conversation, she mysteriously disappeared."

"Yes, I see. Reason enough for disquiet."

If you only knew the full story, Sherry thought, picturing Fanny's childish face.

"Very good, sir," Sloane continued. "I shall pass the information to his lordship."

"You might also tell him I'm going to Oxfordshire."

• • •

Sherry kept riding long after dark had fallen and reached the Woodgates Inn in Oxfordshire going on ten. He heaved a sigh and stepped down from the saddle, bone-weary, not having made such a long trip by horseback in quite some time. Twenty-two miles was a hard day for a saddle horse, and he knew General, his big bay gelding, was done up. They both could use a good night's rest.

Once he'd seen his mount to the stables and had arranged for its care, Sherry entered the inn and bespoke a meal and a room. He consumed a hearty country stew and a half bottle of good port before heading upstairs to his room and collapsing on the inn's very respectable featherbed.

He was roused from slumbered by a ruckus in the Inn's courtyard. It was still dark outside the window, and Sherry groaned. He had not been asleep for more than a couple of hours. He rolled over and closed his eyes again, but the shouting continued, and the report of a pistol brought him rearing out of bed. He leapt to the window and stuck his head out. "What the bloody hell is going on?" he shouted.

No one heard him. A noisy crowd from the tavern, offering advice and encouragement, had gathered around three gentlemen wrestling with a fourth man—obviously deep in his cups—and attempting to take charge of the pistol he was flourishing.

"Robin, for God's sake," one of the three men pleaded. "Give it up."

"No-o-o, sirre-e-e," slurred their inebriated and belligerent companion. "No way. I'm gonna kill 'im." Following this declaration, one of Robin's acquaintances yanked the pistol from his hands, and they let him go. He staggered and fell on his face. As the crowd burst into laughter, his friends picked him up and dunked his head in the horse watering trough.

Sherry shook his head and went back to bed. He didn't even care what the row was about.

• • •

The next time he woke it was light outside, and the inn was quiet, except for sounds from the stables where the lads were harnessing horses for guests who'd chosen an early morning departure. He stretched and rolled out of bed. He had much to do that day.

After hurried ablutions, he entered the public rooms downstairs, bespoke breakfast, and asked the proprietor if he knew a man named Percival Pembroke.

"I don't, sir, but the wife and I only bought the inn three months ago. You might ask one of the locals. They usually start coming in for a pint by late afternoon."

Tables began to fill quickly with tradesmen, hostlers, and departing guests, and the owner excused himself to take orders. Sherry's meal arrived, and he was lingering over a final cup of tea, trying to figure out what to do rather than wait for the late afternoon crowd to come in, when the young man whose antics had woken him during the night entered the room. Despite the man's youth, no more than twenty Sherry gauged, he looked very much the worse for wear from a combination of liquor and lack of sleep. His cravat was rumpled, and his clothes looked as though he'd slept in them. Sherry supposed he had. The young man slumped into a chair at the table next to Sherry's, calling for coffee and a pint of ale.

Sherry chuckled at the combination—hedging his bet, so to speak. From experience, Sherry thought he'd do better with biscuits and rashers.

The gentleman glanced up and caught Sherry looking. He gave a wry smile. "I suppose you heard that dreadful display last night."

"Hard not to, but I only caught the end of it," Sherry owned. "By the by, I'm Andrew Sherbourne."

"A pleasure. Robin Thornton here. I do beg pardon for waking everyone."

"From what I saw from my bedchamber window, you were, um, a trifle disguised."

Thornton laughed. "Kindly put, but I was completely castaway. If not for my friends, I might have done worse than make a fool of myself."

"You *were* rather intent on killing someone."

"My cousin. He took that filly right from under my nose. Still makes me angry after I'd had my eye on her for months."

Sherry wasn't sure whether they were talking about a horse or a woman, but probably it didn't matter. Both were of equal interest to most young bucks.

"You're not from around here," Thornton said, setting aside his grievances with his cousin. "Just passing through?"

"Up from London. Are you from around here?"

"I am. I guess I refused to go home last night, so they put me in a room here." Thornton put a hand to his forehead, bemoaning last night's activities.

"I'm looking for a man who lives around here. Perhaps you know him? Percy Pembroke."

Thornton shook his head and eagerly sipped the hot coffee the barmaid set down. "Some Pembrokes live north of here. Maybe three miles, a little more. His name is Hugh, but he might know this Percy fellow."

"Thank you." Sherry rose and paused beside Thornton's table. "I hope that head of yours gets better. No offense intended, but no filly is worth killing your kin."

"Hell, I know that," the young man mumbled. "Leastways I do when I ain't drinking."

Leaving his horse to rest, Sherry rented a gray gelding from the stables. The animal proved to be a steady goer, and with the help of further directions from two farmers along the way, Sherry arrived in due course at Pembrokes' well-kept home, a yellow, square, three-story structure built in the last century.

He presented his card at the door, asked to speak with the master, and was ushered into an old-fashioned but scrupulously clean and neat parlor. Despite the tidy appearance, he failed to find any sign of a recent woman's touch. More likely the owner was a widower with an excellent housekeeper. Having made those assumptions, he was not surprised when an older man entered the room and introduced himself as Hugh Pembroke. Graying black hair and mustache, but the figure of a man still active; his black eyes held a note of query.

"How may I help you, sir?"

"I have ridden from London, hoping to speak with Percy Pembroke."

"That would be my eldest son. He lives about five miles to the northwest. May I inquire what this is about?"

"I've come about Maria—"

"Where is she?" Pembroke interrupted, taking an eager step forward. "Is she well, unharmed?"

"The Maria Pembroke I know was well when I saw her two mornings ago."

"And my granddaughter?"

"She is safe."

"Thank the Lord." Pembroke's tense shoulders relaxed a bit. "Do sit, sir, may I offer you tea or ale?"

"Tea would be most welcome." Sherry took a chair and watched the older man pour two cups. If he was Maria's father—which seemed likely, given his age—his concern for her and Fanny appeared to be genuine. So, why had she left home? Sherry pondered how much he should reveal. Until he understood their relationship a bit better and what this man knew of Maria's past and present activities, he'd have to tread carefully.

Pembroke handed him one of the cups and sat, eyeing him intently. "What can you tell me about them? Where are they now?"

"I was hoping you could tell *me* of Maria's whereabouts. She has unexpectedly disappeared. Before I go any further, please describe Maria, her relation to you, and the child's name. I have no wish to offend, sir, but I need to know we are talking about the same woman."

"Maria is my daughter, Fanny my granddaughter." Hugh Pembroke described both mother and child. "Is that sufficient?"

"I am more than satisfied. What sent her to London?"

Pembroke's dark eyes narrowed. "How do you know my daughter? Are you a friend of hers?"

"We used to be friends…in France, but I had not seen her for nearly three years until she came to my London lodgings the day before yesterday."

"Then you know she was with the French Resistance?" Pembroke asked.

"Yes," Sherry said, but he didn't elaborate.

"She has spoken of an Andrew. Is that you?"

"I cannot say if I am the Andrew she mentioned—not knowing what she has said. Much has happened since we parted rather abruptly in Paris."

Pembroke nodded, his eyes revealing his understanding. "She told us."

"Told you what?" Sherry was getting frustrated. He and Pembroke were both being cautious and talking in circles. He asked bluntly, "How much do you know of her activities in France?"

"I dare say I know most of it. Enough to realize why you question whether you are friends or not." The older man sighed and steepled his fingers. "Perhaps it would help if I tell you what happened to Maria after she left Paris."

"Please do. I would welcome your candor."

Pembroke nodded. "When Maria returned to us three years ago, she was frightened and withdrawn. Within weeks it was obvious she was carrying a child. She refused to talk about it, but we still did our best to protect her, even found a suitable local lad who was willing to marry her. She refused."

"For God's sake, why?"

"She said it would not be fair to burden him with a child when she was still in love with another man."

"The father? Did she tell you his name?"

"No, but she gradually opened up about other things: her work with the Resistance, her friend Lisette, you, and that final day. Did you know about the French officer she killed during her escape?"

"Not until Monday. She said his brother was in England looking for her."

Pembroke frowned. "So that is who he was. A Frenchman came here asking about her."

"Did he give you a name?"

"He may have, but I do not recall it now. After I told him she no longer lived her, he was rather persistent in knowing where she had gone, if she was visiting relatives, or if she had moved to London. I figured I'd already said enough and asked him to leave."

"What did he look like?"

"Shorter than you, older—about forty, dressed in typical riding clothes for a tradesman, dark hair. I am afraid that is all I recall. It has been more than five months."

"Pardon? Maria left that long ago?"

"Nearly six months now."

"I had the impression she had only recently arrived in London. Where has she been the last five or six months?"

Pembroke gave him a troubled look and shook his head. "I have no answer for you. Perhaps I should finish with what I *do* know. Maria's parents died when she was young, and my own wife is gone now, but her Uncle Percy and I raised her. Naturally, we have supported her and Fanny in every way we could. I believe they were happy here until a letter arrived from France, and the haunted look returned to Maria's face. She would not tell me what was wrong, and the next day, she and Fanny were gone. She left a note saying only she was sorry and that she loved us." Pembroke paused. "We sought them everywhere but found nothing. We even appealed to Bow Street, but because she left on her own, they would not look for her." He spread his hands. "That was the last I knew of her until you walked in here today, bringing me hope."

"I have little I can tell you in return," Sherry said. "Maria came to me with Fanny Monday morning, told me they were in danger from this Frenchman, and asked me to protect Fanny. Before I could determine how best to handle the situation, Maria slipped out of the house, and she has not returned. I don't know where she is, but Fanny is safe with a nanny in my London home."

"Is she yours?"

"Frankly, I don't know, sir. Maria said she was, but she may have said that—unnecessarily, I assure you—to convince me to protect Fanny. I intend to find out as soon as I locate Maria. As she is not here, I shall return to London and continue my search if she has not been found in my absence." Sherry rose. "I will send word when I find her. If you should hear from her…"

"Yes, of course, but what of Fanny?" Pembroke protested as he also came to his feet. "What will happen to her?"

"For now, she is under my protection. If she is mine, I shall, of course, provide for her and raise her in Maria's absence. You shall always be welcome in her life."

"But what if you conclude she is not yours?" Pembroke asked anxiously.

"Then I will bring her to you, if that is what you wish."

"It is, sir. My dearest wish."

Chapter Six

Sussex, October 1812

Lucien and Salcott wasted no time in putting their plans for the Dowager Countess into action. Several kinswomen were already supported by the estate, and Salcott went through those names and quickly found a suitable companion, Cora Lamb, a widowed second cousin in her forties of sturdy constitution and agreeable character living alone in a boarding house two counties away.

An invitation was promptly carried to the widow, and her response expressed delight at the proposed change in her living circumstances. Cousin Cora went on to say she would begin packing immediately and should arrive by Friday.

All that was left was to convince the Dowager Countess. Lucien and Salcott set out for Dower House well pleased with their efforts to date.

"Surely she will see reason," Lucien said, suddenly uncertain as they crossed the garden path to the conservatory where the dowager was sitting in a sunny spot.

"With Mother, you never know."

How right Salcott proved to be. The moment they proposed closing Dower House, she objected...strongly and insistently. For twenty minutes or more, she regaled them with all the reasons it would not suit. Lucien and Salcott managed to counter every volley, stressing the advantages to the estate, to Cousin Cora, and even the lighter workload for her own household staff. Not once did either of them mention their concerns for her health or well-being.

She finally grew quiet, eyeing her son. "You are determined to do this, Arthur?"

"Yes, madam, I am. To do otherwise is inadvisable for all concerned."

"So you say, but why now, after all these years?" She threw up her hands. "Never mind, you have already blamed it on your accountants. Such frugality seems overdone, but very well, if you feel this is best, I shall gracefully accede to your wishes. When can I expect to be removed from my home?"

Lucien and Salcott exchanged a look over her head. Graceful it was not, but it was done.

"As Cousin Cora will arrive on Friday, it would be fitting for you to be in residence to greet her as the lady of the house."

• • •

Upon returning to Salcott Hall, Salcott excused himself to attend to urgent correspondence from London. "It appears my colleagues in Parliament are working on new legislation, and there is a goodly amount of disagreement."

"Isn't there always? I will leave you to it, sir, as I have a letter of my own I should write."

"To Lady Anne?"

"Matchmaking, father?"

"I did not think I had to. Your attention appeared rather fixed."

"Did it? There is no such understanding between us. She has returned to Warwickshire to care for her ailing mother. I do not think she plans to return to London in the near future."

"I am sorry to hear that. She is a lovely woman."

"Yes. I thought to write and inquire after her mother's health."

Salcott nodded. "An excellent idea. Surely the civil thing to do."

Lucien gave his father a quick look. Was Salcott putting him on?

"Shall we meet later for a drink when we have completed our correspondence?" Salcott asked as he headed toward his study.

"I shall see you then."

Lucien suspected his father's swift departure had hidden a smile. Well, he supposed his true reason for writing to Anne was rather obvious. He missed her. Was he just prolonging the inevitable loss of contact over time? Perhaps, but a simple note of courtesy could do no harm. And she would be pleased that his relationship with his father had continued to improve, and he could tell her how grateful Miss Eleanor had been over their efforts last summer regarding the disappearance of her niece.

Consequently, he was soon seated at the desk in his room, pen in hand.

Dear Lady Anne,

I hope this letter finds you well and that your mother's health has improved. You may be surprised to learn I am at Salcott Hall in Sussex...

Chapter Seven

Oxfordshire to London, October 1812

After his meeting with Pembroke, Sherry returned to the inn, collected his horse, and set out for London. The solitary ride gave him ample time to worry about Maria and Fanny…and what the future held for all of them. Some questions he just could not answer, leaving him more frustrated than before and prone to dwell on them over and over.

If he was Fanny's father, why had Maria not come to him when she realized she was with child? If not then, why not six months ago when she first suspected she and Fanny were in danger? Why now? She said the Frenchman had found her twice. Presuming the second time was in London, exactly where had she been living? Where was the Frenchman now? And where the devil was Maria?

"What the—?" Sherry's normally well-mannered mount was shaking his head and prancing. Realizing he had inadvertently tightened the reins in his growing anxiety, he loosened them, and General smoothed his pace, settling into a ground-eating stride. "Sorry, big fellow."

Sherry drifted into thought again. Why had Maria taken off, leaving Fanny behind? Regardless of his hurt and angry feelings toward her, he would have protected them both from the Frenchman whether the child was his or not. He frowned as he reached the same conclusion he'd come to a dozen times before—something was going on that Maria hadn't told him.

Near midnight, he stopped at a country inn along the way to rest his horse and get a few hours of sleep, but he lay awake, restless and discouraged, his thoughts jumbled. He finally got up and sat in a chair staring out the window at nothing and going over yet again everything Maria had said and done, trying to see the situation through her eyes. Why would a mother part with her child? Perhaps she planned to confront the Frenchman and knew how dangerous that would be. Or was she on the run and felt she could move more quickly without the child? And what of the Frenchman—was he so obsessed by thoughts of revenge that he would dare to enter a country at war with his homeland in order to hunt and kill a woman and child?

Dawn was lighting the sky with fingers of white and purple when he flopped on the bed, his mind and body begging for sleep. He dozed fitfully until woken by the sounds of a busy stableyard as coaches got back on the road. Relieved the night was over, Sherry dunked his head in a bowl of water before grabbing a light meal, retrieving his horse, and continuing his ride to London.

He rode into his own stable shortly after midday on Thursday. Leaving his tired mount in the groom's care, he entered the back door of his residence and had just reached the main hall when Archibald nearly pounced on him.

"What? Have you been watching for me?" Sherry exclaimed.

"Yes, m'lord. Two constables were here last night with questions about Miss Pembroke and Fanny, and the house has been watched since dawn, maybe all night. I fear something is dreadfully amiss."

Sherry felt a sharp stab of unease. "We've had no word from Maria?"

"No, sir."

"What did the constables say?"

"They asked for you, and I explained you were away. They then asked if Miss Pembroke had been here and if we knew the whereabouts of Miss Fanny. I told them nothing, only that it was not my habit to gossip about my betters."

Sherry could imagine him looking down his long nose at them as he said it.

"They left then but said they would be back," Archibald finished.

Sherry took a steadying breath. It had not missed his notice that the constables had *not* asked to see Maria. "Well, we shall discover how urgent their mission is. If they are watching the house for my return, they should be here soon."

Indeed, in less than a half hour, they had a caller. With more than his usual stiffness, Archibald showed in a large, burly man. Sherry knew immediately this was no ordinary constable. He was dressed in the casual clothes of a tradesman, but the suspicion in his eyes gave him away. He was a runner.

Archibald announced, "Albert Haskett from Bow Street Station, sir."

At Sherbourne's silent scrutiny, Haskett took off his hat. He was nearly bald with a thin ring of dark brown hair.

Sherry took command of the conversation. "I assume this is not a social call, Constable Haskett."

"I've come about Maria Pembroke."

Sherry lifted a brow. "What about her?"

"So, you don't deny you know the woman."

"No, should I?" Sherry smiled, maintaining a casualness he was far from feeling. "What is the problem?"

"When did she last visit here?"

"I don't believe I said she had."

Haskett's eyes turned hard. "If you don't cooperate, sir, I'll be thinking you have something to hide."

Sherry gave him his best Lucien imitation. "While I am grieved you might think poorly of me, I can hardly cooperate without knowing why you are here." He crossed his arms and leaned against the fireplace mantel.

Haskett's jaw jutted out. "Maria Pembroke was found dead yesterday morning."

"Dead?" Sherry straightened, staring at him. Of a certainty, he had not expected that...but perhaps he should have. "What happened to her?"

"You might tell me, *milord*." Haskett made the last word sound like an insult.

"How would I know? I've been out of town."

"Since when?"

"I left London two days ago, mid-morning on Tuesday."

"Ain't that a coincidence," Haskett said with a sneer. "The doctor says when they found the body, it had been dead a day or so—about the time you left town. Don't suppose you know where the child is? The victim's landlady—a very helpful woman—told me Miss Pembroke was bringing her fatherless child to you. But I reckon the chit wasn't fatherless at all, was she?"

"I know nothing of Miss Pembroke's death, officer. Indeed, I am very sorry to hear of it." Sherry was thinking fast. This sounded bad...for him, and he wasn't going to help Haskett build a case against him. He gave the runner a haughty look. "The landlady has told you a Banbury tale."

"I don't think so. Where is the child? Did you get rid of her too?"

"See here, Haskett. No one comes into my house making such spurious and outrageous accusations. Leave at once, or I shall have you shown out."

Haskett clenched his jaw, nearly snarling. "You're gonna regret this. I'm going...but not for long."

The moment Archibald shut the front door, Sherry ordered that clothes be packed for himself and Fanny. "We're leaving, immediately."

"For how long, sir," Archie asked anxiously.

"I do not know." Sherry shrugged. "Pack light. I shall be on horseback."

"Does that mean you are not taking me? Perhaps I can join you somewhere?"

"Not this time, Archie. It is best if I go alone and that you do not know where. If anyone inquires, I have gone to the country."

"But, sir—"

"I'm afraid serious trouble is coming, Archie, and I prefer you are not caught up in it. Maria Pembroke is dead, and Bow Street appears to believe I killed her."

"Good Heavens." Archibald's eyes revealed his shock. "She was unharmed when she left here, and so I shall tell them."

"Thank you, Archie, but since you cannot vouch for where I went after I left the house on Tuesday morning, Haskett is unlikely to accept your assurance of my innocence. I must hurry now, and I need you to do a few other things for me. Send the nanny home so she is not here for them to question. In fact, since I've not admitted Miss Pembroke was here or that I have any knowledge of the child, it might be a good idea if you close the house. I do not want any of you to feel you must lie for me. I also need a letter dispatched to Lord Ware in Sussex with all haste. Please see it off yourself."

"I shall take care of it all, my lord, but I shall be staying. The house cannot be unattended."

Sherry looked at him, saw the determination and worry on his face.

"Buck up, Archie, and get to it. If you are choosing to stay, I suspect you will have to deal with more runners and constables within the hour."

"I shall manage, sir," Archibald said, once again the inscrutable manservant rising to the challenge. "You only need concern yourself with getting you and Fanny to safety."

"You're a good man."

Within minutes, Sherry went out the back carrying the child. Fanny was unusually quiet, as though she knew something was amiss, and they departed on horseback without fuss. He half expected to be accosted any moment, but Haskett must have come alone, or anyone left behind was watching the front entrance.

In any event, they were away without being chased by the constables, and once Sherry was confident he wasn't being followed, he turned his horse toward Hays Mews. It hadn't taken long to decide where to go. Although Lucien was away, his servants were certain to take them in until their master could be reached and further arrangements made.

He wasn't wrong, of course. Hughes and Talbot accepted them without question. Talbot took Fanny to what had once been a nursery for earlier owners; the valet appeared happy to have someone to fuss over while his master was away.

When Talbot returned once Fanny was safely settled and had fallen asleep, Sherry called the two men into the study and explained his predicament. Lucien trusted them implicitly, and thus so did Sherry. At all events, they had to know the circumstances to ensure no one mentioned Fanny to outsiders. He also warned them Bow Street runners might come to the door.

"They would be cautious about demanding entrance if Lucien were here, but in his absence they may be bold enough to question you or insist on searching the house."

"We know how to keep secrets and manage encroaching visitors, sir," Hughes said when Sherry had finished. "Bow Street shall not get past the front door."

Talbot nodded. "You are safe here, sir. If that is all, I should look in on Fanny again. It would not do to have her wake alone in a strange place."

"Thank you, Talbot." The valet left and Sherry sighed wearily. He turned to find the butler standing at the sideboard with his back to Sherry. "What a pother I'm in, Hughes. I suppose I have made it worse by evading the runners, but I could not tolerate the thought of wasting time in Newgate while Maria's killer is on the loose. More importantly, there is Fanny. They would have sent her to one of those dratted orphanages."

"Here, sir," Hughes turned and handed him a glass of brandy. "This always helps his lordship when he has serious thinking to do."

"Ah, Lucien's best brandy." Sherry grinned at the butler. "I am going to tell him you made me drink it."

"Very good, sir. Although I scarcely think it is the first time you have."

Sherry chuckled and took a long swallow. "Thank you again, Hughes. As you say, I have some thinking to do."

"Very good, sir." Hughes started for the door and stopped. "I assume you have written to Lord Ware."

"Yes, of course. I could use his cool head to help sort this out."

"And Lord Rothe?"

Hughes was aware of their intelligence work during their four years in the war and was just as familiar with their recent inquiries on behalf of the Prince Regent.

"I have not. I cannot ask for his help. My situation will be embarrassment enough with the runners chasing one of his agents."

Hughes cleared his throat. "I understand, sir, but perhaps a word of warning would not be amiss before Bow Street descends on him."

"Egad, you're right. Where is my head?" Sherry sighed. He was weary from his journey and apparently too distracted by recent events to be thinking with clarity. "I shall send him a note right away, but no one can know it came from this residence."

"I shall see to it and be discreet, sir."

Sherry stifled a yawn. He downed the rest of the brandy and stood, crossing to the desk. After writing the note, he handed it to Hughes. "I'm going to lie down for an hour or two before I drop to the floor."

"We shall endeavor not to disturb you, sir."

• • •

Sherry woke to the sound of fists pounding on the front door and morning sun streaming across the bed. *Bloody hell.* He had fallen asleep and slept all night. It sounded as though the runners had been busy and already found him. He bounded out of bed and threw on his robe.

Talbot met him at the bedchamber door. "Hughes will handle them, sir. Just you wait and see."

"They must not be allowed to take Fanny," Sherry said, alarmed despite Talbot's confident assurance. "If they push their way inside to search the house, can you get her away to safety?"

"Of course, sir, but such action will not be necessary." Talbot continued to be unruffled by events.

Sherry slipped into the hall to listen to the heated conversation at the entrance. Haskett was demanding entrance, and he had two constables with him.

"Give way, or we will force the door," Haskett blustered.

"I told you Lord Ware is not in residence," Hughes said equably. "He went to the country several days ago. If you need to speak with him and cannot await his return, you shall find him with the earl at Salcott Hall in Sussex."

"Is that so?" The runner sneered, but he sounded less certain at the reminder he was demanding entrance at the home of the Earl of Salcott's heir. Salcott's prominence and power in the House of Lords was not unknown, even to ordinary citizens and constables. "If you let us look around, we'll be on our way."

Hughes' voice grew implacable. "I am sorry, sir. I cannot allow it. His lordship would be most displeased if I were to allow strangers to tramp about his home in his absence. You must wait for his return."

"And just when would that be?"

"I cannot say with any certainty. Lord Ware's stay at the earldom is indefinite at present due to his grandmother's illness."

Sherry peeked through the railing. Hughes was looking down his nose at Haskett's booted foot planted in the doorway. "If you will kindly move your foot, sir, I shall inform his lordship of your desire to see him upon his return."

"I do not wish to see him," Haskett snarled. He tried to peer around Hughes. "I am here to take Andrew Sherbourne into custody."

"This is not the town residence of the Baron of Sherbourne's family," Hughes responded. "If you desire the correct address, I can give it to you."

Haskett's face darkened. "You think I haven't already been there? He is gone, making him a fugitive from justice. It is your duty as a citizen to assist us."

"Surely Lord Sherbourne's servants can give you his son's present direction."

Haskett snorted. "Said he'd gone to the country."

"Then I would look for him there. If he is not at the Sherbourne country home, perhaps you might inquire of him with Lord Ware at Salcott Hall."

Sherry choked back a laugh. Even Haskett would not be so bold. He would not dare confront the baron or the earl with his demands.

"Notify me the moment Lord Ware returns," Haskett snapped. With that churlish command, he acknowledged defeat and pulled back his foot.

Hughes shut and locked the door. Turning away, he dusted his hands together as though ridding himself of a pesky problem. He stopped at the foot of the stairs and looked up where Sherry and Talbot now stood and unbent his dignity long enough to say, "All is well, sir."

Chapter Eight

Sussex, October 1812

After two days of frantic activity, the dowager's household—without Barnes, the aging butler, who would be overseeing Dower House—was moved to Salcott Hall, and Cousin Cora arrived late on Friday morning. At first, the dowager treated the other woman with reserve, but they soon came together in their enthusiasm to claim the second parlor as their own private sitting room and to redecorate it with new furnishings. Delighted at this turn of events, Salcott told Lucien the cost of improvements was a small price to pay for such an easy transition.

By Saturday morning, feeling they an earned a day of jaunting around the countryside on horseback, Salcott collected a hunting party of like-minded neighbors, and father and son spent the better part of four hours chasing the hounds. Upon their return to Salcott Hall, they were dirty, tired, and hungry—and pleasantly satisfied.

The butler met them at the door and handed Lucien a letter. "This came while you were out, my lord."

Lucien glanced at the handwriting on the outside, and the smile on his face faded. Sherry? His friend was an indifferent correspondent. With a sense of foreboding, he unfolded and read the brief note. *Mr. Simon Grey's presence is urgently requested at his London residence.*

What the devil? At my home? Was Sherry staying at his townhouse? Something must be seriously wrong...something involving the War Office or more likely their shared past. Lucien had not gone by Simon Grey since his spying days in Paris.

"Bad news?" Salcott asked, studying his face.

"I'm not certain what is amiss, but I am needed in London immediately. I apologize for such an abrupt end to a pleasant stay, sir, but I must leave within the hour."

His father lifted a brow. "Do as you think best, my boy. Anything I should know as a member of Parliament?"

A year ago, before Salcott knew of Lucien and Sherry's past and present work for the War Office, he would have been offended by the sudden departure, assuming the summons was frivolous, an empty excuse for Lucien to get away from the estate. This was a promising change.

"Sherry's note is rather mysterious, but nothing indicates there is a threat against the country. If I learn differently, I shall, of course, send word. I must hurry, but I will say a proper goodbye to you and Grandmama before I leave." Lucien paused in the hall long enough to send word for his carriage to be brought around and then dashed upstairs.

After a swift wash up and change of clothes, he left a servant to finish packing his belongings and to take his bag to the coach. Descending the staircase, he located the dowager countess and Cousin Cora in their private parlor deciding on colors. He was relieved to discovered his grandmother was so absorbed in her new project that she didn't ask many questions about his sudden departure.

"It was delightful to see you," she said kissing his cheek. "I know there are other demands on your time, but do try to come back soon."

"I shall. I promise, my dear." He bowed over her hand with a grin. "I must return to see what the two of you do with this room."

Having taken leave of the ladies, Lucien headed for his father's study.

"A last drink?" Salcott offered as Lucien entered.

"Sorry, sir. I dare not delay. Sherry's message was urgent."

"Then I shall walk you out."

"I spoke with Grandmother," Lucien said. "She looks better already. There is a bit of pink in her cheeks."

The coach was waiting when they stepped outside. Lucien's red-haired groom stood at the heads of the frisky, snorting team of chestnuts. Lucien grinned at the small man. "They appear well rested, Finn."

"Aye, m'lord. It'll be a lively beginning to our trip."

Lucien nodded and turned to his father. "Well, sir. It is time."

"Safe journey, son. I hope it will not take another three years or a crisis to bring you again." Salcott cleared his throat. "I confess I am a bit embarrassed you had to sort out the situation with Mother. I should have been more attentive."

"Hardly your fault, sir. She was not at all forthcoming," Lucien reminded him. "The fact that I could help at all proves that you and the dowager are a less contrary combination than you and I." He swung up into the carriage.

Salcott's lips twitched. "Perhaps, but this time, we did not do so badly."

Lucien stuck his head back out before closing the door, nodded, and tipped his hat. "As you say, sir, and I shall not stay away so long."

Salcott's lips stretched into a smile. "Anytime, my boy. This is your home."

• • •

Lucien's carriage drew to a stop before his London townhouse late morning the following Monday. He had slept little on the return trip, mostly pondering Sherry's note, wondering what it meant. He had gone over in his head the people he'd known from his days as Simon Grey and the complications left unresolved due to their hasty flight from France.

With a mixture of curiosity and unease, he jumped down from the coach and strode toward the front entrance. The door swung open before Lucien had the opportunity to knock, and his butler greeted him with a bow. "Welcome, my lord. We are very glad to have you home."

"Thank you, Hughes. Is Sherry here?"

"He is, my lord. I believe you will find him on the third floor."

"The third—" A child's laughter interrupted his train of thought. He looked at Hughes. "Is that a child I hear?"

"It is," Hughes confirmed. "It believe it would be best if Sherbourne explained."

Lucien didn't stop to ask further questions but hurried up the staircase. Following the laughter, he was amazed to find Sherry sitting on the floor playing with a small female child of two or three. For a moment they didn't notice him, and he stood in the doorway dumbfounded by the sight. He had never thought of Sherry with children, but his partner appeared quite comfortable in the role.

"Well, I can see much has happened while I was away."

"Lucien, thank God you have finally arrived." Sherry leapt to his feet. "I, ah…may I introduce you to Miss Fanny Pembroke. Fanny, this is my good friend Viscount Ware."

Pembroke? Related to *Maria Pembroke?*

The infant with dark ringlets surrounding a pixie face scrambled to her feet and curtseyed charmingly. Her face was solemn, and her big eyes held a question.

Lucien smiled to reassure her and bowed in return. "I am honored to meet you, Miss Fanny."

She still appeared uncertain and looked at Sherry. "Does that mean he likes me?" she whispered.

"I think so," Sherry whispered back.

Fanny presented Lucien with a bright smile. "I like you too."

Lucien's smile broadened. What a charmer. "Thank you. I hope we will be great friends."

"Me too." With another grin, she plopped on the floor and picked up the doll she'd been playing with when he came in. "This is Betty."

Big button eyes seemed to stare at him. "I am honored to also welcome Miss Betty to my home."

Fanny gave him another smile and cuddled the doll.

"Welcome home, my lord," said a familiar voice from the corner of the room as his valet stepped forward.

"Ah, Talbot. I wondered where you were. Have you been attending our small visitor?"

"I have, but now that you are home—"

"You shall continue as you are. If you will excuse me, Miss Fanny, I must divest himself of all this dirt and then take Sherbourne away for a brief chat."

Fanny shrugged her small shoulders. "Talbot will play with me."

Lucien chuckled and turned to Sherry. "Give me twenty minutes. My study? I can hardly wait to hear what's taken place while I've been gone."

"It's been eventful for sure. I'll see you there."

Lucien wanted a bath, but it would have to wait. He was keen to know who Fanny was and why she and Sherbourne were living in his household. He splashed his face and hands with water, changed clothes, and smoothed his hair. When he arrived in the study, Sherry was lounging in a chair before the fire.

"You must have quite a tale to tell," Lucien said as he entered.

"I am sorry to impose in this way," Sherry said, straightening and spreading his hands in apology. "I didn't know where else to go."

"Nonsense." Lucien strode across the room to the sideboard. "No apology is needed. My house is yours whenever you need it. Allow me a moment to pour us a bit of brandy—assuming you have not emptied the cellar in my absence," he added with a grin, "and then tell me what has occurred."

"I think I left a bottle or two." Sherry's tone was equally good-humored, but the underlying tension said his heart was not in it.

"So?" Lucien prompted, when they were both settled.

"This will take a while."

"I have all day."

Lucien listened in silence as the story unfolded. In truth, he was too stunned to ask questions or offer helpful comments. Every time he thought he had heard the worst of it, Sherry made another startling revelation.

"That is the entire confounded story," Sherry concluded. "You are harboring a fugitive being sought by the Bow Street runners."

"Good to know." Of all the questions running through his head, Lucien started with those he considered most critical. "How and when did Maria die?"

"I believe the body was found last Wednesday morning, but I dared not leave your townhouse to discover the details and risk being taken up by the runners—not until I knew Fanny was safe. I have laid low waiting for you."

"It would not take much for the runners to learn of our friendship. Have they not been here?"

Sherry laughed. "Of course, they have, but Hughes ran them off. He can be quite formidable when he wants."

"I am aware." Lucien's smile faded to a worried frown. "Nonetheless, you will not be safe here for long. If Haskett is as tenacious as you say, he will be on our doorstep as soon as he knows I have returned. I can hold him off a day or two with haughty indignation, but eventually it will be obvious that I am denying him entrance for a reason, and he will return with a warrant."

Sherry nodded. "Yes, I will need to find safer accommodations, but I must stay free to hunt for Maria's killer because Haskett won't. He is so determined to arrest me that he is not looking for anyone else. However, Fanny's welfare comes first. I will not have her end up in an orphanage."

Lucien grew thoughtful. "If you plan to stay on the run and sleeping in some two-penny casual, you cannot take Fanny into such a place. We must find someone who will provide care for her, yet someone Bow Street would not suspect."

"Not my family or yours," Sherry said.

"Granted. Sophy might take her for a day or two," Lucien said, knowing what a tender heart his former mistress had. Even though he and the Widow Stine had parted romantically, they had remained close friends. "But we would have to move Fanny again. I cannot conceive that Sophy or her lady's maid could endure the demands of a child confined inside their house longer than that."

"I could send her to Emily in the country, but that would

require an explanation I am not able to give her, not until I know if Fanny is mine."

Lucien gave a short bark of laughter. "I'd hesitate too, my friend. Not only would you have to explain to the lady you are courting, but as she lives only a few miles from your family's country estate, she would be bound to talk with your mother."

"Egad, yes." Sherry looked horrified, then he flashed Lucien a rueful smile. "I hope they both would understand…but, uh, Fanny *is* a complication."

"What about Fanny's grandfather?"

"Too risky. Maria left Oxfordshire because she believed they were in danger from the Frenchman, and he knows where Hugh Pembroke lives. Besides, if she is mine, I want her raised within my family and to keep her safely under my protection. I can only do that if she is hidden close by; nor do I have time for another trip to Oxfordshire. I must track down Maria's killer, and time is not on my side. I've already lost too many days."

Lucien's throat tightened. Everything Sherry said was true…as were the words unspoken—he could not avoid the runners forever. Time was indeed limited.

They continued to discuss friends and acquaintances who might be suitable caretakers, rejecting each person for one reason or another.

"Have you talked over the situation with Rothe?" Lucien finally asked in frustration. "Maybe he could call off Bow Street."

"I forewarned him they might call upon him, but I cannot ask him to use his influence. It would weaken his standing with Bow Street, and I'll not place him in that awkward position."

"With due respect for your admirable feelings, Sherry, I'm running out of other ideas." If Lady Anne were here, Lucien thought, she would know what to do with a small child. He straightened. "What about Miss Barnett?"

"Lady Anne's friend? What would she know about raising a chit like Fanny?"

"She has the advantage over us of having been one, and if her parents agree to shelter the child at Barnett Park, I'm sure Mrs. Barnett would assist with Fanny's care. She is a very motherly lady, and we could hire a nanny to ease the burden."

"Actually, I had one," Sherry said, as he appeared to warm to the idea. "A young niece of my cook. Jane was good with Fanny, and I wager she'd be willing to go wherever we ask."

Lucien stood and stretched, still stiff from the long coach ride. "I think we have a plan. Do you wish to approach Miss Barnett on your own, or should we do it together?"

"You know her much better than I do. For such a huge request, I think I shall need your support."

"You shall have it. Since I am famished, a light meal is in order first, and then we can ride to Blinker's Marsh after mid-day."

• • •

Sir George Barnett gave them a warm welcome. It had been nearly four months since the three men had seen each other. When Lucien was investigating a missing woman in the neighborhood last summer, Lady Anne had urged her friend Margret Barnett to invite him to the Barnetts' house party. Before his inquiry was resolved, his partner Sherry and the entire Barnett family—including Captain Wycliff who was courting Margret—were involved in the events of a major crisis. During those critical days, the group had become rather close friends.

Lucien didn't delay long in raising the reason for their visit, and after a brief but pointed discussion, Sir George gave his approval for them to approach Miss Barnett and Lady Barnett with their request. Lucien and Sherry found the ladies in the family sitting room.

"I can vouch that she is a charming chit," Lucien assured them, after Sherry had presented his appeal and related part—but not all—of the story behind it.

"I am sure she is," Lady Barnett said with a smile. "We shall welcome her for as long as needed. Indeed, it will be delightful to have a young child in the house again. I confess I miss the days long past of pretend tea parties…and singing a small child to sleep."

"Now mama," Miss Barnett said with a smile. "Don't get all sentimental on us."

Lady Barnett blushed. "Shush, my dear. You will understand one day when you have your own babes." She turned a motherly eye on Sherry. "I am truly sorry for your troubles, sir. I hope they will be settled soon."

"As do I," he said. "I cannot thank you enough, ma'am. It will lift a burden from my mind to know Fanny is in your care. I am most anxious to get her to safety, and if today is not too soon, I shall return with her and Nanny Jane within three to four hours."

Lady Barnett's smile widened. "Oh, my, well, yes. That would be perfect. I shall have just enough time to prepare the nursery."

"If it matters, I promise to do my part too," Miss Barnett said with a laugh.

Satisfied with the results of their visit, Lucien and Sherry left the Barnett estate and returned to London, riding through the village of Blinkers Marsh. A few of the villagers recognized them from last summer and waved. It was a friendly place, a perfect shelter for Fanny.

Her placement, however, had not come without a price. Although they had kept their explanations brief to the ladies, they had given Sir George the whole bloody story. He was shocked at events to be sure, and he disapproved of Sherry evading the runners, but in the end he conceded that Lucien and Sherry had the better chance of solving the murder. They were certainly more motivated.

Nonetheless, Sir George had wrested a promise from Sherry— should the matter remain unresolved at the end of two weeks from now, he would turn himself over to authorities.

Lucien was determined it would not come to that.

Chapter Nine

While Sherry was escorting Fanny and Nanny Jane to the Barnetts, Lucien paid a visit to the Whitehall War Offices. Mr. Sloane, the Marquess of Rothe's private secretary announced Lucien, and Lord Rothe stepped into the outer office, which housed the clerks and under-ministers, to meet him.

"Ware, how was your trip to Sussex? I trust the earl is in good health."

Lucien assumed Rothe's uncharacteristic effusive greeting was for the benefit of the office staff, a pretense that nothing was amiss—as though they could keep Sherry's situation quiet. "Yes, sir. He is very well."

"And your grandmother? I understand she was ailing."

"I found her better than expected, sir."

"Good, good." Rothe ushered him into his office, closed the door, and turned with a scowl. "What nonsense is going on with Sherbourne? I knew he talked with Sloane about Maria Pembroke, then I heard she was dead, and now Bow Street is looking to arrest him for her murder."

"That is the crux of it, sir. Of course, he didn't do it, but I am concerned the Bow Street runner in charge has no interest in evidence or finding the *right* man as long as he arrests someone."

"Hmm, yes. Haskett is good at hauling in rascals and cutthroats, but this…well, he is convinced of Sherbourne's guilt. So, what are you doing about it?"

"Frankly, not much yet. I arrived in town yesterday, and we spent this morning finding a secure place for Maria's young daughter."

Rothe returned to his desk and seated himself. As was his habit, the marquess's tall, slender figure was attired in gray, matching the streaks in his dark hair and his steely gaze. He arched an elegant brow. "Ah, yes, Haskett mentioned a child. Is Sherbourne the father?"

"He cannot say for certain."

Rothe nodded. "Tell me the whole of it. If I can offer assistance without openly thwarting Bow Street, you know I will."

It was precisely what Lucien had hoped to hear. Although Sherry disapproved of involving Rothe, they needed the details of the woman's death and what facts Bow Street had gathered if they were to launch their own inquiry. He hoped Rothe could get those details, and consequently, Lucian related the salient events of the past few days.

"We need basic information," he said when finished. "Where she had been living, where she died, the cause of death. Otherwise, we shall be hard pressed to prove Sherry could not have done this."

Rothe grimaced. "You must do better than that—you'll have to catch the murderer." He picked up a paper and pushed it across the desk to Lucien. "Haskett's report is sparce, but it does include where and how. As far as I know, they have not recovered the murder weapon or located a witness to her death."

Lucien picked up the report. "I am grateful, sir, as Sherry will be."

Rothe cleared his throat. "The sooner you resolve this, the better. These accusations against Sherbourne—and his eluding Bow Street—have, well…they put me in a rather untenable position."

"We know that, sir. Sherry did not approach you for that very reason, and he won't be best pleased that I did."

Rothe smiled. "You're a good friend for a man to have, Ware. Keep me informed as you can. If I learn anything else of importance, I shall find a way to get it to you."

• • •

Lucien was in his study that evening reviewing the Bow Street report for perhaps the fifth or sixth time. He had just removed his coat and cravat when Sherry walked in. His partner was smiling and reported Fanny had been giggling and romping with one of Barnett's hounds when he'd left Blinker's Marsh.

"I am mightily relieved," Sherry added, plopping into a chair. "What are you reading?"

"Haskett's official report on Maria's death."

Sherry shot upright. "What? How did you get a hold of it?"

"A visit to Rothe. He was quite sympathetic, I might add."

"I told you to leave him out of it, did I not?" Sherbourne growled, but his eyes were on the paper in Lucien's hand. "What does it say?"

"Maria's body was found early Wednesday morning—while you were in Oxfordshire—in an alley behind her boarding house. She'd been stabbed twice in the back, possibly as early as Tuesday morning. When did you leave London?"

"Tuesday, late morning," Sherry said morosely. "I suppose I would have had time to do it…but not to hide the body. I swear I did *not* kill her."

Lucien frowned at him. "Good lord, Sherry. You don't have to convince me. Did you think I doubted you?"

"Well, no. I suppose not, but—"

"But nothing. Nor can we waste time worrying over what Haskett thinks. The report does not give the doctor's name, but I suspect it was Noah Pettigrew who examined her. He is a favorite with Rothe and many in the constabulary. We need more exact information on when she died—and the murder weapon." Lucien nodded in tune with his thoughts. "The landlady, a Mrs. Martha Doud, must be questioned, and I shall do that one alone."

"The devil you will. She is pointing the finger at me, and I want to know why."

"Of course, you do, but consider the situation. How likely is she to talk with the man she says is a murderer? Would she not go running to Bow Street the moment you approached her?"

Sherry firmed his lips and said nothing.

Lucien eyed his friend. "We cannot behave as though this is a normal inquiry. You have to stay out of sight if we are to keep Bow Street at bay and you out of gaol."

After a moment, Sherry muttered, "I know that, but it doesn't make my idleness any easier."

Considering less said the better, Lucien returned to the content of Haskett's report. "Without the murder weapon or witnesses, he has little real evidence against you. That will not stop him—he seems not to care—but it gives us specific things to look for." He rose, yawning. "I'm for bed. We have a long day tomorrow, starting with Doc Pettigrew."

• • •

Noah Joseph Pettigrew was an educated physician. Nonetheless, having gained much of his experience on the battlefield, he set broken bones, bandaged injuries, and provided all the hands-on treatment for his patients that was usually left to the less-learned surgeons. He was a modest man despite his aristocratic origins and maintained a practice available to rich and poor alike, including indigent women needing care beyond the skills of a midwife. Lucien had first met him examining a corpse in a dark alley at the behest of Lord Rothe. More recently, Pettigrew had assisted Lucien's inquiry regarding a missing woman.

Lucien and Sherry found the young doctor helping his apprentice restock his medicine shelves. He looked up and came toward them with a smile. "Lord Ware, a visit from you is always of great interest. Shall we retire to my office?"

As soon as they were inside, Pettigrew closed the door and turned to his guests. "Since you appear uninjured, my lord, I assume you are hoping to hear my findings on Maria Pembroke."

Lucien was taken aback. "How did you know?"

"Lord Rothe. He sent word you might be calling." He glanced at Sherbourne and back to Lucien. "I'd prefer that you do not introduce your companion. What I do not know for certain, I cannot be expected to report."

Lucien smiled. "What companion?"

"Just so," Pettigrew agreed.

Sherry tipped his head to him as the doctor took a seat behind his desk; Lucien and Sherry settled on visitor chairs.

Lucien leaned forward. "What can you tell us about her death? I understand she was stabbed twice."

"Slashed and stabbed," the doctor corrected. "She was attacked from behind by what I believe was a sword or rapier. There are no defensive wounds. I suspect she did not see her attacker and thus had no opportunity to fight back. The killing thrust was done with considerable force."

"By a man?" Lucien asked for clarification.

"Yes. Or a strong female, although it would be an unusual weapon for a woman."

Not to say rather noticeable to carry about, Lucien added to himself. Where could the murder have occurred that the killer would have a sword handy? No gentleman or even military man would carry one into society except on special occasions—it was not good ton.

"Did she die in the alley?" Sherry asked. "Perhaps ambushed on her way home?"

"Good question, my friend. I found little blood on the ground around her, where I would have expected much more. So, I'd say no. She died elsewhere."

"Time of death?" Lucien asked.

"Not easy to determine. Nights have been cool recently, so I cannot be more specific than eight to eighteen hours before I saw her."

"So, she might have been killed as early as mid-day Tuesday and dumped that night or early the next morning," Lucien said.

"It is certainly possible. She was definitely dead by midnight," he added.

Lucien and Sherry looked at one another.

"I take it that is not what you wanted to hear," Pettigrew said.

Lucien shrugged. "I always want the truth, but the time span goes back too far to be help to us."

It did not exonerate Sherry. Given Albert Haskett's belief in Sherry's guilt, the runner would ignore the more likely possibility she died during the evening. Instead, he would cling to the argument that Sherry had killed Maria before fleeing town late Tuesday morning and that an accomplice had disposed of the body.

• • •

After leaving the doctor's office, Lucien held a brief argument with Sherry.

"I was confident of Pettigrew's silence, but you cannot continue to work out in the open," he insisted. "I intend to poke around the alley where Maria was found, visit her lodgings, and question the landlady. As we discussed before, Mrs. Doud is likely to be hostile or even hysterical if confronted by the man she believes is a killer."

"Do you always have to be right?" Sherry muttered. "I'm no good sitting at home and waiting."

"Spend your time sorting out how we can find the Frenchman."

"I suppose I can do that." Although his agreement was grudging, Sherry got out of the carriage at the rear of Lucien's townhouse and slipped inside the servants' entrance.

Once Sherry was safely inside, Lucien drove across town to Gerrard Street.

The Doud boarding house—one of the tall, thin row of structures crowding the street—stood in what was considered a middling location just off the east end of Piccadilly and was popular with tradesmen. The structure could use a new coat of paint but was in reasonable condition.

Lucien circled his curricle to the narrow alley tucked between the row houses that faced Gerrard and those facing King Street. It was more a path really, inaccessible by coach and horse-drawn wagons.

Doc Pettigrew seemed certain the body had been dumped there, so how had it been moved? Surely someone had not carried her that far.

Lucien left Finn with the horses and entered the pathway on foot. Street lights would not penetrate the alley at night, he decided. Nor much moonlight either, he noted, glancing up at the canopy of trees overhead. Anyone moving a body would have wanted a lantern, but would they have risked being seen?

He doubted it, and to his knowledge, no one had observed such activity. He'd have to make inquiries for witnesses at every house on Gerrard and King Streets. Even if the constables had bothered to ask around, the general resentment toward thief takers—who'd often arrested anyone handy just for the reward money—had carried over to the runners. Citizen trust just was not there, and they might have lied to get rid of them. Of course, that didn't mean residents would talk to Lucien either—given the normal aversion to getting involved with murder.

He walked the length of the alley and back again. Rocks, weeds, sticks, and leaves lay next to the fence line, but he failed to spot any blood or a discarded weapon. Nor did he meet anyone who could tell him what happened the night Maria died. In truth, he hadn't expected to find evidence the constabulary had missed, but walking the scene gave him a feel for the place.

A movement caught the corner of his eye, and he slowly turned. A tiny, white-haired woman sat in the rear garden of a house on King Street. He doubted she had been there when he'd walked past fifteen minutes ago, although she did blend into the shadows of a large shade tree. She was well-dressed; if not precisely fashionable, her clothes were expensive and made by a proficient seamstress. She held a book in her hand, and spectacles gave her a big-eyed appearance.

He felt a moment of surprise when she lay the book and reading glasses in her lap and gestured for him to come to the fence. He approached and doffed his hat. "Good day, madam."

"And to you, sir. I noticed from the back windows of the house that you appeared to be searching for something. Is this by any chance about the murdered woman?" Her eyes sharpened with interest. "You do not look like a journalist or the police."

"Viscount Ware, ma'am. I was acquainted with the victim."

"Miss Amelia Farnham," she returned with a sparkling smile, then she sighed. "My sympathy, sir. What a horrible thing to happen"

"Indeed. Did you know Miss Pembroke?" he asked.

"Oh, no, but I saw her and her child now and then. We waved and smiled, but never had a proper conversation. What has happened to the little girl?"

"She is safe and well-cared for by family friends. She also has other family who very much want her."

"I am so relieved. It is a dreadful thing for a child to lose her mother." Miss Amelia sighed and leaned toward him, lowering her voice. "I almost saw the killer, you know."

Lucien's interest spiked. "How frightening for you. How did this happen?"

She looked around furtively and whispered, "W-e-ll, I heard him. They say she was murdered somewhere else and brought to our alley. I heard the cart wheels. The sound woke me that night— thump, thump, thump, the sound of a wheel turning that was loose or had a chip in it—but I was too tired to get out of bed to look. If I had only known." She pointed a finger behind Lucien. "The next morning, I saw the constables. Dumped the poor woman right there, he did."

Lucien turned to examine a spot next to the fence directly behind the Doud lodging house. He noted a few scuff marks in the leaves, probably left by the constables, but nothing else. The killer clearly had known where Maria lived, and for some reason, he had brought her home. Had he wanted her body found—and identified? Or was it done merely to get her away from where she had died?

He turned back to Miss Amelia. "Do you know what time you heard it?"

"Let me think. I had quite a bit of trouble getting back to sleep. I must have sensed something was wrong." She hunched her shoulders and shivered before she spoke again. "I lay there a while before the hall clock chimed two. So, he must have been out here about a quarter before the hour." She tilted her head at him. "Are you looking into her death on your own?"

"Just poking around a bit. This path is pretty narrow for a cart and horse."

"Oh, there was no horse," she said decisively. "I heard a garden cart or barrow, bumping along with an uneven wheel."

Lucien furrowed his brow. No one would push a body a great distance in such a conveyance. Had the killer known he would need a cart and brought it in a coach with the body, or was the cart stolen from a neighbor when the killer realized his coach could go no further? Unless Maria was killed in the neighborhood, and the murderer used his own gardening cart.

"Oh, dear, my nurse Beatrice is coming for me. She makes me take naps," Miss Amelia said, as a middle-aged woman came out of her house. "I hope you find him," she whispered in an obvious attempt to keep Beatrice from hearing their conversation.

"One last thing," he said while the nurse was still at some distance, "did you tell the police what you heard?"

"Certainly not. I would not converse with the likes of them, but you seem such a nice, well-bred young man."

Lucien smiled and made a bow just as Beatrice arrived. "Thank you, Miss Amelia. I've been honored to meet you. Enjoy your book, and have a wonderful day." He continued down the alley as Miss Amelia picked up her cane. He glanced back to see the two women moving slowly toward the house.

Miss Amelia had given him two important pieces of information: the approximate time the body had been deposited in the alley and that the likely conveyance used was a garden hand cart with a distinctive sound pattern. A search for the cart might lead to the murderer or at least to the place where Maria died.

Lucien returned to his curricle and took the reins from Finn.

"Any luck, gov?"

"Some." He told him about the cart as he drove around the corner and stopped in front of the Doud boarding house on Gerrard Street. "Now for the landlady. Wait here."

He entered the front door and located Mrs. Doud's rooms on the first floor. Her door swung open before he knocked, and a large woman with suspicion written across her rather angular face scowled at him. "What do you want? I saw your fancy curricle and toadeater, so I'm pretty sure you're not looking for a room."

Lucien stifled an immediate distaste for this ill-bred, snippy woman and produced a smile with difficulty. "Mrs. Martha Doud? I am Viscount Ware. May I have a moment of your time?"

"I'm Mrs. Doud all right, but what do you want with me? If you are one of the busybodies meddling in a murder that don't concern them, you can be on your way."

"I was a friend of Maria Pembroke."

"Oh, yes?" Her voice bristled with disbelief. "Then you should know she no longer lives here. She was murdered, and I cannot tell you a thing about it."

"May I step inside?"

"What needs to be said can be said out here." Her tall, sturdy frame filled the doorway, blocking his entrance.

"Very well. I hoped you could answer a few questions about Maria. I wasn't aware she had moved to London. How long had she been with you?"

"If you're the friend you claim to be, why don't you know?"

"We lost touch after she left Oxfordshire about six months ago. I very much would like to know what happened to her since that time." He lifted a brow and looked at her steadily until she gave a sniff of resignation.

"Can't say there is much to know. She'd been a lodger since late April—she and that child of hers. Quiet, stayed at home most nights. She still owes a week's rent, claimed she hadn't been paid yet."

"How much are you owed?" he asked, thinking money might loosen her tongue. When she stated a reasonable sum, he reached into his pocket. "I'll pay it, if you'll answer a few more questions."

Greed flashed through her eyes, and she nodded. When Lucien placed the required coins in her hand, she stared at them as though she wished she'd stated a larger amount, and then stuffed them in her pocket. "Tell me again, why you are asking about her?"

"I thought it might help me—and her family—to accept her loss, if we knew how she spent her last few months."

Martha Doud shrugged. "Can't see how it will help, but don't dawdle, ask what you want. I have other things to do."

"Did she have many visitors? Perhaps friends she saw regularly?"

"None I recall. Maria kept to herself, like I said, just her and Fanny. I watched the chit for her during the day."

"While she was working, you mean?"

"That's right."

"Where was she employed?"

She hesitated a moment. "With the Edingtons on Brewer Street. Maria looked after Mr. Edington's elderly mother."

Brewer was not far away, well within the distance of a brisk, ten-minute walk.

"You seem an observant woman, Mrs. Doud. Was anything bothering Maria those last few days? Was she fearful? Had anyone given her trouble, threatened her?"

She shook her head, and her face grew pinched and wary again. "Why would you ask that? The constables know who killed her. 'Twas that Sherbourne fellow. Maria went over there to take him his by-blow that morning. They must have argued over whether he was going to do his duty and pay up what was required."

"She told you Sherbourne was the father and that she intended to ask him for money?"

"Why else would she be taking Fanny to him? Besides, she needed the funds to settle up with me."

"But did she say so?" he persisted.

"I told you, it was obvious."

"Yes, I see," Lucien said, knowing he was losing her. "Before I go, may I take a look at Miss Pembroke's room?"

"Absolutely not. It has been cleared out, and I have a new tenant. He would not wish to be disturbed. Now, if that is all..."

"What about her belongings?"

"Police took them." She closed the door before Lucien could ask anything else.

He frowned and returned to the curricle. It was doubtful the police had taken Maria's things; more likely the landlady had sold them. His first impression of her had born out—an unpleasant, sharp-tongued woman. While most of her language was that of one bred into a middle-class family, her attitude verged on the vulgar.

Nonetheless, he had collected another fact he hadn't known before—the name of Maria's employer.

Chapter Ten

Lucien stood on the far side of the cobblestone road designated as Brewer Street and studied the house where Maria had worked. The Edington residence was substantial in size, but the family had suffered a visible setback in fortune. The three-story building had a bay window in front, intricate wrought iron fencing, beautiful stained glass over the door, but the roof needed repair, the second story had a cracked window, and the cream paint on the front door was turning yellow.

He crossed the street and knocked on the door. When a footman answered, Lucien handed him his engraved card. "Good day. Viscount Ware to see Mr. Edington."

The footman straightened upon hearing Lucien's title. "If you will wait in the parlor, my lord, I shall see if he is available."

Lucien stepped inside, and the servant took his hat before hurrying away to locate his master. Looking around the parlor, Lucien spotted signs of neglect similar to those he had noted outside—good rugs with worn spots, same with the upholstered chairs, and heavy drapes several years out of date.

"Lord Ware," a feminine voice spoke from behind him, "my husband is not at home. Perhaps I can help you. I am Olivia Edington."

Lucien turned and bowed as a slender woman, a bit taller than average, entered the room and moved gracefully toward him. A heavy perfume tickled his nose. "A pleasure to meet you, Mrs. Edington. In truth, you may be the more appropriate person with whom to speak."

She arched her eyebrows. "Now you have made me curious. Shall we step into the drawing room? I have ordered a fresh tea tray." She turned and walked briskly across the hall to a large room with better furnishings. Any household improvements in the past few years had clearly been done in there. The room was light and airy, done in cream and a pale green. Mrs. Edington sat in one of the chairs in a four-chair grouping near the bay window with a view of Brewer Street. Lucien sat opposite her.

"I was sitting by the window and observed your arrival, my lord. You are a careful man." Her voice held a question.

She had obviously seen him studying her house. He smiled and offered an explanation. "I was debating how to approach someone I did not know and ask them about a murdered member of their household."

The woman's face tightened. "Miss Pembroke. A disgraceful affair."

"Most distressing. I am an old acquaintance of hers but had not been aware she was in London until I heard of her death. I understand from Mrs. Doud that she had been working for you."

"You spoke to Martha? Well, yes, I suppose you would. It is true…Maria worked for us the past five or six months. She served as companion to my husband's aging mother."

"But she was not living in the house?" he said acting puzzled.

"Mother Edith can do for herself with her maid's assistance, she just needed companionship during the day, and Miss Pembroke, being an unmarried woman with a small child, well… I am sure you understand I could not allow them to live in our household."

"If you felt that way, I am surprised you hired her."

"Mother Edith insisted. Heaven knows why, but she was drawn to the woman during the interview, before we knew her circumstances." Mrs. Edington sniffed. "I guess Maria's murder has once again sadly proven her true nature. I can only image what she must have done to provoke such violence."

Lucien bit back a sharp retort. "Had Miss Pembroke acted afraid or worried those last few weeks?"

"Not at all. She was the same as always, a rather withdrawn young woman. I did not see her appeal, but due to Mother Edith's uncommon attachment to her, I fear we shall have trouble finding a new companion she will accept." She shook her head in obvious annoyance. "I do not mean to seem unfeeling, but her death has been most inconvenient."

More so for Maria, Lucien thought. Interesting how Olivia Edington could overlook Maria's presumed failings as long as it was useful to her.

"Did anyone come to see her? Friends, acquaintances, a young man, perhaps?"

At a sudden rattle of a side door latch, Mrs. Edington's head swiveled in that direction, and Lucien turned to see a stooped, white-haired woman with a cane.

"Ah, Mother Edith. Do join us." Olivia said. "You can help me answer Lord Ware's questions. My lord, this is my mother-in-law, Mrs. Edith Edington."

"Eh, how is that? What questions?" The elderly woman leaned heavily on the stout, wooden cane, her boney fingers gnarled from inflammation of the joints, as she shuffled slowly toward them. Despite her obvious frailty, her eyes were bright with interest.

"Dear Mother Edith, you should have called a maid to help you." Olivia Edington frowned at her mother-in-law but made no move to lend a hand.

Lucien rose and crossed the room to assist her.

"I miss Maria," the old woman said querulously, staring at her son's wife. "She was so helpful." She looked up at Lucien as he offered his arm. "Who did she say you are, young man?"

"Viscount Ware. May I escort you to your chair?"

She returned his smile with a coquettish look. "Of course, you may. Thank you."

When she was settled, Olivia Edington told her why Lucien had called. "He is asking about Maria's friends. Did she mention anyone to you?"

The older woman shook her head. "Not anyone in London. She talked mostly of Fanny and sometimes mentioned Martha— Martha Doud. She watched the child during the day, but Maria didn't like her much." When Olivia cleared her throat, Mother Edith went on, "Otherwise, it was always family or friends back home, her father and an older brother, I believe."

"Did she mention Andrew Sherbourne?" he asked.

"I don't believe she did."

Olivia Edington's head whirled to stare at him. "That is the man the runners say killed her, is it not?"

"Is it?" Lucien said vaguely. "I have not yet spoken with Bow Street." He shrugged off the question and returned to his conversation with Mother Edith. "Was Maria happy here?"

"Oh, we got along very well, if that is what you mean."

"I am certain you did," Lucien said with a smile. "I was thinking in more general terms about her move to London. She was a country girl."

Mother Edith pursed her lips in thought. "I would not say she was unhappy, but she missed Oxfordshire. And like I said before, she fretted over leaving Fanny with Martha."

"Now Mother Edith, "Olivia Edington protested. "Why would you say that?"

"Well, it's true, but she did not have much choice, did she?" Her gaze flicked to her daughter-in-law and back to Lucien.

"She was lucky to have Martha." The younger woman sniffed, making a sour face, and closed her lips firmly.

Lucien watched the interaction with interest. Such underlying animosity. What might Mother Edith tell him if they were alone?

He gave the elderly woman a sympathetic smile. "Tell me about the day Miss Pembroke died. Did she say or do anything you considered unusual?"

Mother Edith shook her head. "She wasn't here. Maria had taken off several days to hunt for more suitable lodgings and child care."

Lucien lifted a brow at Olivia. "You hadn't mentioned this."

"I assumed you knew. I'm sure we told the constables."

Perhaps, but oddly enough, Mrs. Doud had also failed to mention it. Had she hoped to conceal the fact that Maria was unhappy with her, or did she not know? Another interesting detail, but was it relevant?

"Did she actually say she was dissatisfied with the boarding house or could something else have been bothering her?" he asked.

Olivia shook her head. "I'm sure she never said that. It must be some oddity Mother Edith got into her head. Maria acted perfectly happy with her lodgings, and I should hope she was grateful that Martha was willing to watch such a chit. Not everyone would, you know." She flipped the edge of the handkerchief she held as though to emphasis her point. "Maria did not tell me why she needed the week off, and I did not ask. She said something about important matters. I only agreed to allow it because Mother Edith was worried Maria might quit otherwise. I regret the indulgence now. If Maria had been working that day rather than getting into whatever trouble she was in, well ... we would not be having this unpleasant conversation." Upon that note, Olivia stood, ending the visit, and Lucien excused himself.

As he walked toward the front door, he heard male voices coming from behind a closed door he assumed was a study or library. It sounded as though Mr. Edington was at home after all. Lucien strained to hear what they were saying, but the sound was too muffled, and he could hardly stop to press his ear against the door with the footman watching. He walked on by as though he'd heard nothing of consequence—but he was intrigued.

Why had Mrs. Edington chosen to lie rather than simply admit her husband was engaged with a prior caller? Very odd behavior— socially bad form, and so unnecessary that it roused his suspicion. Whom or what were the Edingtons so determined to conceal?

Collecting his hat and cane, Lucien exited the house, climbed into the curricle, and drove around the corner before stopping again. He hopped down and handed the reins to Finn.

"Someone was visiting the Edington house while I was there, and they went to some pains to deny it. I am going back to see who leaves. It should not be long."

"Aye, gov. The horses is getting' restless, so we'll take a short jaunt if ye donna mind and come right back."

"All the better."

Finn grinned and flicked the reins.

Lucien smiled at his groom's obvious pleasure in driving the big bays. Since Lucien frequently chose to drive himself, Finn didn't often get the opportunity.

Walking back to Gerrard Street, Lucien strolled slowly until he could see the front of the Edingtons' house, and then he leaned against the trunk of a large tree, as though he was waiting for someone to join him. Ten minutes later, a man emerged from the residence and walked in the opposite direction, away from Lucien.

Bloody hell. His mind spinning with the possibilities, Lucien swiftly returned to his waiting curricle. He had not needed a second look to recognize Reginald, the house manager of Cade's Gentlemen's Club and close associate of its owner, Charles Cade, the crime lord known throughout London as the Gentleman Thief.

A troublesome development. Lucien gritted his teeth and leapt aboard the small carriage, urging the horses into a trot. Why the devil did Cade keep showing up in his life?

While Mr. Cade's history was shadowy, he was believed to have been a street urchin—and possible by-blow of a titled gentleman—who rose to power as a ruthless leader in London's underworld. And yet, his claimed heritage, his fashionable attire, and his impeccable manners had afforded him grudging acceptance by Society—not the high sticklers, of course, but most everyone else.

Lucien had neither met the man nor visited his club until the hunt for a spy last winter had brought them into conflict. Despite frequent clashes during that inquiry and a second, subsequent investigation, the two men had formed a wary tolerance due to their mutual loyalty to England. That certainly did not mean Lucien wished to pursue the acquaintance. Nor did he consider Cade a good man. Reginald's visit to Nigel Edington implied that things were seriously amiss in that household.

The bigger question, of course, was whether it had anything to do with Maria's murder.

• • •

Sherry met Lucien in the front hallway upon his return to Hays Mews. "What took you so long? You've been gone for hours."

"One thing led to another," Lucien said, heading into his study. "Port or brandy?"

Sherry waved a casual hand. "Whatever you're having. Tell me what you've learned."

"Patience, my friend. It has been a long day."

Lucien poured two glasses of port and sank into a chair before the fire. He took a long swallow, then began, "I started at the alley where Maria's body was found." Relating things in the order they happened, he covered the day's activities and discoveries, including the witness who heard a cart in the alley and the landlady's sour attitude. "Doud might be hiding something or just be a disagreeable woman. Hard to say, but from there, I went to see Maria's employer." He described his conversation with Olivia Edington and Mother Edith, leaving the best part to last. "As I left the house, I was sure I heard Mr. Edington speaking with another man in the study. Curious who he was, I waited outside. Imagine my surprise to see Mr. Cade's man, Reginald, walk out the front door."

"Egad." Sherry shot up straight in his chair. "Did Cade order Maria's murder? How would she get entangled with him?"

"We don't know that she was." Lucien shrugged. "Given Cade's abhorrence of violence toward women and children, it seems unlikely he had anything to do with her death…but I don't like finding Reginald at the home of her employer. At the very least, it raises questions about the Edingtons and what they have been doing that drew Reginald's attention."

Sherry's eyes widened. "You're not going to ask Cade, are you? No matter how helpful he has been in the past, you have also been kidnapped and shot for what he perceived as interfering in his business. I would rather not pull my partner's body out of the Thames."

"More likely you would never find it, and I must correct you— the shooting was accidental," Lucien said. "But no, I see no reason to approach Cade, not unless we unearth a motive for him to have ordered Maria's death. However, I cannot promise Cade will not demand to see me. I imagine he already knows I have been to visit the Edingtons."

Sherry swore under his breath, slumping back in his chair. "You are probably right about that. *Bloody cit.*"

"Bite your tongue. The man has a family crest on his coach."

Sherry snorted.

"In any event, it might not be a bad thing if he wants to chat. It would give me an opportunity to ask about Reginald. Nonetheless, forget Cade for now," Lucien said. "He'll do whatever he wants. Let us discuss what *we* need to do."

For more than an hour, they went over the various lines of inquiry that needed to be followed. At times the conversation grew heated. Sherry wanted to be part of every inquiry; Lucien wanted him to remain in hiding at Hays Mews or another secret location. Sherry finally gave in and agreed to stay off the streets, confining his role to chasing down information on the Frenchman, mostly by mail or courier.

Clearly chaffing at the restrictions, Sherry leapt to his feet and stalked to the study door. "I'm going to ask about the mail...again."

"Sherry..."

"Oh, don't worry, Lucien. I am not planning to do anything stupid."

Lucien stood and stared after him. When all he heard were murmured voices and then his partner's boots on the stairs, he sighed, shaking his head. He understood Sherry wasn't angry with him, and he didn't take his sour mood personally. It still worried him that Sherry was so overwrought and impatient. Just one impulsive act could lead to disaster.

When an hour past and Sherry had not returned to the study, Lucien sought reassurance from Hughes that Sherry had not gone out. Learning he was in his room, Lucien left him alone to come to terms with the situation.

• • •

Early that evening a courier arrived for Sherry. A half hour later he came downstairs with his equanimity restored.

Lucien handed him a glass of port while they waited for dinner to be announced. "I heard a courier was here. Good news?"

"Yes, from Mr. Sloane. I'll be leaving town for a couple of days."

Lucien arched a brow. "To where?"

"Hertford. Do you remember Pierre Leflore and his wife Yvette?"

"The names are vaguely familiar."

"Should be. They worked with me in France in the four months you were on assignment in Spain."

"Oh, yes. Now I recall. What about them?"

"Sloane has located the LeFlores living here in England. They stayed in Paris a few weeks after we escaped, and I'm hopeful they heard about the French officer Maria killed. If they can tell me his surname, it would be a tremendous help in the search for his brother. As Pierre is a cautious man, he is more likely to talk with me in person than answer questions in a letter. I leave for Hertfordshire early in the morning."

"That *is* good news," Lucien said, grinning at him. "Not only about the LeFlores, but I cannot deny it will be a relief to have you out of London and beyond Haskett's easy reach."

"Short-lived relief, I'm afraid. I should not be away more than two or three days, back on Friday at the latest."

"Nonetheless, it gives me time to make inquiries without worrying about you, my friend. Perhaps I will have news of my own when you return." Lucien smiled and lifted his glass. "Tonight, however, I am to attend a musical soiree where I should see Miss Barnett and discover how Fanny has settled." Hopefully a good report on the child would relieve some of Sherry's anxiety. By meeting Miss Barnett casually at a social event, he should avoid drawing Bow Street's attention to the Barnett family and exposing them to Albert Haskett. While Sir George was more than capable of putting a flea in the runner's ear, Lucien wanted to spare the family from that necessity.

• • •

The moment Lucien walked into the soiree, Miss Barnett came over with Captain Wycliff on her arm as though she had been watching for him. "Lord Ware," she whispered in a hiss, "is it true Bow Street is about to arrest Lord Sherry for *murder*? You did not tell us that."

"Good evening, Miss Barnett." Lucien gave a deliberately languid sigh. "I see the gossipmongers have been busy. While he is a suspect, I assume you know he is innocent. They are wasting their time on the wrong person while a murderer goes free."

"Well, yes, of course." She acted slightly taken aback by his manner and looked around again before lowering her voice to ask, "Did he know the dead woman?"

"Margret, my darling," Wycliff said quietly, "if you must quiz Lord Ware, this is not the place."

"Then where?" she demanded. She turned to Lucien, her eyes narrowing. "Surely you agree my family has a right to know what is happening."

Lucien kept his voice down and met Miss Barnett's inquisitive eyes. "Your father knows everything, and Wycliff is correct, I cannot discuss it here."

"Then let us stroll in the garden," she suggested. "It is not too chilly, and I could use a breath of air. Captain, if you would get my shawl?"

Wycliff looked at Lucien and shrugged. Knowing she would persist even in the crowded drawing room, Lucien gave a nod. The shawl—a dainty, pink piece of fluff not intended to actually provide warmth—was retrieved, and they stepped outside.

Miss Barnett turned to him. "Well? Tell me what this is all about."

Lucien kept it brief. "Sherry and I knew Maria Pembroke three years ago in France. We hadn't seen her again until she showed up at his home with Fanny. While Sherry was out of the room, Maria slipped away, leaving Fanny behind. Sherry left town the next day to find her family in Oxfordshire, and upon his return, a runner told him Maria was dead and accused him of killing her."

Miss Barnett's face scrunched up in disbelief. "Why him? What reason would he have? Did he not explain he was out of town?"

"Slow down, Miss Barnett," Lucien urged. "I can only answer one question at a time. Sherbourne *did* tell them he'd been away, but their theory is he killed Maria *and* Fanny because he couldn't face the responsibility of a love child, and then he fled town."

Miss Barnett's gaped at him, and she latched onto the part she knew was false. "But Fanny is not dead."

"Yes, well, they do not know that. Sherry denied knowing anything about Fanny for fear they would remove her and place her in an orphanage. His denial led to Haskett's wild conclusion."

"What a pother." Miss Barnett stamped her foot in annoyance. "So, is Fanny truly his?"

"He doesn't know,"

The captain sighed. "You should not ask about such things, Margret."

"Oh, fustian. How am I to understand if I do not ask? While a love child is not quite the thing, why would the runners think he would kill over such a trifle?"

The captain shook his head in resignation, but Lucien was more tolerant of Miss Barnett's forthright comments. His acquaintance with Lady Anne had gotten him rather used to curious females who asked inappropriate questions.

"Haskett believes she was blackmailing him. It makes no sense, not if you know Sherry or understand Society, where an illegitimate child is rarely grounds for blackmail, but Haskett does not appear to be bothered by facts or the improbable." Lucien's mouth twisted in distaste. "Not to mention that killing her and arranging for someone to move the body would have meant such a late departure from London that is would have been nearly impossible to make it to Oxfordshire and back in the time allotted—and certainly not without killing the horse. Haskett would no doubt argue a man fleeing from a murder charge would not worry about his horse."

"Lord Sherry would," Miss Barnett declared.

"Yes, but setting that aside, why would a guilty man who had gotten away return two days later? He would not, of course, but Bow Street is not listening to reason. Sherry will not be cleared unless the killer is found."

"What is Rothe doing?" Wycliff asked.

"Nothing official. He cannot be seen to thwart Bow Street, but he has given me access to Haskett's report, and he agreed to pass on anything else he hears."

The captain pursed his lips. "I perceive you could use some assistance."

"Are you offering?"

"I am. What do you need?"

"For starters, a reliable go-between with Whitehall and other local sources of information. At present, we are sending notes and letters, resulting in delays and potentially creating dangerous correspondence."

"Consider it done, but surely there is more I can do."

"A friend, indeed," Lucien said with a smile. He went on to relate their lines of interest so far—the Frenchman, the cart, the Edingtons, and Reginald. "It's hard to predict what might give us the break we need. Sherry is out of town attempting to identify the Frenchman, an inquiry that should keep him clear of Bow Street for a day or two. I've asked Finn to talk with servants near the boarding house in hopes of locating the cart. If you could interview the families in the same area, there may be another witness who heard or saw something they did not tell the constables."

"Am I free to mention the murder?"

"Go ahead. I doubt if our interest is a secret any longer, and if word of it gets back to the killer, all the better. I want him to know that someone is still looking for him. Nervous people can make mistakes."

"What can I do?" Miss Barnett asked.

"You can get inside," Wycliff said. "You are shivering, my dear."

"It is a bit chilly," she admitted, pulling the flimsy shawl a little tighter, "but I honestly want to help."

Lucien urged his companions toward the house. "Of course, you can. Listen to what is being said at social events, particularly the gossip going around. Report anything that you feel is important. Perhaps you could also throw cold water on the worst of the rumors about Sherry. He will need his reputation intact when this is over."

"Oh, I can do that," she said, her eyes sparkling, then she gave him an arch look. "Have you asked Mrs. Stine about the latest on-dits?"

Well…so she knew about his friendship with Sophy. Then Lady Anne must know…not that it mattered now.

"Not yet, but I will. I shall also be exploring the connection between Cade and Edington. Reginald's visit is a very odd coincidence."

"I agree," Wycliff said. "In fact, I find it more than odd. Very suspicious, I would say."

Chapter Eleven

Chadley Hall, Warwickshire October 1812

Lady Anne Ashburn slipped onto the window seat of her family's private sitting room clutching the two letters that had just arrived. She glanced back and forth between them deciding which to read first, but there really was no doubt. She had not expected to hear from him again. She swiftly broke the seal and read the letter from Lord Ware.

When she finished reading, she put it down, surprised she felt so disappointed. It was a thoughtful letter, courteous, friendly. What had she expected? A man of his stature would never declare himself in a letter—not that she expected him to. Heavens, no. With her at Chadley Hall and him in London, it was unlikely their relationship would progress. Yet, he *had* written. Was that not promising?

She turned to the second letter, this one from her friend, Miss Margret Barnett, who lived three miles outside of London and attended many town events.

Dearest Anne,

You will not believe what happened today! Viscount Ware and Lord Sherry were here and asked us to care for the most darling infant. She is no older than two or three with big dark eyes, shiny black curls, and the cutest dimples! Apparently she was in Sherbourne's care— why, I wonder?

No one said who she was—beyond her name, Fanny Pembroke— but I believe Father knows more. Do you suppose she's Sherbourne's love child??? Mother says I shouldn't say that, but who else could she be?

And to add to all this mystery, he is in some kind of <u>big</u> trouble. I heard them mention Bow Street. Yes, I was listening at Father's study door, but I couldn't hear much. Do you suppose he has been questioned by the runners? What could he have done? Maybe a duel? I intend to find out, and oh, how I wish you were here to help me.

In any event, Fanny is a darling child. Mother dotes on her already, and Captain Wycliff sat on the floor and played with her when he visited this evening. Perhaps he will make a good father someday? ha ha What do you think?

I shall be sure to write when I know more. I should mention we are not supposed to tell anyone Fanny is here, but I knew you would keep the secret. Is this not fascinating?

Anne glanced at the rest of Miss Barnett's letter. Margret rambled on about Captain Wycliff—they were officially courting now—recent social events she'd attended, the latest *on-dits* regarding mutual acquaintances, and once again expressed regrets for missing Georgina's wedding to Lord John. She asked that Anne write and give her all the wedding details.

Deciding she would read the letter more thoroughly later, Anne lifted her gaze to stare out the window. She had loved this room since childhood, when she'd often sat there for hours watching the birds and butterflies in Chadley Hall's extensive flower gardens. This time she paid little attention to the garden or its inhabitants.

While Margret's news regarding Sherry was both alarming and intriguing, Anne had been unsettled by both letters. They had brought memories of Lord Ware sharply to mind. Since her return home, she had determinedly put thoughts of him aside and had immersed herself in the country life surrounding Chadley. It was doubtful she would see the viscount for many months or years—maybe never again. She sighed, remembering the thrilling and occasionally perilous moments they'd shared during two of his inquiries for Whitehall.

She stared out the window for a long time before a tap on the door brought her back to the present. The butler entered. "Lord Allerton is here to see you, my lady."

"Thank you, Staves. Please show him in."

Moments later, Daniel Allerton, heir to Baron Allerton, strode into the room with a wide grin on his handsome face, warmth in his hazel eyes. As usual, his fair hair was disheveled from the ride between his father's estate and Chadley. "What is this? You have not changed for our morning ride?"

"Oh, I apologize, Daniel. I have been reading correspondence and woolgathering." Anne rose, set the letter aside, and returned his smile. The two had been on familiar terms since six-year-old Anne had followed the older boy—her senior by three years—around with adoring eyes. He left for the war when she was seventeen, and upon his return last January, they had slipped into old habits again. "Would you mind very much if we went for a stroll in the gardens instead?" she asked. "The weather is mild this morning, and the autumn flowers are much to be admired."

"Of course, Annie. As you like."

They stopped in the hall for a warm pelisse, then he held out an arm, and she linked hers with his. The past two months, Daniel's company had been a welcome respite from watching her mother slowly fade away.

Lady Chadley had been an invalid more than ten years, following a bout of scarlet fever that had severely damaged her heart. A late cold spell this last spring had given her a chill and fever. She'd shaken the fever two weeks later, and her spirits returned. Sadly, her strength had not recovered, and the doctor had privately told Anne and her father of his growing concern.

"How is Lady Chadley today?" Daniel asked, once they'd reached the far end of the gardens and were circling back toward the house.

"No better, I fear. She is sleeping more, but the extra rest does not add to her strength. It is heart-rending to see her like this."

"I know," Daniel squeezed her hand. "I wish I could spare you this grief."

"You *have* helped, so much—the rides, the visits. I know you must have other responsibilities you are neglecting."

"Nothing as important," he assured her. "I would be here more often, if you would allow me."

Anne didn't respond. Daniel had made similar oblique hints the past two weeks, most particularly after escorting her to her cousin Georgina's wedding, but only engaged couples were allowed to visit so frequently. She could not even think about such a commitment with her mother so ill. She was fond of Daniel—he was a wonderful friend who had been getting her through a very low period in her life—but was she fond enough to marry him? Her morning letters had only added to the confusion, reminding her how much Lord Ware had stirred her feelings—memories she had tried to forget, but she was not so inconstant she could easily set them aside.

Daniel gave her a worried glance. "Why the sudden silence? Have I said something I should not?"

"I'm just worried about Mother. I know," she said turning on a bright smile, "a race to the fountain is just the thing to cheer me up."

Daniel laughed. "We are no longer children, Anne, but if it will please you, let us do it."

She lifted her skirts and sped along the path. Daniel didn't really try, loping slowly behind her, letting her win. There was a time when he would never have allowed a girl to show him up in anything. She sighed. Perhaps they *had* grown too old for such frivolous behavior. Was it so wrong she wanted to break the monotony that had become her life these past weeks?

"Shall we have tea?" she asked blithely. "Afterward, I must see if Mother is awake. I am reading the first two cantos of Lord Byron's *Childe Harold's Pilgrimage* to her. They say it mimics the author's life. Have you read it? Everyone is."

"Honestly, Anne, I have no time for Byron or his poetry."

"A pity, Daniel. He writes so vividly of his travels." She gave him a fleeting smile—they could not always like the same things—and turned the conversation to a topic she knew would please him. "Tell me about the new colt you bought."

Chapter Twelve

London, October 1812

Lucien strode toward the stable, impatient to get started on the day. A week had already gone by since Maria's body was found, and he was keen to follow-up on the progress he had made yesterday. It was too early for most of the things he wanted to accomplish, but one part could be set in motion without leaving home.

He found his groom Finn cleaning harness. The everyday task was abandoned the moment Lucien suggested Finn might help him catch a killer by locating the garden cart used to move the body.

"Gardeners or stable lads around the boarding house may know something they won't share with the constables…or me. Are you interested in giving it a try?"

The small man's face lit with excitement, his blue eyes eager under his mop of red hair. "G'or, m'lord, 'course I am."

Lucien smiled at his enthusiasm; Finn was ever begging to assist in his inquiries. In truth, his appealing grin and the blarney that were so natural to him often brought results when other approaches failed.

"Take care you do not mention Sherry or Fanny to anyone," Lucien cautioned.

"Aye, got it. I'll find yor cart, m'lord. By G'or, I will." Finn tipped the felt cap he habitually wore and set out at a jaunty strut.

Lucien shook his head in amusement and returned to the house. His next task was to visit with Sophy, but she would not be receiving for at least an hour. That left time for a meal and a cup or two of coffee.

The footman had just cleared Lucien's plate away when Sherry wandered in looking sleepy-eyed. He stifled a yawn. "I thought I heard you outside."

"You did. I was speaking with Finn. He'll be spending the day looking for the cart."

"Uh, good." Sherry began filling his own plate from the sideboard. "Were you able to talk with Miss Barnett last night?"

"I did. Fanny is doing very well indeed." Lucien chuckled. "In fact, she has Lady Barnett doting over her, and Miss Barnett is hinting you may never get her back. It is safe to say the Barnett household has taken to the chit."

"Capital, though I'm not surprised." Sherry set his plate across from Lucien, and the footman filled his teacup. "Did you hear anything else?"

"The usual gossip. I recruited Wycliff, well, actually, he offered to help with the inquiry. So did Miss Barnett, of course. I asked the captain to interview the other residents on Gerrard and King Streets within a five-minute walk of Doud's boarding house."

"It was good of him to offer. I owe him…and you, of course," Sherry said. "I should be doing this myself—"

Lucien interrupted. "But you cannot, so your friends will do it for you. If you tried, Haskett would have you in custody before the day was out."

"I know. All the more reason for me to be on my way to Hertfordshire. By the bye, I have written my father explaining what has occurred—"

Lucien interrupted. "And to Emily, I trust."

"Well, yes, of course, but I'm not worried about her charging up to London and yelling at me—and at the Bow Street runners. I hope the letter to my parents will convince Father to stay at home."

"You seriously believe that will work?"

"It should. I told him I was leaving London and for him to wait until I write again. I failed to mention how soon I was returning. There is nothing he can do in town except worry, and he might as well do that at home with Mother."

"I pray he listens to you. He would only get in the way and slow the inquiry." And they had no time to waste. "Take my coachman Gregory and the bays. They'll get you to Hertford by nightfall. And best use the closed carriage. No sense risking a chance sighting by someone who'd report it to Bow Street."

"I had thought to ride horseback, but…I appreciate it." Sherry frowned, looking uncomfortable.

"Stop before you embarrass us both. You would do the same for me." Lucien rose. "Now, I must be off while I can still catch Sophy at home. I thought she might know something useful about the Edingtons. You know how passionate she is in staying up to date with the latest gossip. On my way out, I'll tell Gregory to prepare the carriage. I assume you still plan to return day after tomorrow?"

Sherry nodded. "If I'm delayed beyond Friday, I will send word."

Lucien nodded. "Good travel, my friend, and good fortune to us both." He turned toward the stableyard door and spoke over his shoulder. "Take good care of my horses."

• • •

With a sense of relief that Sherry was on his way out of town, Lucien set out for the home of Mrs. Sophia Stine. Upon arrival, he found her composing a letter in her front parlor. Lucien smiled as he entered the room. She made a lovely sight, beautiful, as usual, with her shining black locks arranged fashionably around her soft features. When she looked up, her green eyes—their color enhanced by her pale emerald gown—widened with curiosity.

"Lucien, darling, what brings you out so early?" She rose and came to meet him, extending her hand which he took in his and lightly kissed her fingers. "I heard the dreadful news that Sherry is being sought on murder charges."

"He did not do it, you know."

"I did not imagine he had. Please convey my hopes for a swift end to his troubles."

Lucien smiled. "You are assuming I know his whereabouts."

Sophy laughed softly. "Of course, you do, but I am not asking where. Come, darling, sit and tell me why you are here."

Seemingly aware this was not a casual call, she gave him a speculative look. They had ended their affaire two years ago because they felt they would not suit as husband and wife. It was never about a lack of attraction, and they had since endeavored to meet only in public, thus avoiding the temptation of falling back into intimacy.

She seated herself on the sofa, and he took the chair next to it.

"I am in need of information, whatever you can tell about the Edingtons, Olivia and Nigel. They employed the dead woman as a companion for his elderly mother."

"Are they suspects in the murder?"

He shrugged. "Not according to the constables at Bow Street, and I have no cause at present, but until I know better…"

"You suspect everyone," she finished. "Yes, I remember that is your approach. Well, I cannot tell you much. They've only been in London about a year. He inherited the house from a distant kinsman, although…" Sophy paused in thought. "I have a vague memory of a problem surrounding the inheritance, but I do not recall what. In any event, they live on the fringe of Society and rarely mix within the better social circles except at the largest events, those where it seems everyone in town is invited. The recent Torrington Ball, for example. If I am not mistaken, funds are an issue, but mostly they are dull and socially inept. They are considered to be country bumpkins."

"How very judgmental of you, Sophy."

"I was quoting others," she said defensively, then laughed. "Oh, you were teasing me. I suppose the designation is apt in some ways, but it does not convey the rather uncomfortable impression they give."

"Yes, I have met the wife. There is something about her…" he agreed. "Cold, self-absorbed, and she lied to me about her husband not being at home. I heard him talking in the study, so I waited to see his visitor. It was Reginald, one of Mr. Cade's men."

"O-oh," she said, her eyes widening. "I supposed her social lie might be excused, but having one of Mr. Cade's men in her home is, well—don't laugh at me, Lucien—but it is bad ton."

"A sad commentary, indeed." His lips twitched for a moment. "But was this a social lie? Why not just say he was busy? I suspect she was trying to conceal Reginald's presence, and I would surely love to know why he was there."

"Will you ask Cade?"

"Not unless I must." He got up and started to pace. "I doubt if he'd tell me, and I would rather not tip my hand regarding my interest in the Edingtons just yet. Of course, with his web of spies, Cade may already know. Confound it, Sophy. Information is so scarce. Reginald's presence may have nothing to do with Maria, and I'm just wasting precious time."

"Or," she said patiently, "it could be very important, and therefore, you cannot ignore it."

"Precisely."

"I am sad to see you so troubled, Lucien. If you wish, I can ask around about the Edingtons, but I doubt if I learn much more. And, darling, no one can tell you about this business with Reginald, except Reginald—or Mr. Cade."

"Reginald wouldn't talk without Cade's permission, and I am hesitant to pursue the matter with him. The prior contacts with Cade were at Whitehall's behest. This is personal."

She tilted her head. "Hmm, yes, it *is* an extraordinary relationship you have with Cade."

He stopped pacing in mid-stride and gave her a sharp look. "I would scarcely call it a relationship."

"No? What would you call it?"

"The man is a crime lord," he began somewhat grimly. "He has been a useful informer on behalf of his country, but nothing more. If anything, I suppose I find the contradictions in him to be...interesting."

She smiled. "I daresay he sees the same in you."

Lucien frowned. "Why are we talking about Cade? I came here to discuss the Edingtons."

"Yes," she said amiably, "and I have told you all I know. "

Lucien sighed. "So you have. Thank you, my dear. Pardon my unruly tongue. I fear talking about Cade brought out the tension plaguing me."

"There is nothing to pardon. You are ever the gentleman no matter how sorely vexed."

He snorted softly, but bent over her hand. "Dear Sophy, always so generous. I owe you."

"Yes, you do." She gave him a flirtatious smile as he went out the door.

• • •

Considering what Sophy had said about the Edingtons' questionable finances and standing in Society, Lucien thought to pursue his inquires in the lesser clubs in town, gaming hells frequented by those who could not meet the high standards for membership at the exclusive gentlemen's clubs such as White's, Boodle's, and Brook's. But it was much too early to visit such places, and he had planned another stop that kept more business-like hours.

Benjamin Sloane, Lord Rothe's secretary at Whitehall, was always a wealth of information. The Edingtons might have come to his notice, and if not, the duplicate public files Sloane maintained for Rothe's spy unit could, at least, provide basic information.

Sloane looked up from his desk and stood, his face solemn. "Lord Ware." He kept his voice low. "I am grieved by the accusations leveled against Lord Sherbourne."

"As am I, Sloane. It has been a rough few days, but I finally have an angle or two to explore, and I need your help. What can you tell me of Olivia and Nigel Edington? Are you familiar with them?"

"Not right off, my lord, but there should be something in our files. I assume this is on Sherbourne's behalf?"

"Yes, is that a problem? Will this compromise Lord Rothe?"

"No, no, just my curiosity. There is no reason for anyone else to know you were here."

Lucien nodded his understanding. "The dead woman, Maria Pembroke, was employed by the Edingtons as a day companion for his mother. I called upon them as a matter of course and saw Mr. Cade's man Reginald leave the residence. Granted, it could be a coincidence, but it's unlikely. In any event, I thought the couple worth my attention."

Sloane's eyebrows rose ever so slightly. "Just so, sir." He picked up a pen and paper from his desk. "Nigel and Olivia Edington, correct?" When Lucien nodded, he wrote it down. "And where do they live?"

Lucien gave him the address on Brewer Street.

"Are you looking for a particular type of information?"

"Anything you can give me. The recent inheritance, their finances, associates, whatever."

"Then let us see what we can find. Tax and property records are always a good bet." Sloane stepped over to a row of cabinets and thumbed through the files inside.

Due to heavy taxation to support the government and the extravagancies of the Prince Regent, England kept extensive records on property owners. Any change in ownership was duly recorded and thus those reports were accessible for Whitehall's varied interests.

Sloane pulled a packet of papers from the back of the third drawer. "Here we are. Nigel Edington," Sloane murmured, skimming over the documents. "He inherited the London property one year and four months ago, and also a small country estate in Worcester."

"Worcester is up north and adjacent to Warwickshire, is it not?"

"You are correct, my lord. Is that significant?"

"No, probably not. I was just trying to place it." In truth, it had occurred to Lucien that Lady Anne must live close by and might know the Edington family. "Does it mention if there was some claim on the estate or question about Edington's inheritance?"

"No. There is a lengthy time gap between the former owner's death in 1805 and Mr. Nigel Edington taking possession in 1811.

It might be significant but not necessarily so. Sometimes it takes years to contact heirs." He frowned. "They have unpaid taxes. Not uncommon, but it is a large deficit and could mean the estate is in serious debt. That is all I can tell you from this record—unless you are interested in the exact amounts of taxes, property descriptions, and so on." At Lucien's negative shake of the head, Sloane put the papers away. "I could inquire about other records, but it might take days or weeks to get them."

"Don't bother, yet. Official records may not contain what I need."

Sloane nodded, then hesitated. "I hope you will not find it presumptuous if I ask you to let Sherbourne know we have faith in him."

"Of course, I will tell him. He needs to know he still has friends." Lucien heard muffled voices from Rothe's office and glanced in that direction.

"Did you wish to speak with Lord Rothe?" Sloane asked. "His meeting should be over soon."

"No. I came to see you. In fact, it would be better if Lord Rothe and I do not discuss this any further than we have. Sherry is adamant to keep his lordship as far from his trouble as possible. He realizes how awkward it is."

"It has been unfortunate."

"Has Bow Street been here?"

"More than once."

Lucien sighed. "They are tenacious—someone is keeping watch at my house. I should go. Thank you. If you hear anything, you know how to reach me."

"Indeed, I do."

• • •

Lucien found Robert sitting on the side of the curricle, dangling his feet and looking bored. While Finn was about his own inquires, the footman had been pressed into service to ride along that day.

"Cheer up, lad, we are going home," Lucien said.

"I cannot say I'm sorry, sir. I like horses, but I do not consider them good company."

Lucien chuckled and flicked the reins. "Finn should be back to take over his duties this evening, but I may need you again tomorrow."

"Very good, sir. Whatever you need, of course, but I must say looking after horses is rather hard on my boots." Robert frowned at a smear of manure on the tip of his footwear.

Lucien was still smiling at Robert's discomfort when he entered the townhouse a few minutes later. With Sherry and Fanny both gone, the place was quiet, but it was a relief not to worry about what Bow Street might find if they descended on Hays Mews again; Hughes would have seen that all evidence of their visitors was removed—a wise precaution, as Haskett had not given up. When Lucien crossed from the stable to the house, he'd noticed a familiar face loitering on the far side of the street. The same man had been there every day since his return from Sussex.

Hughes met him in the hallway. "We had unwanted visitors while you were away, my lord."

"What? Bow Street again?"

"Yes, Mr. Haskett and two others. They insisted upon entry, and I escorted them through the house this time."

"I trust they found nothing."

"Just so, my lord."

"And Sherry got away without incident?"

"He did. We disguised him as a groom, and he sat beside Gregory on the coach. A constable stopped the carriage in the street—"

Lucien scowled, incensed by this added intrusion. "*The devil he did*. Brazen fellow. He will rue the day he tries that again if I am aboard."

"He peered inside the coach but paid no mind to Gregory and Sherbourne on top."

Lucien nodded, somewhat placated that Bow Street had been so easily dupped. "Well, now they have invaded both my house and carriage, I pray that was the end of it. Bloody persistent, these runners." He turned and started up the stairs. "I shall be in my study, composing a letter that must go out immediately."

"I shall notify Robert, my lord."

Lucien poured himself a glass of port and sat at his desk to write to Lady Anne and inquire about the Edingtons of Worcester. No doubt she was already privy to a bit of Sherry's situation through letters from Miss Barnett, but he could not be certain how much she'd been told or how accurate Miss Barnett had been. With that in mind, he began by setting forth the pertinent events of the last week with particular detail on Olivia and Nigel Edington, and then he asked what she knew of the family—their reputation in the community, their finances, and any gossip about the inheritance.

When Lucien concluded his remarks on Sherry's behalf, he asked after Lady Chadley's health, and then he paused, pen in hand, as he debated whether to say more. But what more did he have to say? After a moment, he finished with his usual hurried signature.

At the last minute, he added a sentence at the bottom letting her know the Grande Chiffre, Napoleon's complex war code, had recently been broken, due in large part to the assistance Anne gave Whitehall's codebreakers last winter. She would be pleased to hear that, he thought, a smile tugging at his lips. Affixing his seal, he rose and rang for Hughes.

"This letter must go out on the next mail coach headed north."

"Yes, my lord. Robert will see to it directly." Hughes bowed and hurried away.

Lucien moved to a chair by the fire, his thoughts already moving on to which clubs were most likely to yield information on Nigel Edington.

• • •

Lucien had just finished dinner that evening when Hughes appeared in the archway and announced Captain Wycliff. The captain strode into the room with that unmistakable military bearing, and Lucien rose to greet him.

"Captain, an unexpected pleasure to see you." He held out a hand, briefly sharing a firm clasp.

"I beg your pardon for interrupting your dinner."

"Not at all. I was just finishing. Do join me. Have you dined? I'm sure the cook can serve up more of this very fine goose."

"Thank you, but no. My own dinner will be waiting." Wycliff pulled out a chair, and both men seated themselves. Lucien nodded to the footman who poured a glass of port and set it in front of Wycliff. "I wished to pass on what I learned today in hopes it would help Finn in his search—unless he has already found the cart?"

"He is not home yet, so I assume not."

"Ah, then this may be useful. Mrs. Tolliver, a widow lady who lives on the corner of Gerard, three houses east of the boarding house, heard the cart in the alley that night."

"I trust she was more curious than Miss Amelia," Lucien said leaning forward with keen interest.

"She was," Wycliff said. "However, it was too dark for a useful description of the cloaked figure she saw. Nevertheless, she is clear it was a barrow that was being pushed in the direction of the boarding house. What I also found interesting was she kept watching and listening...and it did not return."

"So, the killer entered from the east but left the alley going west," Lucien said, catching on quickly.

"Just so. I shall visit houses on the west tomorrow. Perhaps there is another light sleeper who noticed someone out that night and got a better look at him. Once rid of the body, the killer might have been less cautious in concealing himself."

"This is excellent news, captain. Are you sure I can't offer you something to eat?"

"No, truly, I must go. I will be stretched to eat a meal and still attend a friend's soiree as promised. Is there other progress?"

"Bits and pieces only. Sherry is still out of town, and I intend to make the rounds of the gaming hells tonight to learn what I can about Nigel Edington. I cannot help but dwell upon his meeting with Cade's man."

"It looks bad," Wycliff agreed, "and probably is, but it may have nothing to do with Miss Pembroke."

"Granted, but it must be pursued. The incident says *something* about Edington's character—I'm just not sure what that is."

"Well, good luck tonight. We shall no doubt speak again tomorrow." Wycliff rose and made his way out.

Lucien lingered over his port, thinking about the killer pushing the laden barrow through the alley that night. Unless the scoundrel had nerves of steel, he must have been fearful every step, cringing at the noises the wheel made, dreading that someone would see him, even accost him. Why take such a frightful risk to bring the body home? Had he just panicked, desperate to get rid of her body, and the dark alley was the first place that came to mind? Had he hoped that if she was found along a public path her death would be blamed on footpads?

He frowned. That is precisely what might have happened—it was the constables' first conclusion—until Mrs. Doud pointed them in Sherry's direction.

Which raised another question—why had Maria told Mrs. Doud about Sherry? The landlady certainly wasn't the type to whom he would have confided, and Edith Edington had said Maria didn't like Mrs. Doud, that, in fact, she had intended to move and change caretakers for Fanny. Had she merely thrown out Sherry's name to fob off a nosey landlady?

Hughes' cleared his throat from the dining room doorway, claiming Lucien's attention. "Finn has returned, my lord. He was unsuccessful in finding the cart. He was anxious to tell you himself, but as he was cold and hungry, I sent him to the kitchen to eat first, knowing he would be needed tonight. He should be up soon."

"Very good, Hughes."

He did not have long to wait for Finn's report—no more than twenty minutes passed before the small man of half-Irish descent presented himself, cap in hand.

"Sorry, milord. I dint learn much. One lad thought he heared somethin' that night, but he dint look. An' no one so far is missin' a cart."

"Which street were you covering today?"

"King. East of the boardin' house."

"Captain Wycliff found a witness who saw a barrow in the alley that night." Lucien repeated what Mrs. Tolliver had said, and Finn nodded eagerly.

"Aye, it helps to know it be a barrow and which way it come from. You want me to go all the way t' Brewer Street?"

"If need be. Unless you find the barrow's owner before you reach the Edingtons' property, find out if *they* own one or did on the night of the murder. That is a task for tomorrow, however. Tonight, we visit the gambling clubs."

Chapter Thirteen

Lucien made the rounds that evening, starting with White's and Boodle's. As he suspected, no one in those exclusive clubs was familiar with Nigel Edington beyond a passing acquaintance. He was not a member of either, and Lucien quickly switched to the lesser establishments, the gaming hells that welcomed everyone with coin in their pockets.

He avoided Cade's Club all evening, even though it was the most likely to yield the information he sought. His own odd association with the club owner held him back. The thought of getting drawn further into Cade's unsavory world or being associated with his activities was more than distasteful. Lucien would have cut the connection long ago if Lord Rothe had not encouraged him to maintain it for the benefit of Whitehall's inquiries. But this was not a Whitehall inquiry—it was private, personal—and Lucien was loathe to deal with Cade on that level.

Nonetheless, at four in the morning he entered Cade's Club as a last resort. He was tired, frustrated, and he'd had too much to drink. Even though he had not finished most of the drinks at each stop, he had consumed more than usual over the last six hours. He would have preferred to seek his bed at this point, but once he had decided this visit had to be made, he wanted to put it behind him tonight.

He nodded at the man on the door and headed straight to the gaming tables. With any luck, the notorious owner would have retired for the night and thus would remain unaware of Lucien's visit until he woke in the late morning.

As he entered the gaming room, Lucien swept his gaze over the crowd. A surprising number of games were still running with full or nearly full tables. He chose a large round table with five men playing Hazard. They were doing quite a bit of drinking and talking—precisely what he wanted. He smiled and pulled up a chair, nodding to the one man he knew, and introduced himself to the others.

"Room for one more?" he asked.

"Of course, Lord Ware." The rest of the amiable group nodded in welcome.

"We could use some new blood, and the deeper the pockets the better," one fellow joked.

Lucien returned the smile. "I should warn you, I won't be easy pickings."

"We shall see about that."

Laughter from around the table.

An hour later, Lucien was breaking even and had learned not only that Edington was a frequent patron at Cade's but also a frequent loser. What he could not ascertain was whether Edington was able to cover his losses or was running up significant unpaid debt. Gentlemen were loath to discuss debts, even when foxed.

He surreptitiously studied the man sitting directly across the table. If Barnaby Thrup was as close to Nigel Edington as he claimed when Lucien had tossed the name out, he should be able to answer many of Lucien's questions, but he was deep in his cups, more likely to pass out than hold a sensible conversation. The lines on Thrup's face suggested he was a decade or more older than Lucien, but they might just as well be attributed to years of debauchery and over-indulgence. He was certainly a sloppy drunk, leaning on the table and slurring his words. He had been losing heavily since Lucien arrived.

"That's it, sir." The house banker shook his head at Thrup. "No more IOUs tonight."

"How dare you? I pay my debts," Thrup said angrily, but no one took his protest seriously. He had arrived at the fall-down drunk stage.

"Sorry, sir. We have a nightly limit, and you have already surpassed it."

To Lucien's knowledge, there was no such limit—entire fortunes had been won and lost at London's gaming tables—but the better clubs often stepped in when patrons were this stupefied by spirits. He wasn't surprised Mr. Cade followed their example, as he strove to compete with the likes of White's and Brooks.

"Come, sir." Lucien stood and helped Thrup to his feet. "Your luck is out tonight. Perhaps it will improve if you try another day."

The man mumbled something, and Lucien deposited him in a chair by the fire. He stood looking down at him, wondering if it was worth his time to question him. After a moment, he shook his head. Thrup could barely sit upright, clearly too far gone to make sense.

Lucien turned to leave and caught sight of Reginald headed in their direction. Was Thrup about to get an escort from the building...or was Lucien the house manager's quarry? He halted to wait and see.

"Lord Ware, if you would be so kind, Mr. Cade wishes to speak with you."

Lucien lifted a brow. That was the most courteous invitation he'd yet to receive from the Gentleman Thief. Others had been delivered at the point of a gun, but then, Cade would not want trouble inside his club—bad for its reputation.

As Lucien wasn't looking for trouble either, he gave a short nod. "I am agreeable, but someone needs to puts Mr. Thrup in a coach."

"I see that, sir. A hackney will be summoned." Reginald gestured to a footman, then turned back to Lucien. "If you will follow me..."

They climbed the stairs, knocked on the office door, and Cade called for them to enter.

Lucien had been in the private office before—fashionable mahogany furnishings, Persian rugs, a sideboard well-stocked with spirits...and upon this occasion something he had not seen before, a tea tray. Mr. Cade stood next to the sideboard, filling a teacup. The dainty porcelain looked out of place in his hands. He was a well-built man, shorter than Lucien, in his mid-thirties with swept back brown hair and a trimmed mustache. As was his habit,

Cade's attire was expensive and fashionable but conservative, not one hint of the dandy about him.

He turned his pale blue gaze on Lucien. Often cold and penetrating, his eyes revealed nothing of his mood this morning. "Tea or something stronger?"

"Tea would be most welcome."

"I thought as much. You have had an unusually long night of drinking."

Lucien suppressed a frown at this blatant demonstration of Cade's knowledge of his movements, but he had learned long ago that the club owner had spies all over town—mostly ordinary people: street venders, pub owners, dock workers, doubtless a constable here and there. He would not be at all surprised if someone inside White's or Boodle's was on Cade's payroll. "Why the interest in my activities?"

"I was ready to retire, when I heard you had entered the club. Naturally this rare occurrence pricked my curiosity, and I made some inquiries as to what might have led you here." He handed Lucien a warm cup. "Please…have a seat, and tell me the reason for your interest in Nigel Edington."

"I am more intrigued by yours," Lucien countered, "although I have no objection to telling you mine. Andrew Sherbourne has been accused of killing a woman who worked for Edington. I intend to clear his name by finding the actual killer."

"And you believe it is Edington?"

Lucien shrugged. "I cannot say…yet. At this point he is someone of interest, along with everyone in his household." His lips twisted in a frown. "And dozens of other people, unfortunately."

"Why not footpads as the authorities first claimed?"

"She was not stabbed in the alley. Ordinary thieves would not have moved the body."

Cade lifted a brow. "Moved it, eh? I had not heard that. I assume Bow Street is claiming the child was Sherbourne's motive?"

Lucien eyes flashed to meet Cade's, his voice harsh. "What do you know of the child?"

"Less than you, I am sure, only what is on the streets. But if she is his...and unwanted—"

Lucien nostrils flared. He straightened and set down his cup. "You go too far, Cade. Sherry is an honorable man. If the child *is* his—which is still in doubt—he will provide for her. In fact, he appears rather pleased at the possibility."

Cade waved a placating hand and spoke with equanimity. "Do not take offense where none is intended. It is a motive the courts will surely be asked to consider. I, however, am willing to accept your assessment of Sherbourne's character. More tea?" When Lucien declined, Cade set aside his own empty cup. "What reason for murder do you attribute to Nigel Edington?"

"None, as yet. Maria had only been in London for six months, living a quiet life with few acquaintances, and I shall scrutinize them all." Lucien paused before adding, "I must say, Edington's association with Reginald caught my attention."

Cade gave him a thoughtful look. "It took you long enough to get to the point. I assume you discovered Reginald was there the day you spoke with Mrs. Edington."

"She did not tell me, if that is what you think. In fact, she told me her husband was away, but I heard men talking in the study... and I saw Reginald leave."

"I see how that might make one curious." Cade shrugged. "Mr. Edington has run up considerable debt at my gaming tables. Reginald was reminding him it must be paid."

Lucien thought that over. "If he was out of funds, did *payment* of his debts have anything to do with dispatching Miss Pembroke?"

"Now you insult me." Cade's voice was mild but those pale eyes had gone cold.

"Not intended," Lucien said, remaining equally casual. Yet he felt the sudden tension in the room and kept an eye on the other man's slightest move. "I was merely seeking clarification."

The silence stretched a moment longer before Cade said, "Akin to your friend Sherbourne, I do not make a habit of preying on women and children."

"Habits do not preclude exceptions. Your rules, yours to break."

Cade gave a short, humorless laugh. "Not this time. I had no quarrel with Miss Pembroke, and if Edington did, I have no knowledge of it. Is that plain enough?"

"It is." He felt the tension ease but was compelled to press his own point. "However, it does it exonerate Mr. Edington."

Cade nodded. "I grant you that."

"Can you tell me more about Edington, beyond the fact he is a poor gambler?" Lucien waited to see what Cade would say. It was hard to predict whether or not his unique moral code would include discussing a club patron in order to clear Sherry's reputation.

"I know little of the man. The estate he inherited—after several delays—has more debts than funds. By now, most would consider it a burden rather than an asset."

"What caused the delays?"

"A missing heir. In truth, I did not inquire further. Reginald may have the details." Cade rose, spoke to his men in the hallway, and returned to his seat behind the desk. "As Reginald met with Edington, he can give you his impressions of the man, and perhaps he made additional inquiries before his visit."

Lucien was taken aback by the offer. Perhaps Cade approved of justice after all—as long as it was not aimed at his activities—or he simply did not fancy a woman's killer going unpunished.

A knock on the door announced Reginald's arrival, and he stepped inside. Even dressed as a gentleman, the man's stocky figure and bulldog expression bespoke his roots in London's dockyards. "You wanted to see me, sir?"

"Lord Ware is interested in Nigel Edington. I thought you could give him an honest assessment."

If Reginald was surprised, he didn't show it. "In a word, he is a poltroon, sir. The wife controls everything, regulating most of her husband's activities. His one rebellion appears to be gambling— maybe to avoid going home. He is far into dun territory, and I wouldn't wager against debtors' prison in time."

"A dim future," Cade muttered. "But Ware's particular interest is if he is capable of murder."

"Isn't everyone? I doubt he would kill on his own. Perhaps in league with others or if the wife ordered it, but it would not be an affair of honor—rather a shot from hiding or a stab in the back."

Interesting he should use that wording. "Would he kill a woman?" Lucien asked.

Reginald cocked his head. "If he was primed to kill, I doubt he would care whether it was a woman or a man."

"You have painted quite a rogue," Lucien remarked.

"I may have overstated the matter," Reginald said thoughtfully. "He is weak and mostly does what he is told. Perhaps it is Mrs. Edington I found so wanting in character."

"What do you know of his dealings with Maria Pembroke, a woman who worked for him?"

Reginald's face cleared as though he finally understood the questions. "Ah, yes, the murdered woman. I know nothing except what I read in the news sheets. I was not aware Edington was her employer." Reginald frowned and showed the first sign of curiosity. "Is he a suspect in her killing?"

"Not as Bow Street sees it," Lucien said. "I have not dismissed the possibility."

The house manager snorted. "I would not overlook that wife of his." He switched his attention to Cade. "Was there anything else, sir?"

"What about the inheritance?" Lucien asked before the man got away.

"Yes, we were curious to know what caused the long delay in awarding the estate," Cade added.

"I don't recall. As the matter had been resolved in Nigel Edington's favor, the estate's finances were my main concern, and I didn't look into his past." He swung his gaze back to Cade. "Do you wish me to inquire, sir?"

"No. Thank you, Reginald. I believe that is all."

"Yes, sir. Lord Ware." He nodded at both men before leaving the room.

Cade gave Lucien a doubtful look. "I am not certain that was of value to you, but I wish you well in finding the killer."

Lucien readily accepted the dismissal and stood. "Thank you."

The club owner tipped his chin in acknowledgment. Lucien smiled as he stepped into the hallway. Despite Cade's outward indifference, the matter had caught his interest. What would he do if his web of spies reported anything useful to Lucien's inquiry? Would he pass it on? Lucien shrugged.

He pursed his lips, thinking over Reginald's candid remarks. He had more than hinted that the lady of the house deserved a longer look—and he would do that—but this inheritance thing kept coming up with no answers to its lengthy delay...could it be important? Was it not settled months before Maria entered the Edingtons' household? And yet...it nagged at him.

As he boarded his curricle and headed home, he wondered if, on the other hand, he was spending too much time on the Edingtons. Seeing Reginald there had heightened his suspicions, but now that had been explained to his satisfaction. As far as he could tell, Edington's gambling debts had nothing to do with Maria—suggesting Reginald's appearance had set Lucien onto the wrong track.

That would bring him back full circle to the mysterious Frenchman, the man Maria had said was hunting her and who had a strong motive. Sherry should be back in a day or two. If he had procured the Frenchman's name, perhaps all they had to do was find him and put this whole sorry muddle to rest.

Chapter Fourteen

Hertfordshire, October 1812

Sherry arrived in Hertford just as night settled, and he put up at the White Owl Inn. It was too late to visit the LeFlores, so after a simple meal and a pint of ale, he took to his bed. For the first time in days, he slept free of worry that the runners would burst in during the night.

The next day dawned under a cloud of dense fog, but with directions from the innkeeper, he found his friends' cottage just as the sun broke through the mist. Pierre threw open the front door the moment the coach stopped in the lane, and Sherry descended to be wrapped in the man's enthusiastic embrace.

"*Bonjour*, Andrew. So delighted to receive your message. Come in, come in." Pierre steered Sherry toward the house and called to his wife, "Yvette, he is here."

She came hurrying out the door, wiping her hands on a towel, her black hair swirling loose around her face. She was a bit plumper than the thin young woman he'd last set eyes on. Life outside the world of intrigue must suit her.

"*Mon cher*, it is so beauteous to see you." She kissed him on both cheeks and tugged on his arm. "Come, please. I have made your English tea and biscuits. Is that not what is served here?"

Chatting merrily in a combination of French and English, Yvette seated him in the homey cottage kitchen, quickly placing tea and a plate of tarts and biscuits in front of him. Sherry had recently had breakfast, but it would have been churlish not to sample the food she had obviously prepared to welcome him.

"What a feast, Yvette." The tarts really were very good. "Do tell me what brought you to England and to settle in Hertfordshire."

The three of them talked for nearly an hour about present activities and the old days in Paris before Pierre finally raised the reason for Sherry's visit. "Your letter said you wanted to talk about Maria. Has something happened to her?"

"I'm sorry to say she is dead."

"*Mon dieu*. What happened?" Pierre asked, drowning out Yvette's startled denial.

"She was murdered...and the authorities believe I did it. I did not, I assure you."

"Stupid fools. You would not do such a thing. Does your English *Sûreté* know nothing?" Yvette was indignant and reached across the table to clasp his hand.

"It is unthinkable," Pierre added. "My friend, do you need a place to hide?"

"No, no. Nothing like that." Their support was heart-warming, but he finally cut short their indignant reaction and told them the rest of the story.

"We, your true friends, will help prove your innocence," Yvette said, when he was finished. "But how?"

"I must locate the Frenchman who Maria said was chasing her. He may well be her murderer. My efforts to find him have come to nothing, mainly because I do not know his identity. As you were still in Paris after her escape, I thought you might have heard the name of the French officer she killed."

"Ah, o*ui*, of course. We heard of his death, did we not, *ma petite*? The tale was all around Paris." Pierre looked at his wife uncertainly. "But his name, it escapes me.

"Louis. No, not Louis. Francois. This is it." Yvette smiled in triumphant. "I do not recall, how do you say, his *famille* name."

"It will come to me," Pierre said. "I remember the story...two brothers from a prominent French family—one found stabbed to death in his lodgings, the other seriously injured in battle two days later." He lightly tapped his fist on the edge of the table. "What was their name? Perhaps we should talk of something else. It is right here." He touched his fingers to his mouth.

"*Oui*, Pierre's brain will work on it if we speak of other things. Do you see your friend Simon?"

The LeFlores had only known the two Englishmen as Andrew and Simon, and Sherry left it that way. "Frequently. We are still friends. He is doing well." He described his own life in London, minus the continuing inquiries for the War Office. He even told them about courting Emily Selkirk, and Yvette's eyes danced.

"Shall we soon hear you have become, as our English neighbors say, leg-shackled?"

"I don't know," Sherry admitted. "It was already complicated, and now there is Maria's child."

"Your Emily, she does not understand?" Yvette asked with sympathy. "I hear the English are not so agreeable in these matters."

"That is true, but I have not told her about Fanny…or Maria, for that matter. Before having that conversation, I must free myself of the murder charges and discover if the child is mine."

"I think that is very wise." Yvette said, nodding as she poured Sherry another cup of tea.

Pierre had been quiet for a while, and now he turned the conversation back to the murder charges. "Surely Simon is helping you. He would not desert you, would he?"

"Good lord, of course not. We remain close friends, and he is gathering evidence in London while I am away. He took Fanny and me into his home and—"

"Breguet," Pierre blurted. "Francois and Gaston Breguet. Francois…he was the officer who died, and it must be Gaston who has come to England."

• • •

Although Sherry wanted to return to London with all haste and start the hunt for Gaston Breguet, the LeFlores argued he should stay overnight before such a long journey. He might have politely set their concerns aside if the coachman Gregory had not agreed, reminding him that Lucien's prized bays needed a day of rest.

Stifling his impatience, he settled in as his friends brought out the wine, and they were soon reminiscing and often laughing over their adventures in France. The passage of time had added a touch of humor to incidents of narrow escapes and missed opportunities that had once been matters of life and death. If Sherry occasionally felt the urge to grab a horse and ride hell-bent for London, he didn't let it show.

Chapter Fifteen

London October 1812

After coming home from Cade's Club near dawn, Lucien slept restlessly, plagued by unanswered questions. It was late morning before he called for his curricle and hurried to keep his noon engagement with Wycliff. They planned to complete the Gerrard and King St. interviews of neighbors with Lucien taking one side of the alley and Wycliff the other.

With Robert the footman on the back of the curricle, Lucien had gone only two streets from home when he heard his name called. He looked over his shoulder and saw Finn running down the middle of the road.

"Lord Ware! Wait, milord."

Lucien brought the horses to a halt. "Is something wrong?"

Finn stopped as he reached the curricle, gasping and bending over with his hands on his knees to catch his breath. "I found it, milord."

"The barrow?"

"Yes, sir. I know where it was stole an' where it went."

"Excellent work, my lad. Get up behind, Finn, and show me."

"Does this mean I can go home?" Robert asked. "Hughes had several errands for me, and—"

Lucien chuckled and shook his head at Robert's eagerness to be off. "Yes, by all means, go."

With Finn happily settled in his customary place, Lucien tooled the small carriage toward Lille Street, the first road south of Gerrard and out of sight of the boarding house. They found Wycliff on horseback waiting for them, and Lucien quickly apprised him of the latest development.

"How do you want to do this?" Wycliff asked. "Clearly you need to speak with both households involved. I could go with you, but I'm thinking it would be more useful if I completed the other neighborhood interviews. It has to be done at some point."

"Yes, unless these two households tell us something startling, but before you begin, tie your horse on the back, and we'll drive down King and Gerrard so Finn can show us the two houses involved."

As they drove slowly past the alley where Maria's body was found, Finn pointed out the backyard where the barrow was stolen, three houses east of the boarding house on the Gerrard side of the alley, and then the other backyard—two houses west on the King Street side and just past Maccles Lane—where the barrow was dumped. Once they had identified both properties from the front, Lucien brought the curricle back to Lille Street. He and Wycliff leapt down, leaving Finn to watch the horses.

"If anyone starts paying too much attention or actually comes out to question you, move the curricle," Lucien instructed, "but not too far." He handed Finn his spare pocket watch. The one thing he had taught his groom—and most of his servants upon employment—was how to tell time. It avoided a host of mistakes and misunderstandings. "Beginning one hour from now, come back to this spot every fifteen minutes until I return."

"Yes, sir. I be here when y' need me."

Lucien and Wycliff walked east to the corner, turned north and parted when they reached Gerrard. Wycliff turned west to finish the interviews on Gerrard; Lucien took Maccles Lane toward the house on King where the barrow was abandoned.

He stopped first at the alley for a closer look at the backyard in question. Nothing particularly remarkable about it; like most of the properties, it had an alley gate with a simple latch, easy access for the killer. He retraced his steps to Maccles Lane and went around the corner to the front door.

A footman answered his knock, and Lucien presented his card. "Is your master or mistress at home?"

"Please step inside, my lord. I shall inquire if they are available."

A gray-haired, rather distinguished looking man appeared only moments later and introduced himself as the owner, Carlton Morehouse. "May I inquire the reason for your visit, Lord Ware?"

"I understand you found a barrow on your property a few days ago that belonged to one of your neighbors."

"My gardener found one, I believe." Morehouse looked perplexed. "Is there some problem? Was the barrow damaged?"

"Not to my knowledge, sir, but it may have been used in a criminal act," Lucien said. "May I speak with your gardener?"

"What kind of crime? Are you telling me my gardener is a criminal?"

"No, I have no reason to believe so," Lucien said. "I merely wish to know where he found the barrow and its condition at the time."

Morehouse frowned. "You have not said what crime was committed, nor what it has to do with you, sir."

Lucien hesitated. He had hoped not to explain any of this—nor raise speculation that might get back to Bow Street—but Morehouse left him little choice. "I believe it was used to transport a dead body before it was left in your yard."

"A corpse? Why I never! How dare the scoundrel." Morehouse appeared affronted that his property had in any way been associated with such a heinous crime. "I've a mind to have that gate removed. I shall certainly install a lock, but how will the gardener get in if I do? Oh, my, I shall have to sort it all out." Morehouse finally looked at Lucien. "What is it you wanted?"

"The gardener, sir?" Lucien prodded.

"Oh, yes. That would be Sam Hunt. We all hire him. I believe he was next door this morning when I put the dog out. It is Thursday, is it not? The Abernathys' day."

Lucien left Morehouse still fussing over the ill use of his backyard and returned to the alley. Approaching the Abernathys' rear gate, he spotted a man in a laborer's clothes trimming bushes.

"Are you Sam Hunt?" he asked, leaning on the fence.

"I am, sir. You needing a gardener?"

"No. Just a few questions about the barrow you found."

"Oh, that thing. It's already been claimed."

"Yes, I know." Lucien explained it's possible connection to the body in the alley, and Sam expressed an eagerness to help.

"Found it right behind that shed," he said, pointing at the small building close to the back fence in Morehouse's yard. "Just enough room to stuff the barrow between the shed and the fence." Hunt scratched his head. "I knew right away that something wasn't right. Like most folks around here, Morehouse don't have a barrow, and I always brung my own. It smelled funny too, all covered with that dark stain." He rolled his eyes. "Now, that you tell me what happened, I reckon it was blood."

"Was anything left in the barrow?"

"A piece of stained canvas in the bottom. I dint touch it. Most of the smell was from there, and it looked a bit soggy." He shrugged. "Told Mr. Morehouse's man up at the house, but it weren't nothing to do with me, so I left it where it was."

"How did you locate the owner?"

"Dint. He found me. The next day I'm working down the lane, and Mr. Browns's man Ed from over on Gerrard comes along. He says they is missin' their barrow. So, I showed him the one in Morehouse's backyard, and he said it was theirs." The gardener lifted his shoulder again. "That was that."

Lucien thanked him and cut through to Gerrard Street and was admitted to the barrow owner's house by a tall, extremely thin manservant.

Lucien introduced himself. "Are you Ed?"

"Yes, Edward Sweet." He looked puzzled.

"I would like to speak with you and your master regarding the stolen barrow," Lucien said.

"A strange occurrence to be sure," Sweet allowed. He gestured for Lucien to enter the front parlor. "I will see if Mr. Brown is available to see you."

In was a full ten minutes before Sweet returned, pushing a portly, gray-haired man in a wheelchair.

"I apologize for the intrusion," Lucien said.

"No trouble at all," Brown said, appraising his visitor. "Nothing much to do all day now my Nettie is gone. Married twenty years we were. But that's not why you're here. What is this about the barrow?"

"I believe it was used to transport the body found in your alley a week ago," Lucien said bluntly.

"You don't say. Are you certain?" Brown appeared dumbfounded, but a glint of interest lit his face.

"I am rather confident," Lucien assured him. "Can you tell me when it went missing?"

Brown turned his head to look up at his manservant, and Sweet hurried to answer. "Not the exact day, milord. We hadn't used it in a while."

"It was late last week when Sweet told me it was missing," Brown said. "A couple of days after the constables were about. I sent him out right away to find the thing, and sure enough, he brought it back within an hour." He beamed in satisfaction. "Barrows are not cheap, you know."

"They are not," Lucien agreed, although he had no knowledge of what a barrow cost. Obviously, it was a significant amount to a man of middling means. "What was the barrow's condition?"

"It had a loose wheel that I had to fix, and well, it was very, um, dirty," Sweet said, giving his employer a sideways glance. "But otherwise, undamaged."

"Dirty?" Lucien repeated. "That hardly seems an adequate word, considering Sam Hunt's description."

Sweet pulled at his collar, obviously uncomfortable. "I, uh, well...

"Quit blathering and answer the man," Brown interrupted.

"Well, milord, I had not mentioned the dried blood or the bloody rags to Mr. Brown. I did not wish to upset him. It was a right ghastly task to clean it. I figured someone had hauled away a dead dog or maybe rats."

"You should have told me. I am not so delicate you could not," Brown said with a frown. "It is annoying that it was taken without permission and left it in poor condition, but to think it was used in a murder…" He broke off. "I suppose there is no chance it was animal blood, is there?"

"Probably not," Lucien said.

Brown shook his head. "Disgusting. To think a dead woman was carted around like so much garbage." He straightened. "Get rid of it, Sweet. I do not want the dratted thing on my property."

"But sir— I have cleaned it."

"No, Sweet, I will bear the cost to replace it. I would think of that poor woman every time I saw it. Get me a new one. Bright and shiny."

"Yes, sir."

"May I see it first?" Lucien asked.

Brown shrugged. "As you like, my lord, but knowing how thorough Sweet is, I doubt there is anything to see."

While Brown stayed inside, Sweet showed Lucien into the backyard. His master's prediction proved true when Sweet opened the garden shed to reveal a barrow that had been scrubbed shiny clean except for a little rust and a few small dents from age and use.

"Looks almost new," Lucien said. "You may be able to sell it."

"I thought so too, sir."

"Dare I asked what happened to the bloody canvas?"

"Burned with the other trash."

Lucien turned toward the rear gate. "Thank Mr. Brown for me. I think I'll slip out the back gate."

"Very good, sir. Uh, there was one other thing."

Lucien looked back at him. "Yes, something you forgot?"

"Not forgot…but when I removed the canvas…well, sir, a pair of bloody gloves fell out. Leather gloves."

"Don't tell me—you burned them too."

"I did, sir. They were ruined." Sweet looked concerned. "Did I do something wrong, milord?"

Lucien stifled a sigh, but there was nothing to be gained by chastising Sweet. "You couldn't know they might be future evidence, but perhaps you can describe them."

"Certainly, sir. They were very fine deerskin. Winter dress gloves I believe. Nice enough a gentleman or even a lady might have worn them, but I remember thinking it odd they had been needed in such mild weather."

They had not been used for warmth, Lucien thought. Someone had not wanted bloody hands.

Having learned what he could about the barrow, Lucien returned to Lille Street where he found Finn waiting as arranged—and Wycliff with him.

"Captain, I had not expected to see you so soon."

"I had only five houses to do, and two had no one but servants at home." He smiled. "Nonetheless, I do not return with nothing. A young buck was making his way home on King Street around two the morning Miss Pembroke was found and saw a carriage on Maccles Lane obviously waiting for someone. He thought it was odd, but being well into his cups, he did not give it another thought until I asked."

"Anything to identify the carriage or horses?"

Wycliff shook his head. "As I said, he'd made a heavy night of it at the clubs. All he remembered was a light closed carriage with two horses, definitely not a hackney. The coachman was fiddling with the harness, so he didn't get a look at the man's face. Not much to go on, but it might indicate we are searching for a gentleman killer."

"That it might," Lucien agreed as Wycliff retrieved his riding horse from the rear of the curricle. "A theory that is supported by the pair of bloody, well-made gloves that were found in the barrow. Could belong to the Frenchman, or some other gentleman Maria got entangled with, but I would certainly like to know what type of coach Nigel Edington owns—and where he was when the body was being dumped."

"Have you discovered a motive?"

"Not yet, but I wonder if she saw or heard something she should not."

"You know," Wycliff said suddenly, "if that coach is involved, it would mean more than one person took part—while one man got rid of the body, the other moved the carriage to the far end of the alley."

"Or woman," Lucien said. "Under your theory there were at least two, maybe three. A trusted coachman, for sure, and there could have been another accomplice inside the closed carriage." He smiled at Wycliff. "I am eager for Shery to return. We have much to discuss."

Chapter Sixteen

Chadley Hall, Warwickshire, October 1812

Recognizing the strong masculine handwriting, Lady Anne Ashburn gripped the letter in her hand. Her heart beat a bit faster in her impatience for her maid Jenny to finish straightening her dresser and leave. To be honest, Anne was of two minds about the letter that had arrived a short time ago. It had raised disconcerting emotions…and numerous questions. Oh, there was no doubt of her reading it, but why would Lord Ware be writing to her again so soon?

The moment Jenny clicked the door closed behind her, Anne broke the seal and unfolded the letter. To her surprise, it was long. Could it be about Sherbourne's situation? She frowned. Surely that would be an odd thing to share with her—unless he needed her help. Nonsense, what could she do from Warwickshire?

With an unladylike snort, she quit speculating and started to read.

Dear Lady Anne,

I shall come right to the point—I need your assistance, once again. I am certain you have heard some of what is happening with Sherry, but before I make my request, I must apprise you of the full facts as I know them and the results of my inquiries up to this moment.

Anne's eyes widened in shock. He *did* need her help. The most amazing part was not that he felt she could do something from so far away—but that he had asked.

She had received a second letter from Margret telling her of the horrifying charges against Sherbourne, but she had assumed the matter was resolved by now. How could it not be? The charges were ridiculous, and it was hard to imagine that Lord Ware had not yet uncovered the guilty person. She shivered, thinking of the possibility that Sherbourne might be hanged if Bow Street caught up with him.

She read on, nodding once or twice at his description of what they were doing, then shaking her head at the small progress. "Edington," she said aloud when she came to the name. The elderly couple she knew had died, the wife, some dozen years ago, and he, maybe two or three years later.

"Oh, I see. Yes, of course," she murmured to herself as Lucien explained he was inquiring about the new heirs, that they had employed the murdered woman, what he'd learned about them thus far, and finally asking her what was known about them in the community.

She stopped for a moment and considered what he had not said. Surely they were suspects…and perhaps the main suspects. Otherwise, why would he be showing so much interest? Any information she could provide might help him prove Sherbourne's innocence.

She read on and came to the last line regarding the broken cipher. "Oh, Lucien. Thank you," she murmured, her lips lifting in a smile. "How very thoughtful to let me know." For a moment she was lost in memories of the frightening—and thrilling—events that first brought them together.

Anne finally rose, determined to do what she could to help solve Sherbourne's troubles. Although she didn't know much about the new Edingtons—well, nothing, really—there was one sure way to find out. She glanced into the looking glass to assure herself her attire was appropriate for a morning visit. The blue trim on her white gown matched the blue of her eyes. She patted her fair curls, her eyes gleaming with suppressed excitement. Yes, she would do.

Hurrying downstairs, she asked Jenny to find her blue pelisse and sat down to wait for Daniel's morning visit. In order to make it a proper call, she would ask him to escort her. Since she had not called on the new residents since her return from London, had she not been remiss in her social duties to represent Chadley Hall?

Anne smiled to herself. How was she to know they were residing in London? Besides, someone must be living there who could answer her questions. Perhaps the steward...what was his name? Oh, yes, Henry. He might be persuaded to tell her about his new employers, and Jenny could question the servants below stairs.

Having decided on a plan, Anne waited impatiently for Daniel Allerton to arrive. He had been visiting nearly every day, and he was twenty minutes late, having promised to be there by eleven. When she finally heard his voice, she met him in the hallway.

"Daniel, I have the most wonderful plans for us." She took his hand, pulling him into the parlor and quickly related selected parts of Lord Ware's letter. She mentioned Sherbourne was in trouble but withheld any talk of murder. Contrary to her own eagerness, Daniel's face told her long before she finished that he was not enthusiastic about the proposed visit.

"It sounds a bit havey-cavey to me, Anne. Bow Street, an illegitimate child. Such matters should not be spoken of—or put in writing—to a gentle lady. I am surprised this Lord Ware would take the liberty."

Anne frowned at him. "Don't be so judgmental. These are friends of mine and very respectable people," she said, her tone having a biting edge.

"I beg pardon if I have offended, Anne. Perhaps his familiarity could be overlooked, but he should not ask a lady to become involved in such a sordid affair."

"He only inquired of what I knew. It was my idea to visit the Edington estate. And why should he not ask me for assistance? I have done it before," she blurted before she had time to think. She had not told him or her parents of her previous adventures in London, although her mother knew some of the less controversial parts. She had not wished to worry her parents, and...well, she was not certain why she had kept it from Daniel. Maybe she had sensed the disapproval that was now on his face.

"What do you mean?" Daniel stared at her. "Are you saying this Lord Ware fellow has already put you in danger?"

"No, of course not." She had done that part all by herself on both occasions. "But he did me the courtesy of listening to my opinions, and Miss Barnett and I picked up a bit of useful information on one matter. Come now, Daniel. Don't look so stern. You know how curious I have always been. Participating in an inquiry even a little bit was rather jolly fun."

His brow finally lightened, the lines smoothing, and he sighed. "I daresay you would think so. Sometimes, my dear, your high spirits threaten to go beyond the bounds. It is time you were settling down."

"That is as may be, but for now, Lord Ware needs assistance, and I intend to find out what I can about the Edingtons…with or without your help."

"In that event, of course I shall go." He smiled, looking more like the childhood friend she knew. "Someone has to keep you out of trouble."

• • •

A half hour later, Anne, Daniel, and Jenny were in the Earl of Chadley's second-best coach pulled by a handsome team of four matched chestnuts.

"Have you met the new residents at Edington?" Anne asked Daniel.

"I have not. I have heard they prefer London. What makes you think they will be in residence today?"

"I just feel lucky."

He gave her an indulgent smile. "Your luck may have run out. Rumor has it they are so disenchanted with the manor that they plan to sell it."

"Truly? How sad. The old couple I knew would be devastated. I believe it has been in the Edington family a hundred and fifty years."

"Regardless, the new owners may have a sound reason. The estate has deteriorated and repairs will be costly. It sat empty too many years, and I doubt if old Mr. Edington did much upkeep after his wife died."

"Would Henry, the steward, not have done whatever was necessary?"

Daniel gave a casual shrug. "The daily care, I suppose—cleaning, gardening—but he would not have the authority to order more costly structural repairs."

"Then the heirs should have stepped in to start fixing things as soon as they inherited. They cannot be without funds. The Edingtons always lived well."

"We shall soon see for ourselves," Daniel said, as the coach slowed, swinging into the curving entrance road, and then stopped at the front entrance of Edington Manor.

Anne looked around as she descended. Daniel was correct, it appeared; the stone and brick house had a slightly shabby look—a canvas patch on the roof, cracked and crumbing brickwork—and the lawn needed new plantings. Nothing that could not be corrected, but it revealed a persistent lack of care.

A maid answered the door and informed them the family was not in residence—which, of course, Anne knew. Daniel turned to leave, but she asked to see the steward before he could stop her, and she was delighted to learn her old friend Henry still held that position.

"Anne, what are you about?" Daniel asked. "The Edingtons are not at home."

"It would be a shame not to visit with Henry now that we are here," she said giving him an innocent look. "Jenny, why don't you go to the kitchen for a cup of tea, while we have our visit?" She turned to the Edington's maid. "Is Henry in his office?"

"Yes, ma'am, but—"

"Please take us to him. I am confident he won't mind the interruption. We are old friends."

"Yes, my lady, just this way."

When the maid tapped on the steward's open door, he looked up from his ledgers with a frown. "What is it?" Henry had developed a slight paunch and his hair was receding, but his lips spread into a broad smile when he recognized Anne standing behind the maid. "Oh, my lady, forgive my manners." He rose quickly. "Lady Anne, it has been years. And Lord Allerton. How delightful to see you both. What brings you to Edington? If you hoped to meet the new owners, I am sorry to say they are in London."

"We just heard. I had looked forward to making their acquaintance," she said. "It must be a relief to finally have a family in residence again."

He gave a doubtful shrug, and Anne latched on to the tell-tale gesture.

"Don't tell me Mr. Edington is a harsh master?"

Henry turned to the maid still hovering in the doorway. "Rose, I'm sure our guests would like a cup of tea. We shall be in the front parlor." When she left, he cast a speculative glance at Anne before answering her question. "I know little of the new master and mistress. They are not *in residence*, nor have they been—at least not here. A year ago, they came to inspect the property on the way to London and left after two hours. We have not seen them since."

"Surely they have corresponded with you regarding household matters."

"I wish it were so. My list of needed repairs has elicited no response. As for household staff, Rose and I are the only live-in servants; Cook comes once a day, and a lad from the village does yard work every two weeks. I have received no instructions, so we are continuing to do what we have always done."

"That is very strange indeed. Are they going to sell?"

"I expect so." He lifted a brow. "I heard there are significant debts to pay."

Anne frowned. "That surprises me. I always thought the family was well situated."

"The old gentleman was." He hesitated. "I suppose I should not say this, but I believe it is a matter of gambling debts incurred by the new owner."

"Oh. How unfortunate."

Daniel cleared his throat as though disapproving of the direction the conversation had taken.

Anne ignored the hint because this was just the kind of information that Lord Ware might need. "There must be things to do if it is to be sold, and staff needs time to find new positions. I wonder why Mr. Edington has not told you of his plans for the manor."

"Nary a word. And, well, his name is not Edington. It is Smythe...or was until recently," Henry added grudgingly. "I suppose it is legally Edington now. They were very distant relations to old Cyrus Edington, and not in the direct line. They changed their name from Smythe to Edington even before the court awarded them the estate."

Daniel cleared his throat again. "Perhaps tea is ready now."

She heard the edge to his voice and wondered at his obvious disapproval. Surely he was not opposed to a bit of community chit-chat.

"A timely reminder, my lord." Henry led them through the house, passing the family portrait gallery on their way to the front parlor.

Anne paused before the painting of a very distinguished gentleman standing behind a seated woman. "I recognize Cyrus Edington. Such a nice old gentleman he was. This must be his wife. I cannot remember her very well."

"She was ill for several years before she died. A compassionate woman, very good to the servants. He missed her dearly. We all did."

Anne skipped over the next painting of someone named Morville—why on earth was it included?—and stopped to study the portrait on the end of a tall slender couple, their countenances rather severe. "Is this the new owners?"

"Yes. Meet Nigel and Olivia Smythe, now Edington. A few weeks after their brief visit, the portrait arrived with instructions to add it to the gallery."

As they reached the parlor, they found Rose setting up the tea tray, and Henry broke off the conversation. "I beg pardon for going on so, my lady. It's just that I have been rather worried about the future."

"I understand, Henry. You have every cause to be concerned." If the estate was out of funds and the property sold, where would Henry go? A maid could always find a new household, but a steward's position was not so easy to procure. What if they did not even bother to give the servants references? Anne sighed. The Edingtons' apparent indifference to the plight of the manor and staff was deplorable.

Anne wanted to know more about the couple, but Henry acted embarrassed he had spoken so freely of his employers. She tried to ease him into the topic again, but each time, Daniel inserted a question about the stables or crops. The conversation lagged and gradually turned to more mundane subjects—her mother's health and local gossip regarding new babies in the village and the vicar's unexpected engagement. As soon as they finished their tea, Daniel stood.

"We should be on our way. We have already taken up too much of your time."

"Not at all," Henry assured him. "I was delighted to see you. We don't have many visitors…as you can imagine."

Anne was far from ready to go, but arguing with Daniel would be the height of impropriety, and she acquiesced to his wishes. They collected Jenny, thanked Henry for his hospitality, and set out on the return trip to Chadley.

As the coach rolled on and minutes passed in unusual silence, Anne glanced at the stony set of Daniel's face. What in heaven's name was troubling him? When he still failed to say anything after she sent several pointed glances his way, she finally asked, "Whatever is it, Daniel? You look quite put out as though ready to ring a peal over my head."

"Not now," he said with a barely perceptible nod toward Jenny. "We shall talk about it later."

"As you wish." If that was the way he was going to be, she'd rather not talk about it—whatever *it* was—at all. She turned away and tilted her head toward Jenny. "Did you pick up any interesting tittle-tattle downstairs?"

"Oh, yes, miss. The cook was quite talkative. She plans to quit, as soon as she gets the pay she's owed for the last four weeks, but she's heard the estate has no money. She only met the new Edingtons once but she didn't like them much. Mrs. Edington was snappish, and her sister complained about everything. He had hardly a word to say."

"Really, Anne," Daniel broke in stiffly, "you should not encourage this kind of gossip about their betters."

"You don't have to listen," she said without looking at him, more than a little annoyed that he would choose to reprimand her in front of her maid. She kept her attention on Jenny. "I had not heard of a sister before. Did the cook mention her name? Or say anything else about her?"

"No, my lady. She couldn't recall if she'd even heard her name."

Henry might know, Anne thought, and that could be important information for Lord Ware. She was all for going back and asking him, but when she suggested turning around, Daniel looked appalled and firmly shook his head.

"Absolutely not. We have already overstepped the bounds of propriety."

Anne stared at him. Is that what he thought? And it truly provoked him? When had Daniel become such a fusspot?

Unfortunately, that was not the end of it. Once they got back to Chadley, and they were sitting in the front parlor with Jenny discreetly doing her mending on the other side of the room, Daniel made clear the extent of his displeasure. "Honestly, Anne, it is no wonder Jenny gossips as she does. You have set a poor example. I was surprised you encouraged Henry to talk about his employers in that manner. No, I misspoke, not just encouraged, it was more akin to an interrogation. Have your months in London made you forget simple country manners?"

Anne's eyes widened. "Have you forgotten my purpose in going was to gather information?"

"Which I voiced an objection to from the beginning. It was unseemly, Anne."

She stiffened at his tone. "Are you giving me a scold, Daniel? Is that not stretching friendship a bit far?"

He looked taken aback and raised his chin. "I did not realize there was such formality between us that I could not speak of it when I observed a flaw in your conduct. If I have overstepped, I beg your pardon, *my lady*. Perhaps I should take my leave before one of us says something we shall regret."

"Perhaps you should," Anne agreed, rising from her chair in a gesture of dismissal.

Daniel bowed stiffly and walked away with a scowl on his face. Anne did not call him back.

When had her fun-loving friend become such a prig? What would he be like in another ten years? A steady man, no doubt faithful and attentive to his wife, but managing...and boring. There, she had said what she had been feeling.

She took in a deep breath. Perhaps she was being too harsh. After all, it was not entirely his fault—she had allowed him to maneuver her into ending today's visit before she had everything she wanted. At the very least, she needed the sister's name, and Henry's tone had suggested there was more to learn about the transfer of the estate to the present holders. Had Lucien not said so too? She should have asked.

And another thing...she pictured Olivia and Nigel Edingtons' portrait in her head and the baffling portrait hanging between it and old Cyrus Edington. Why was it there? Morville had been the name below it. Not an Edington, so who was he? Another unanswered question she should have asked. She sighed again, far from satisfied with the visit. What should she do now—send what information she had to Lord Ware and let the rest go?

She paced across the parlor floor, thinking hard. Lord Ware would not have asked for her assistance if he wasn't desperate. How could she let him down by being less than thorough? The thought of Sherbourne remaining in gaol—or heaven forbid, hanging—because she had not done her part was too horrid to even contemplate.

Anne pressed her lips in a stubborn line her mother would have recognized as trouble. She was due at the vicarage at four to discuss plans for the autumn festival, but tomorrow she would return to Edington manor...and this time, without Daniel.

Chapter Seventeen

Hertfordshire to London, October 1812

Sherry woke early on Friday morning. Despite the late night with Yvette and Pierre…and way too much wine, he was keen to get back to London and resume the hunt for the Frenchman. Now that he had a name—Gaston Breguet—it was only a matter of time before he ran him to earth. As instructed, Gregory had the carriage ready by eight, and after a quick meal and effusive goodbyes, he was on his way before nine, which put them back in the city by mid-afternoon.

Clad once again in the tradesman's clothes he used when they'd left London, Sherry leapt down from the coach the moment it stopped inside Lucien's stable. While Gregory was putting the team away, Sherry saddled and mounted his bay gelding, hoping to get away before Gregory noticed. Although Breguet might already have fled London, there was always a chance something had delayed him, and Sherry couldn't give him another moment to make good his escape. He turned his horse toward the stable door.

"Sir, no," Gregory called, running across the stable and grabbing the reins to detain him. "You must wait for Lord Ware. He told me to make sure you weren't seen around the city. Going off on your own is not safe."

"This is my decision, Gregory," Sherry said. "Not yours. I have to locate Gaston Breguet before he leaves the country. In the event I am unsuccessful, give Lord Ware the Frenchman's name, but I plan to be back by evening. Now step away."

"He is not going to like it." Gregory sighed heavily but released his hold on the reins. He continued to watch with a worried frown as Sherry exited the stable door.

Once outside, Sherry nudged his mount into a brisk trot, turning toward the north.

On the journey from Hertfordshire, he had planned his search—starting with the inns near the northern route coming into London from Oxfordshire. If Breguet had come straight to the city after talking with Pembroke, he likely would have stopped at an inn along that path. Of course, five months was a long time, and he would have moved, probably several times. Regardless, Sherry needed a place to start, and this made the most sense to him.

• • •

By the time he swung out of the saddle at the Red Fox Inn, his lips were tight with frustration. He'd been at this for three hours, visiting a number of inns and boarding houses without finding a trace of a man named Gaston Breguet. Nor could anyone identify any particular Frenchman from Hugh Pembroke's vague description—near forty, dark hair and eyes, medium height, heavy accent. Sherry was getting discouraged, but no doubt he was just tired. This would be his last stop before giving it up for the night.

The Red Fox's public rooms and tavern brimmed with noisy chatter. Sherry made his way to the bar, ordered a pint of ale, and waited for an opportune moment to talk with the bald-headed landlord. Finally, there was a lull and he gestured to the man.

"Another pint, sir?"

"Not quite yet. I'm looking for a man. A Frenchman by the name of Gaston Breguet. About forty, heavy accent."

"Oh, aye. He was here, stayed several weeks. I usually don't take to Frenchies, but he was a tolerable fellow. I hope he's not gotten into trouble."

Sherry straightened with a surge of triumph. "No, it is a personal matter."

"Something to do with family, I wager. He was looking for his brother's widow and their infant child."

"That's the man," Sherry said eagerly. "Do you know where he went from here?"

The publican shook his head. "He was looking for cheaper, more permanent lodgings to allow him to continue his search. That was around three months ago. I sent him to a boarding house on Briar Road and haven't seen him since."

"I've not met Breguet. Is there some way I might identify him by sight?"

"Not that..." The man started to shrug then stopped. "He had a leg injury, right leg. War wound maybe, but I didn't ask, didn't want to know. He hid it well, and the limp wasn't really noticeable until late in the day. As I said, pleasant enough fellow, but his English was so bad it was hard to have much of a conversation."

"Good to know. I appreciate the information." Sherry handed him his calling card. "If you see him again, I'd like to know."

Sherry hurried out the door with a grin on his face, headed for Briar Road and perhaps the end of his search. He was so caught up in considering how to approach Breguet that he nearly collided with Albert Haskett.

Bloody hell. His stomach clenched, and he looked around for a way to escape, but the runner was accompanied by three constables, and one had already circled behind him.

Haskett's face twisted in a mocking smile. "Here now, Sherbourne. Needn't be in such a rush. We must have a word, you and me."

Sherry made an attempt to bluff it out. "Not now, my good man. I have an appointment, but I shall be glad to speak with you tomorrow."

"Surely you would not be going to an appointment wearing those clothes. No, sir, ye won't be putting me off. Take him, me lads. His lordship be stayin' in a cold gaol cell tonight."

The constables grabbed for him, and Sherry instinctively twisted away. He'd only taken a few steps when Haskett struck him in the gut with a wooden baton. He doubled over, and they hustled him into an enclosed wagon. Despite numerous applications of Haskett's baton, Sherry refused to say anything except to assert his innocence and demand that his family or friends be notified of his arrest.

• • •

An hour later he found himself tossed into a drab, stone holding-cell in Newgate Prison. It wasn't just cold, but damp and filthy. His nose twitched at the unpleasant stench of mold, urine, and human feces.

"Bloody hell," he murmured as he got to his feet and glanced at his seven fellow inmates, most of them glaring at him. In general, the lower classes, which formed most of the prisoners in Newgate, were not fond of the privileged aristocracy. His speech and general demeanor might have given him away eventually, but the goalers made it known by repeatedly addressing him as *his lordship*. He might be more in danger from his cell mates than from the gaolers. Those awaiting trial were often intermingled with convicted prisoners facing transportation or execution. Some of those staring at him had nothing left to lose.

Sherry looked away, avoiding eye contact. As he might be there for a while, he had no wish to antagonize anyone. Haskett had refused to allow him to contact Lucien or send word to his father. The runner's clear intention was to keep him hidden until he could extract a confession. Since Sherry knew that wasn't going to happen, his chances of getting out of there speedily were not good. However, Lucien would start looking for him soon, and he'd notify the baron if necessary.

Sherry hunkered in one corner, hoping to make himself appear inconsequential. If he could keep to himself and stay alive in this hell hole, Lucien would find a way to get him out.

He had to believe that.

• • •

Timely passed slowly, giving Sherry ample opportunity to worry and wonder what his family and Emily would think of the charges against him. How soon would the news reach them in the country? Surely his parents would know he was innocent? Would Emily?

After what seemed like hours, his legs began to cramp. He wanted to move around but didn't for fear of drawing unwanted attention. He had heard the whispers and occasionally felt the weight of someone's hostile stare, but so far, no one had approached.

He stiffened at a sudden change in the atmosphere, a stirring among the prisoners, and he glanced up to see a large, bulky man coming toward him. The fellow had the look of a laborer from the docks. His eyes were hard. He had something concealed in his right hand—a weapon, no doubt. A handmade knife? A rock or piece of iron that would break a man's jaw?

"Hey, you. What you in for? Kickin' a dog?"

Some of the crowd laughed, seeming to find this funny. Sherry straightened, keeping his body loose, casual, and he shrugged.

"What's the matter? Cain't talk?"

"I'm not looking for trouble," Sherry said, knowing his continued silence would be seen as disrespect.

"Your rich, top-lofty friends deserted you?" another prisoner taunted, coming up behind the first one. "Why you wearin' those clothes? Pretending' you one of us? I reckon I know who you are? Heard the gaolers talkin'. You done killed a woman a week or two ago."

"Killed a tart, eh?" the first man asked.

Sherry shook his head again, keeping his eyes on the man with the weapon but aware that others were closing in from both sides.

"Why didya kill her? She no good?" The man made a vulgar gesture, leaving no doubt what he meant.

"Maria was no tart," Sherry said, keeping the wall behind him, "and I did not kill her."

This brought more laughter. "Hey, Paddy, he be an innocent man, like all the rest of us."

Paddy, the obvious leader, broke off his laugh, gripped the object in his hand a little tighter, and snarled, "Well I don't believe it, and I don't get on with those that kills females."

Sherry set his back against the wall, shifting his weight to the balls of his feet. When someone grabbed his left arm, he jerked to the right, but a second assailant was waiting. Sherry leapt high enough to kick him in the gut before he was seized by the throat from behind. He let his body weight fall, breaking the man's hold, but he landed hard on the cell floor as others closed in. Sherry tried to roll away, under a hail of kicks from booted feet, but his arms were grabbed, pulled behind him, and he was yanked upright.

Paddy closed in, his sneering face six inches from Sherry's, his breath foul, and his hand came up to reveal a home-made knife.

"All right, ye blighters!" A gaoler banged his baton on the bars, and Paddy's knife disappeared. The gaoler unlocked the door. "Back off. This fellow is off limits. He goes to the Magistrate tomorrow. Wouldn't want no marks on his pretty face." He glared at Paddy. "Y' hear me?"

Paddy shrugged, insolence spread across his face. Sherry pulled his hands free. Paddy and his friends weren't going away. It would be seven to one the moment the guard left, but on his feet with his hands free again Sherry could give a better account of himself.

The gaoler looked him up and down. "You hurt?"

"No," Sherry mumbled, brushing himself off.

"That's good." The gaoler raised his voice. "Mr. Cade sends his regards."

Sherry stilled and said nothing, but he saw the looks exchanged among the other prisoners, and then Paddy abruptly turned and walked away.

Well, *bollocks*, that was unexpected. Sherry snorted softly. Apparently he would survive a bit longer—thanks to Cade, a man Sherry did not know except by reputation. This protection had to be offered because of Whitehall's or rather Lucien's past contacts with Cade. Still, it was odd.

Had Lucien already learned of Sherry's arrest? Had he been forced to go to Cade for help? Sherry gritted his teeth. Whether the intervention had been volunteered or requested, he was indebted to Cade this time. Despite Sherry's certainty he'd regret the help later, at the moment he could only take a grateful breath of relief.

He still would not let his guard down. He had seen Paddy's face—resentful, angry. The man didn't like following orders from anyone. He was sly enough not to defy Cade openly, but if he could take Sherry down without anyone seeing him, he'd do so. Sherry leaned his back against a corner. Any rest tonight would be done with one eye open.

Chapter Eighteen

Lucien returned to Hays Mews early that Friday afternoon in anticipation of Sherry's arrival. He'd barely gotten in the front door when his coachman surprised him by coming down the hall from the back of the house.

"Gregory, good to see you're back. Did the journey go well?"

"I've been waiting for you, milord. It's about Lord Sherry. I tried to stop him, sir. I truly did."

"Stop him from what? Where is he?" Lucien asked with a sense of foreboding.

"He's gone after that Frenchie, milord. He was fixed on doing it. Said to tell you the fellow's name is Gaston Breguet, and that he'd be back this evening…and then he left on horseback."

Damnation! Lucien's chest tightened. "How long ago?"

"Maybe a half hour."

"Did he say where he was going?"

"No, sir. Only to find Breguet."

"Why didn't he wait for me?" Lucien muttered to himself.

"I told him he should, but he was raring to go. Truthfully, my lord, there was no stopping him."

"I can imagine. The bloody fool." Lucien understood Sherry's impatience—he might have done the same if desperate enough—but Sherry had help available, and he hadn't even asked for it. Any of Lucien's people would have gone with him. Going off on his own was dangerous—not only due to the Frenchman, a possible killer, but Haskett—and all the city's constables, not only those at Bow Street—were waiting and watching for just such a mistake.

Lucien rubbed his jaw in thought. Did he have any chance of catching up with Sherry? Where would his partner start? Did he have other information regarding the Frenchman that Lucien didn't know? *Devil it.* He couldn't go chasing around London with no idea of where Sherry and Gaston Breguet might be.

"Thank you, Gregory. Get some rest. You'll need it after such a long trip."

"I'm sorry about Lord Sherry, milord."

"Not your fault. He knew the risk. He will doubtless return by nightfall and wonder why we were concerned."

Lucien returned to the hall to pick up his mail and asked Hughes if he had any additional information on Sherry's activities.

"No, sir. He left straight from the stables. I had no opportunity to speak with him. Surely he will be all right."

"I certainly hope so." Lucien retired to his study in an uneasy mood. He sorted through the day's mail, found nothing of particular interest, and sat down at his desk to answer yesterday's letter from his estate agent, who oversaw his property at Waring. The steward was asking to build two additional cottages and add two workers for an innovative farming project they had been discussing for months. Lucien gave his final approval.

It was almost dusk when he heard someone at the front entrance, and he rushed into the hallway. He was standing at the top of the stairs when his father was admitted.

"Salcott! I did not know you were in London."

"Nor did I expect to be," the earl replied, mounting the stairs. "Were you anticipating a visitor?" He was obviously surprised to find Lucien waiting in the hall.

"I was hoping you were Sherry. But I *am* pleased to see you, sir."

The earl gave him a sharp look as they walked into the study. "I heard he was being sought by Bow Street on a charge of murder."

"He is not guilty. Is this why you're here?"

"It is not why I came to London. I was asked to see what I can do about the equity in the courts bill they propose to introduce next month. The drafters are at an impasse. When I got to town, I heard about Sherbourne…what the devil is going on? Is his father in town?"

"I haven't heard from the baron. Sherry wrote to him and told him not to come because he was leaving London." Lucien poured two glasses of port and handed one to his father. "Which he did, but Sherry failed to mention he was coming right back. He returned today, as a matter of fact, and went out alone—while I was gone—searching for the bloody Frenchman."

Salcott frowned. "What Frenchman?"

Lucien sighed. "I should start from the beginning. Have a seat, sir. It is a rather complicated story." As they sat by the fire, Lucien related the story—from Maria's appearance with Fanny to the Frenchman Gaston Breguet and to Lucien's suspicions of the Edingtons. He held back nothing. Whatever his past differences with Salcott, Lucien had never doubted his father's integrity...or his loyalty.

"What a tangle," Salcott said when Lucien finished. "Be wary of getting caught up on the wrong side of this, Lucien. If both of you end up in gaol, you will not be of much help to one another."

"I know, believe me. Bow Street has searched my house, my carriage, and they continue to watch the place."

"The devil you say. Very brazen of them."

Lucien smiled, noting Salcott's reaction mirrored his own. "I hoped that once they'd had their run of the place in a thorough search they would be done with me. No such fortune. The man across the street is an annoying reminder of how careful I must be."

"See that you are." Salcott rose, setting his empty glass on the table. "Keep me apprised, if you will. I shall think on this to see if there is a way I can be of assistance. I would hate to see the lad end up in Newgate."

Lucien sighed as he listened to his father's footsteps descending the stairs. Salcott's visit had only increased his unease. He continued to listen for the front door to open again, and when it hadn't happened by dark, he was pacing the floor, growing more troubled by the moment.

"Confound it, Sherry," Lucien muttered aloud. "How am I supposed to find you when you left no direction?" Every time he heard a sound on the street, he went to the window. He needed to be doing something, and he considered setting out on a random search just to be doing something, but then he wouldn't be there if Sherry returned or sent a message. So, he continued to pace.

Because he had been listening so intently for Sherry's arrival, he was surprised when Hughes tapped on his study door and said a lad was waiting downstairs with a message.

"Is it from Sherry?"

"He would not say, my lord. He came to the kitchen door and told the cook he had a message for you—and only you."

"Well, show the lad up. Let us see what he has to say."

Only moments later, Hughes announced, "Master Tad, my lord."

A street lad of perhaps eleven entered, holding his tattered cap with one hand and a letter in the other. "You be Viscount Ware?" he asked.

"I am. I understand you have a message for me."

"Yessir. Mr. Cade tol' me to give it only to you."

Lucien sighed inwardly. Cade. Good lord. What now?

"You have done an excellent job." Lucien took a coin from his pocket. "Allow me to reward your efforts."

"Oh, no, sir. Mr. Cade done paid me. He wuldna like it if I took from you."

"If you are certain..." When Tad nodded, Lucien put the coin away. Far be it from him to put the lad in Cade's bad graces. "Then accept my thanks," Lucien said, taking the note.

Tad nodded, plopped his cap back on his head, and scurried out the door, his feet clattering on the stairs.

Lucien tore open the note and read the contents. *Bloody Hell.* Sherry had been taken up by the Bow Street runners.

• • •

Lucien spent hours attempting to discover where Sherry was being held. He went to the Bow Street station, but those on duty denied his partner was there, nor would they admit having seen Haskett. Fearing the over-zealous runner was subjecting his prisoner to unduly harsh treatment or interrogation in secret, Lucien went straight to Newgate Prison. They denied having a prisoner named Andrew Sherbourne, but this time Lucien was certain they were lying—the shifting eyes, the furtive looks were damning. *Devil take them all.* How was he going to get past this wall of silence? Cade's message stated Sherry had been taken to Bow Street for questioning, and Cade was never wrong.

So, then where? Newgate, apparently, but how could Lucien contact him?

Knowing it was a mistake to rouse the Bow Street Magistrate from bed in the middle of the night, but worried Sherry was being tortured for a confession—why else would Haskett conceal him?—Lucien allowed his fears and frustration to take him to the justice's home. Fortunately, the household staff saved him from a social and legal faux pas by refusing him entrance. He was firmly told the master had retired for the night, and Lucien's urgent matter would have to wait until later in morning.

Frustrated and out of options, he returned to his curricle, shook his head at Finn, and took the reins. Where could he go? Who would listen? Rothe? Prinny?

Good lord, what was he thinking? He would be turned away by both at this hour.

Lucien sucked in a deep breath. He had not felt so bedeviled in—well, he couldn't remember when. He and Sherry had saved each other so many times in France—he had never doubted they could get out of any scrap of trouble. But now...he raked a hand through his hair and urged his team forward.

Before he realized it, he was pulling up in front of Sophy's townhouse. It was lit up, a sign she had not retired—or was still out for the evening. He had to talk with someone, and outside of Sherry, Sophy was the one person in London who would understand. He swung down from the carriage and knocked on the door.

When the footman showed him into Sophy's parlor, she rose immediately and came forward, her face showing alarm at this sudden, late-night appearance. "Good heavens, Lucien, what has happened? You look terrible."

Seeing the concern on her face, his frustration came pouring out. "It's Sherry. He has been taken up by the runners, and they've hidden him somewhere." Lucien's jaw clenched. "I fear he is not safe, Sophy, and I cannot find him."

"Oh, Lucien. I am so sorry." She threw her arms around him and held tight, murmuring sympathy and understanding, and he folded his arms around her, taking comfort from her warmth.

He turned his head, finding her willing lips and capturing them in a kiss. After a breathless moment, reason returned, and Lucien pulled back. "Forgive me, Sophy. We cannot do this."

"I know," she murmured, turning away and crossing the room, putting distance between them. "Not now. Not when your heart is elsewhere.

He gave her an appraising look.

"Did you think I did not know?" she asked softly

They had always been honest with one another, and he did not brush off her question and all that it left unsaid. "I beg pardon, Sophy. I misused our friendship."

"Nonsense. Do not make me angry by apologizing. Lady Anne is a fool to stay away so long. But the kiss, my darling, was something we both wanted, just at this moment. And it will be our last, for you see, Lord Castlebridge is going to propose marriage, and I am going to accept."

"Walter Castlebridge? Should I congratulate you or—not?" He gave her a wry smile.

"Wish me well. Oh, Lucien, do understand. Yes, he is older and not very witty, but he is kind and fond of me. He can still give me children—and I'm not getting any younger, you know—and he has the wealth to provide well for me and our children. I shall not live an exciting life, but I believe it will be a good one."

"Then I shall wish you happy with all my heart, Sophy. I know no one who deserves it more."

She smiled and gestured toward the chairs near the window.

"Let us have a glass of wine, and you can explain how Sherry ended up in gaol."

He gratefully accepted her decision to refrain from further discussion of that impulsive moment, but the news of her pending engagement only made the kiss loom as a greater mistake. He had never poached on another man's property...nor sought the arms of one woman when he desired another. If he didn't need to beg someone's pardon, why did he feel so conflicted?

• • •

Lucien left Sophy's at dawn. He was calmer now that she had let him talk until he was talked out. He roused Finn from sleep on the carriage seat, and his groom took one look at his master's face before slipping silently into place on the back of the curricle.

Driving aimlessly through the London streets, Lucien attempted to sort through his jumbled emotions. He set thoughts of Sophy and Lady Anne aside for another time and concentrated on the immediate problem of what to do about Sherry. He arrived at Hays Mews still without a plan other than a determination to locate his friend and get him out of gaol.

Brushing aside Talbot's questioning looks, he bathed, changed clothes, and had just settled in the breakfast room with coffee and toast from the sideboard when Hughes announced Lord Salcott.

The earl breezed in right behind the butler. "I apologize for calling so early, but I heard Sherbourne was arrested."

"It is true," Lucien said, rising. "I was all over town last night, including Bow Street and Newgate, but I cannot find him. They denied me everywhere."

"Sit down, my boy." Salcott turned up his nose at the smell of coffee. "None of that bitter stuff today. Have you no good English tea?"

"Yes, of course, we do," Lucien gestured to his footman to accommodate his father's choice, then sat when the earl did.

"I have a bit of news for you. I have been to see Rothe this morning. Haskett has taken a dislike to Sherbourne, heightened

I'm sure by evading him so long. He intends to play on the public sentiment behind this Equity in the Courts bill to make an example of him. Neither Rothe nor I—nor the prince, for that matter—can officially intervene due to the current public outrage that the aristocracy receives greater leniency from the courts—which is true, of course—but it works against us now. Nevertheless, Rothe spoke with the Magistrate who assured him Sherbourne would be brought before the court this afternoon."

"That *is* good news. Surely the Magistrate will see—"

"No, Lucien," Salcott interrupted. "You must resign yourself to the fact that this appearance is only a matter of form. Haskett has a strong enough argument to see that Sherbourne is held over for trial. However, the hearing will require them to bring him to court."

"What time is the hearing?"

"At two."

That gave him less than five hours, Lucien thought. Whatever it took, Sherry would not be staying in gaol—it was too dangerous—and Lucien would need every bit of that time to make his arrangements.

His father shot him a worried look. "Do not act rashly, Lucien. We will keep working on this."

Lucien nodded, acknowledging his father's good intentions, but he couldn't wait while they were *working on* it...nor could he leave Sherry in Haskett's hands.

Chapter Nineteen

Chadley Hall, Warwickshire, October 1812

Lady Anne pled a headache the morning after her trip to the Edington estate and sent word to Daniel cancelling their daily ride. She supposed he would think she was sulking over their disagreement or even be so thickheaded as to imagine she was embarrassed by her behavior. Well, he could indulge in any interpretation he wished—as long as he stayed away.

As soon as her breakfast tray was cleared by the house maid, Anne slipped out of bed.

"Quickly, Jenny, I wish to pay another visit to Edington. I think the blue morning dress with the white shawl."

"Yes, my lady, but if Lord Daniel isn't coming, who will escort you?"

"You shall, silly. A lady's maid is a suitable companion for such a visit."

"But—"

"No, no protests, Jenny. Hurry now."

As soon as they were ready, the two of them slipped out to the stables, and Anne waited impatiently while the carriage was made ready. The coachman, Timothy, appeared surprised she had not sent word ahead, but she assured him it was a last-minute decision, and he appeared appeased by that.

Worried Daniel might show up despite her note, Anne gave a sigh of relief once they were on their way. She settled back in the seat, organizing in her head the questions she wished to ask. This time she intended to have a heart-to-heart conversation to gather every bit of information Henry had about his employers, including the unknown sister and the mystery surrounding the inheritance.

While she was there, she hoped to satisfy her own curiosity about the portrait of Mr. Morville.

"My lady, you know Lord Daniel will be upset, don't you?" Jenny asked. Since the young maid was first hired ten months ago, the two women in some ways had been more companions than mistress and servant. She was almost as outspoken as Anne could be.

"Yes, if he finds out," Anne said, smoothing her gloves. "*I* certainly do not intend to tell him."

"Nor I, ma'am. You can count on that. But someone at the stable might."

"Then I shall deal with it when it happens." Anne gave her an encouraging smile. "It's almost like old times—off on a secret inquiry."

Jenny grinned in return. "I hope this time is less dangerous. Lord Ware isn't here to rescue us."

"Surely we are capable of rescuing ourselves, but there is no threat of danger. All the villains in this matter are in London."

On this reassuring note, the ladies dropped the subject, and it wasn't long before the coach pulled up at the Edington front entrance. Anne spoke to the coachman as he helped her down. "We should not be long. Half an hour, certainly not much more."

"Yes, ma'am."

"Oh, and Timothy, lest I forget, when we get home, no one needs to know where we have been today—and that includes Lord Allerton."

Timothy allowed himself a brief smile. "Yes, ma'am, I mean, no, ma'am. No one at all."

Lady Anne knocked on the door, and the same maid, Rose, answered it. The girl's brows shot up in evident surprise. "My lady!"

"Please tell Henry I wish to speak with him."

"Yes, my lady. Do come in." She showed them into the drawing room and left.

When Henry appeared a short time later, he came toward her with a worried expression. "Lady Anne, is something amiss? Did you lose something yesterday?"

"No. I have a great and abiding desire to see your gardens," she announced without preamble.

"Um, well, yes, certainly, my lady. Come right this way."

He led them through the house, grabbed a light jacket hanging near the back door, and they stepped outside. The formal gardens were rather dismal looking, not having the care of a full-time gardener, but in all fairness, no one's gardens looked good at this time of year. Anne and Henry turned onto one of the garden paths with Jenny walking a respectful few steps behind.

"Well, my lady, what did you wish to discuss?" Henry asked. "I assume that is why we are pretending to admire this pitiful foliage."

"The design, Henry. You must say I was interested in the garden's design," she said, choking back laughter. "It is quite impertinent of me to impose upon you two days in a row, but well, to tell the truth, I could not speak freely yesterday in Lord Allerton's presence. I should not have brought him along." She stopped on the path for a moment and gave him an earnest look. "I really must know more about your new employers. A friend in London is in terrible trouble, and the Edingtons may be the cause of it. Whatever you can tell me about them or the problems with the inheritance might be helpful in straightening out a dreadful situation."

Henry sighed audibly.

"I know I'm putting you in a difficult position…" she trailed off.

"No, it is not that. I understand," Henry assured her, "more than you know, and I am not surprised to hear your concerns. Were they ordinary employers, I would not speak, but I owe them nothing. And I am afraid we shall all be turned off without reference, and they have taken no steps to maintain the property. As far as I can tell, they neither know nor care about their responsibilities to the estate or its staff."

"No references? Oh, Henry, I or Father will give you a reference. We have known you a long time and can attest to what a conscientious steward you are."

"Thank you, my lady. I appreciate your kind offer."

He seemed truly touched, and they walked in silence for a

moment while he composed himself. Finally, he asked, "Was there anything specific you wanted to know?"

"I thought of at least three questions after we left. The sister you mentioned, can you tell me about her? What was her name? I assume she was never a Smythe, as that must have been her sister's married name. Did she adopt the Edington name too?"

"They never introduced her. Mrs. Edington called her by her Christian name a couple of times—Mary, Margaret, or something similar. Sorry I cannot be more precise. She was a tall, fussy woman, nothing was to her liking."

"Do you know where they came from?"

"Somewhere in York, I believe. No one around here knew they existed. The lawyers discovered the connection during a lengthy search for the heir."

"What happened with that? I thought you looked disquieted, even skeptical, when you said the court had given them the inheritance."

"I gave my feelings away, eh? I must work on that. A good servant should remain impassive."

"A silly notion, is it not?" Anne said. "But you need not be concerned. I notice things that others do not." She never forgot them either.

"The rightful heir was Sir Lawrence Morville."

"The man in the portrait," Anne broke in. "I wondered why he was in the gallery."

"The old gentleman added the portrait of his intended heir. The property should be Morville's now, but he couldn't be found. That is how the present owners came into it. After two years of searching without success, the lawyers looked farther afield for family members and discovered the Smythes, who'd never been to the estate nor met Cyrus Edington. The lawyers still didn't give up the search for Morville—I suspect they weren't impressed with the Smythes—until Nigel Smythe produced a letter from a distant cousin in India, stating Morville had died two years before Mr. Cyrus passed. Upon inquiry in India, the lawyers discovered the cousin whose name was affixed to the letter had also died—a year after it was written."

"How very convenient," Anne said dryly.

"Yes, my lady. What was really strange was the lawyers failed to find other documents to prove Morville's death, and they extended the waiting period another year. When that time was up, they finally applied to the court for the inheritance to be awarded to the Smythes."

"So, when did the Smythes become Edingtons?"

He cleared his throat. "Six months before the estate was awarded, by way of a legal petition. I thought at the time they were very sure of themselves."

"I bit too certain of the outcome, I would say." Anne arched a brow. "What extraordinary good fortune that the Smythes had kept that particular letter all those years."

"Is it not? I can show it to you, if you like. It's in the study desk. Mr. Edington left it laying out after they were here, and I put it in a drawer. You'd think he would take better care of such an important document."

"Now that he has the property, I suppose he thought it was no longer of value. I very much wish to see it, but tell me, Henry, do you think perhaps they wrote it themselves?"

He pursed his lips. "I could not presume to say with certainty, my lady, but from what I have seen, I cannot discount it."

"If it is a forged letter, then Morville might still be alive," Anne mused.

Henry gave her a faint smile. "Would it not be something if he simply appeared one day?"

"Indeed, it would."

Anne stayed for tea and afterwards they went to the study, and Henry brought out the letter.

She inspected it closely, turning it over and back again. "There is nothing unusual about it, except it is rather clean and unrumpled to have traveled so far."

"I thought that too," Henry said, leaning over the desk to give it a closer look. "But I feared I was being too fastidious."

"I do not think so, but it is too bad we don't have another sample of this cousin's handwriting to compare it with," she murmured. "The letter is short and not very chatty. Other than saying the weather had been hot, it appears to be all about Morville's death." She looked up at Henry. "Why would he write to them at such length about the death of a very distant cousin?"

"It does seem strange." Henry suddenly straightened. "Goodness, Lady Anne, they may be no better than swindlers."

"Precisely my thoughts." Her eyes gleamed. "I am certain Lord Ware will be interested in the letter's contents. I shall write to him today. This may support the suspicions he already has." She took her journal from her reticule, used the quill pen on the desk, and copied the letter's pertinent contents to a clean page—including the date of Morville's alleged death, the date of the letter, the cousin's name, and she noted her and Henry's observations.

She had just returned the journal to her reticule when a loud voice boomed from the doorway. "What are you doing in here?"

Anne nearly jumped off the desk chair, and Henry took a step back. A large man's bulky frame blocked the doorway. He wore the clothes of a man of trade, but his blunt face, the crooked nose that appeared to have been broken more than once, and the formidable size of his fists bespoke a history of fighting. Although she did not have the experience to guess whether that past was spent in a professional ring or fighting on the streets, his manner and speech were all too familiar. She would wager her last guinea he was a good-for-nothing from London's dockyards.

She gathered her composure around her and rose. "I am Lady Anne Ashburn. Whom am I addressing?"

"Moe Mullens. And you ain't answered my question, lady. Why are you in this house?"

Anne lifted her chin and stared him down, mimicking Miss Hetty, an old-fashioned stickler from her village, at her most haughty. "Sir, I do not know how it concerns you, but I am paying a call on Henry, the steward of this property. We are old friends."

"Is that so?" Mullens's tone was mocking, bristling with suspicion.

"Yes, that is so," Henry said, stiffly. "What are *you* doing here? How did you get in without being announced?"

"I come in the back." Mullens jutted his jaw toward Henry. "I'm to close the house for Mr. Edington, see that you all clear out and that no one steals his property." He pointed at the paper on the desk. "What's that you were lookin' at?"

"Nothing of importance." Anne shoved the letter in a drawer. "We were talking about the estate's history. I am curious about old houses that have been passed down through established families."

"Nosey, eh? I don't think Mr. Edington would like that. Maybe I should throw you out."

Anne's brows lowered. "Do so at your own risk, sir. Your manners are deplorable, and I am not convinced you are who you say you are. Do you have a letter of introduction from Mr. Edington? If not, I'd suggest *you* leave. If the local constable has to choose between respectable members of this community and a…a London scoundrel, I think we both know how that would end."

Mullens stalked toward her, using his large frame to intimidate her, but Anne stood her ground.

"Look, lady, I got a letter signed by Edington, but it ain't no business of yorn." He pushed her out of the way, opened the drawer, and picked up the letter. Although he squinted at it, Anne was almost certain he couldn't read. If Edington had hired this fellow, he had certainly chosen his representative from the bottom of the barrel.

"Henry, I think I shall be going. Obviously this unpleasant fellow has business to discuss with you."

"Just a minute." Mullens waved the paper in the air. "I want to know what's so interesting about this letter."

Anne lifted a delicate shoulder and decided to test her theory. "I told you I'm interested in the house's history. The letter contains information on who built it, the difficulties they had in establishing the gardens, the first families who lived here. All very interesting to me."

"Mr. Mullens," Henry said, stepping forward with his hand out. "I am the estate agent. If you are authorized by Mr. Edington, show me your authorization. Mr. Edington would not want me to allow just anyone to come in here and take over."

Mullens scowled at him, but he shoved the letter regarding Morville back in the drawer and dug in his pocket until he found a folded paper. He handed it to Henry, who read quickly, and then nodded to Anne. "It is signed by Mr. Nigel Edington."

"I see. Well, now that is cleared up, I shall be on my way." She lifted a dainty brow at Mullens. "If you would please step aside, sir..."

He stared down at her and finally moved. "Mr. Edington will be hearin' about this. I suggest you don't come back, m'lady. This house is being closed and readied for sale."

"I shall see you to the door, Lady Anne." Henry gestured for her to precede him. They quickly exited from the room and hurried down the hall before Mullens changed his mind.

Anne let out a breath of relief. For a minute there...

"Will you be all right?" she asked anxiously as they neared the front door.

"Have no worry about me, my lady. I've known men like Mullens before. I shall give him no cause to become a problem."

Anne wasn't so sure that was possible. "If you need to, you can come to us at Chadley. You'd be very well there until you can find a new position."

"Thank you, my lady. I hope it won't come to that." He handed her into the waiting carriage. "I shall send Jenny to you." He squared his shoulders as though marching into battle and returned to the house.

Within moments, Jenny came running and climbed into the carriage. "My lady, are you all right? Such a brute. Rose and I tried to stop him."

"Oh, no, Jenny, you should not have done that. Well, never mind. We are safely away. I have to confess it was quite a disconcerting end to the visit," Anne said as she and Jenny settled for the ride home.

"Mr. Mullens' appearance makes the character of the Edingtons even more doubtful. Who hires a ruffian like him? It may not prove anything, but it certainly does not feel right."

"He terrified me, my lady. When I heard him shouting, I thought he might hit you."

"The thought crossed my mind too," Anne admitted. "Not a gentleman of any sort."

Jenny sniffed. "A thatch-gallows for sure."

"Jenny, you should not use cant terms so freely, but I agree he was an exceedingly unpleasant fellow. I am not sorry we went, however. Henry told me some very interesting things before Mullens interrupted."

"I couldn't hear what Mr. Henry said during your walk," Jenny said. "Was any of it helpful?"

"Oh, yes, and then there was the letter." Anne went over the key points of the conversation in the garden and showed Jenny the notes she'd written in her journal regarding the letter.

"Just the oddity of keeping the letter so long—and its pristine condition—makes me wary of their claim. See here…I wrote down the dates. The letter was supposedly written on the thirteenth of September in 1803, stating Morville died two months earlier on the seventh of July. Why would one keep a letter for six or seven years?"

"I might keep a love letter that long," Jenny said with a cheeky grin.

"Well, maybe that," Anne conceded, "but not this letter. It was no better than a death notice. And if *they* were notified of Morville's death, why wouldn't old Mr. Edington have known it too and informed his lawyers? He didn't die for another two years."

"I cannot imagine, my lady, unless it was all just humbug."

"Absolutely right. And…why did they wait nearly two years after they were notified of Mr. Edington's death before presenting the letter to the lawyers? I am convinced it is a fake, and I suspect Lord Ware will agree with me. I shall write to him tonight and inform him of all we have learned. I cannot say how this might have led to Miss Pembroke's murder," Anne said, "unless she was about to expose the fraud. In any event, I hope what we have gathered will assist Lord Ware in keeping Sherbourne out of gaol."

Anne leaned back on the cushion seat with a chuckle. Daniel had been right about one thing—Lord Ware's acquaintance could be risky. Every time she had gotten involved in one of his inquiries, someone had threatened her. Her smiled faded as she realized what Lucien would say regarding her encounter with Moe Mullens. The viscount hadn't asked her to poke around the estate, certainly not go there twice, but it wasn't her fault that Daniel had been so difficult or that Mullens had showed up at the wrong time.

Mullens' reaction had been strange, had it not? Even for a bully, his attitude had been excessive, hostile out of all proportion to finding them in the study, as though he was aware there was something to hide.

She could, of course, omit the encounter from her letter and avoid Lord Ware's certain annoyance with her. And yet...she frowned as it occurred to her the incident was strange enough that it might be important. What if Lucien didn't know Moe Mullens existed? She had no doubt that Mullens was a dangerous man, one who could cause trouble and wouldn't shy from violence... even murder. Anne sighed. Oh, botheration. She would have to tell Lucien and risk a severe dressing down...if for no other reason than to warn him.

A thought suddenly twitched her lips. In truth, how severe could he be? His lordship was much too far away to deliver a proper scold.

Chapter Twenty

London, October 1812

Lucien went straight to Whitehall after his father told him Sherry was likely to be bound over for trial at the afternoon hearing.

"I am sorry, Ware," Rothe said, a frown showing his frustration. "I cannot overrule Bow Street on this. Besides, it has gone too far, the magistrate would not listen to me at this point."

"They'll hang him."

"It won't come to that. If he is found guilty—and that still is not a certainty—it is more likely he would be transported or given a prison term. His father and yours can exert enough pressure to make that happen."

"Not good enough," Lucien snapped. "You know he is not guilty! Nor is he safe in gaol. After all he has done for this country, how can you—" He cut himself off. Railing at Rothe would not help Sherry. "Very well, sir. I shall seek help elsewhere."

"If you are thinking of appealing to the Prince Regent, I wouldn't. He cannot show that kind of favoritism, not with the present cry for equity and the anti-government sentiment exhibited around Lord Perceval's assassination in May."

"I did not have Prinny in mind."

Rothe gave him a piercing look. "Careful, lad. I would hate to lose you both."

After Rothe's lack of support, Lucien found the warning presumptuous. Why would they ever agree to work for Whitehall again? He and Sherry would have to talk it over—but not until his partner was cleared of the charges. He gave a curt half bow and strode from the office, clenching his teeth to keep control of his temper.

As he leapt into his curricle and took the reins from Finn, he knew what he had to do. If the magistrate's hearing—which sounded more like a mock hearing to Lucien—ordered Sherry returned to gaol pending trial for murder, there was only one recourse.

• • •

Mr. Charles Cade narrowed his eyes and puffed on his cigar, studying Lucien. The silence lengthened in the club owner's office, and Lucien felt the tension mount. If the man turned him down...

Cade let out an audible sigh. "Naturally, it can be done, but have you considered the consequences?"

"I know what could happen if Sherbourne remains in custody. I see no other way. I appreciate that you used your name to provide some protection—but it cannot last, and I do not trust Haskett." He twisted his lips in a scowl. "Or any other gaolers at this point. They want a confession. And there are a dozen other things that could go wrong with him inside."

"The bribes will be costly."

"No matter. I shall pay them."

"And what about my payment?"

Lucien shrugged. "Name it. I shall sign over my estate in Waring, if that is what it takes."

"I do not want your property or your money," Cade chided. "At some time in the future, I may need a favor."

Lucien tightened his lips. "I will not kill for you, but ask anything else within my power..."

"Do not be foolish." Cade knocked the ash off his cigar. "Contrary to public gossip, murder is not my first choice in settling differences. Nor would a well-recognized viscount, such as yourself, be my choice of assassin."

Lucien swallowed the anger that had him so on edge. "I intended no offense, but there is one more thing...this debt is entirely on me, not Sherbourne. He will owe you nothing."

A faint smile played across Cade's lips. "I agree. Now, there is much I must do in the next three hours…unless you want to change your mind about this escape."

"Absolutely not." Lucien spoke with the conviction he felt. He had no reservations, not one regarding the need to arrange an escape. The cards were stacked against Sherry, and Lucien needed more time to prove his friend's innocence. Leaving him in gaol—where he might be murdered or die of gaol fever—or trusting him to the less than tender mercies of Haskett were not risks Lucien could take.

Yes, the Bow Street Magistrate was known to be a fair man, but he could not make a just ruling without the proper evidence before him, and Haskett wasn't even looking. Given enough time, Lucien was confident he could unmask the killer and thereby assure Sherry's long-term freedom.

"Very well, Ware. Leave it in my hands."

"Is there nothing I can do?"

"Definitely not. You must have an unimpeachable alibi for the court hearing and the hours beyond. Make yourself visible to potential witnesses. Once Sherbourne is free, he will be brought to private rooms here at the club that are known only to a select few. Wait until late tonight before coming around."

Lucien nodded and rose. He was uneasy with whom he had made this devil's bargain, but to do nothing was unacceptable. "Thank you, sir. I will not forget my debt."

"I have no concerns about that."

• • •

The Magistrate's Court at Bow Street was busy as usual but not overcrowded when Lucien arrived several minutes before two that afternoon. Baron Sherbourne and Salcott were already present, standing together, and Lucien joined them.

The elder Sherbourne, an older version of Sherry with a slight paunch and grey streaks in his auburn hair, stood rigid, his face stony as though he couldn't allow himself any expression for fear of emotion taking hold. Salcott, elegant and composed as always, nodded at Lucien's arrival.

"We should move forward to the rail," Lucien suggested, "so Sherry will know we are in court to support him." Lucien had taken Cade's advice to heart, and he was determined that not only he but others who might fall under immediate suspicion should remain visible to the public eye for the next few hours.

The baron and Salcott murmured agreement to his proposal, and the three of them pushed forward to the wooden rail that separated the trial participants from observers. Lucien firmed his jaw and let out a quiet breath. Doubts had recently crept in—not whether drastic action was necessary but worry that something might go wrong, that Sherry might be injured or killed doing the escape. He hated placing control of events in anyone else's hands... particularly Cade's.

The trial before Sherry's hearing was nearly over, the accused shackled and standing in the dock. An old woman finished telling her side of the story, and the magistrate's gaze lifted to the alleged chicken thief. "Did you do what she says?" he asked.

The defendant hung his head, "My children was hungry."

"And was the chicken eaten?"

"Yes, sir."

The magistrate nodded. "While I am relieved your children were fed, I cannot allow you to steal food that belongs to another." He found him guilty and sentenced him to thirty days in Newgate.

There was a stir in the room, and Lucien recognized two journalists among a dozen better-dressed bystanders who had pushed their way into the back of the courtroom, and then Sherry was brought in, shackled, pale, and rather scruffy in his worn, wrinkled clothes. He stood tall and kept his eyes on the Magistrate, not looking toward the crowd nor searching for familiar faces.

Albert Haskett entered the courtroom ushering Mrs. Doud.

So, the two of them were to be Sherry's accusers. Lucien's lip curled. It was not unexpected, but he'd hoped the disagreeable landlady would not want to be bothered. No doubt Haskett had insisted. He was not a man to accept "no" for an answer.

Lucien saw Reginald slip quietly into the back of the room. Even in gentleman's clothes, he still looked a bit shady, and bystanders instinctively stepped out of his way. Lucien's chest tightened. Reginald's appearance to await the verdict added reality to what Lucien had set in motion. The next few minutes would determine if Cade's man would give the go-ahead for the escape attempt—or not—depending on whether Sherbourne was held over to stand trial for murder. Lucien turned his head toward the front of the room and didn't look at Reginald again.

Instead, he studied Sherry's face. The dark circles under his eyes attested to restless nights. He had a bruise on one cheek but no other sign of injury. He stood immobile, expressionless. His eyes finally flashed toward Lucien as though he had felt his gaze. In that brief moment of contact, Lucien saw the fear in Sherry's eyes...and knew he'd done the right thing.

The hearing lasted less than fifteen minutes. Haskett gave his version of what happened to Maria—the crowd gasping at his description of her body dumped in the alley—and provided Fanny as a possible motive, suggesting the child might also be dead. More gasps. It did not appear to matter he had no proof. Haskett theorized that Sherry had hightailed it to Oxfordshire *after* the murder, hoping to provide himself an alibi, and he ended with Sherry's avoidance of the arrest warrant as evidence of guilt. Mrs. Doud told the same story she had given Lucien, that the last time she saw Maria, she was taking her bastard child to Sherry.

Haskett concluded the prosecutions' case by pointing a finger at the accused. "That man is her murderer."

The crowd murmured angrily, the Magistrate boomed, "Quiet!" and a hush fell. Showing no other reaction to the proceedings, the Magistrate addressed the prisoner. "What have you to say in your defense, Andrew Sherbourne?"

"I am innocent." Whatever he was feeling, Sherry's voice was calm and confident. "I did not do this deed. I last saw Miss Pembroke when she left my residence Monday morning. I know nothing about her murder and was not aware of it until Officer Haskett told me on Thursday when I returned to town."

"Where is the child? Can you bring her before the court?"

Sherry hesitated. "I could, sir. She is safe, but I will not have her placed in an orphans' home. Miss Pembroke left Fanny in my care, and I have spoken to her grandfather. She has family who will provide for her."

"Is the child yours?" Haskett interjected.

Another hesitation. "I do not know."

"Then you, in fact, have no legal responsibility to care for her," the Magistrate said.

Sherry's chin came up. "I have a moral responsibility to honor the trust Miss Pembroke placed in me, sir."

The crowd murmured their approval but the Magistrate glared at them until they grew quiet again.

"If he won't bring her here, how do we know the child still lives?" Haskett asked.

The magistrate looked at Sherry. "Well, sir, can you provide proof?"

"I could bring in witnesses," Sherry said.

"Are they here today?"

"No, sir." Sherry did not even glance in Lucien's direction.

Although he was tempted to speak up, Lucien knew any testimony about Fanny would make no difference in whether Sherry was held for Maria's murder, and coming forward now would draw unwanted attention to himself at a time when he needed to be prudent. If Sherry had wished for him to come forward today, he would have said so. He knew as well as Lucien that their close association would make any statement by Lucien ineffective without tangible proof, and they didn't yet have it.

The Magistrate gave an audible sigh. "I am not convinced of your guilt, Sherbourne, nonetheless, there is sufficient cause to hold you over for trial when the court shall determine your guilt or innocence in the murder of Miss Maria Pembroke."

Baron Sherbourne gave a low groan, and Lucien's hands gripped the railing. He had known the inevitable outcome, thought he was ready for it, but he felt a punch in the gut and knew the baron and Sherry must be experiencing the same. It was an unimaginable situation.

Sherry was hustled from the room, and the journalists made a quick exit to get the news in the latest edition. No one approached Baron Sherbourne—perhaps it was the scowl Lucien turned on anyone who glanced in their direction.

Once Lucien knew the Magistrate and the crowd were aware of their presence, he urged his father and Sherbourne to retire to White's for a drink. They both agreed, and he led the way through the lingering by-standers outside, arriving at the gentlemen's club without incident. He ordered a bottle of brandy, determined to keep the two men surrounded by potential witnesses until he had word of Sherry's situation.

As one would expect, the primary topic of conversation at their table was Sherry—and probably at every other table—but their emphasis was no doubt a bit different—disgust with the perfunctory hearing, how pale Sherry looked, and what they might do to improve his chances at the future trial.

"Proving the child is safe will be easy," Lucien said. "She is staying with the Barnetts just outside town. They would testify or bring Fanny in if necessary."

"Is the child my granddaughter?" the baron asked.

"You heard what Sherry said, sir. That is all I know."

"We will care for her, raise her as our own," the baron said with an obvious tremor in his voice, "in the event my son should be unable."

"Don't lose heart," Lucien urged. "I still hope to name the killer before the trial begins."

After downing two quick glasses of brandy in the next few minutes, the baron muttered, "I have half a notion to break him out of gaol and send him to the Continent or even to America."

"Be careful where you say that," Salcott warned. "You never know who may be listening." He shot a quick look at Lucien.

Lucien hid his surprise at that speculative glance. Had Salcott guessed that something was in the wind? Perhaps Lucien's own relative calm over the court's decision and his somewhat obvious efforts to keep the men at White's had roused Salcott's suspicions. If the baron weren't so overwhelmed by events, he too might have thought something was amiss.

After a third drink, Salcott was looking concerned over the baron's loquaciousness, and Lucien decided they needed to leave before Sherry's father said something that might later be misinterpreted as fore-knowledge of the escape.

He rose. "I believe I'll see if I can get in to talk with Sherry. We should discuss what witnesses are needed for trial."

"I'm coming with you. I have a letter from Miss Emily that might cheer him." Sherbourne stood, and Lucien was pleased to see he was steady on his feet. Apparently the man could hold his brandy if not his tongue.

"I'm expected at a meeting in Parliament, or I would accompany you," Salcott said. He turned to Lucien. "I shall call upon you this evening."

"We could be wasting our time," the baron continued pessimistically. "They may not let us in to see him. Wouldn't last night."

"That was Haskett's doing," Salcott said. "I doubt if your son is held in seclusion again. The Magistrate is aware of him now and of what happened yesterday. Besides, Haskett lacks motivation as he has already achieved what he wanted."

They started across the room, coming to a halt at the sudden surging crowd and excited voices at the entrance.

"I tell you, he was taken away," someone said. "Kidnapped by masked men. Pistols were fired, and the guards were knocked down. Sherbourne was hauled into a waiting carriage. I'd swear he was fighting them."

"Good heavens! Was anybody injured?"

"I don't understand. Was it an escape or a kidnapping?"

Nobody seemed to know for sure. The two gentlemen who were relating the events said it all happened so fast it was hard to say. "I don't think anyone was shot. I'd swear they were firing into the air."

"I say! What has happened?" the baron's voice boomed. "My son has been abducted? Good lord, they'll kill him."

"No one is going to kill him," Lucien said, trying to calm him. "If he was abducted, someone wanted him alive, and if it was an escape, it appears he got away safely."

The baron swung on him. "What do you know about this?"

"Sir. I have been here with you."

"Keep your voices down," Salcott warned sternly. "We should get out of here."

The baron nodded that he understood, but he gave Lucien a long and rather angry look. "I'm going to Bow Street and discover for myself what has happened," he said in a quieter voice.

"As am I," Lucien said.

"As if you don't know," the baron said in a low grumble. "If he is killed, Lucien, I shall not forgive you."

Salcott placed a hand on Lucien's shoulder. "We shall talk... later, I must get to Parliament...unless you feel I am needed."

"Not presently, sir. The baron and I shall attempt to discover what has transpired."

As they parted at the entrance to White's, Salcott turned, stepped in front of Lucien as though he would detain him, and said quietly, "Tread carefully, my son."

Lucien met his gaze. "As ever, sir."

Salcott made a soft sound like a low laugh as he walked away.

• • •

When Lucien and the baron arrived at Bow Street, the building was bustling with constables, by-standers, and several journalists. Lord Sherbourne pushed his way inside, ignoring those who called his name, and Lucien followed in his wake. Albert Haskett was talking with the Magistrate, and the runner spotted them before they reached him.

"There they are! Come to gloat, did you? I've a mind to lock you up, Ware, until you tell us where he is." Haskett shoved others out of his way as he stormed toward them.

"Just a moment, constable," the Magistrate said. "Let us hear what they have to say."

"What do you mean by 'what *we* have to say?'" Lord Sherbourne demanded. "What have you done with my son? Where is he?"

"You tell us," Haskett said, getting right in the baron's face. Then he turned to glare at Lucien. "One of you did this, maybe both. Don't think you can hornswoggle me."

"Constable," the Magistrate repeated. "Show a little decorum."

Haskett took a step back at the sharpness in those words, but his expression held no remorse.

"We could hardly be a part of whatever happened," Lucien said calmly. "We have been at White's, and there must be thirty witnesses who can prove it."

"That doesn't mean you didn't set it up."

"Set what up?" Lucien demanded. "The way I heard it Sherbourne was kidnapped, dragged into a carriage against his will. He may be in danger as we stand here talking…from those who believe your absurd accusation that he murdered Maria Pembroke."

"You know he is guilty," Haskett growled.

"I know he is not," Lucien countered.

"This is wasting time," the baron said angrily. He glared at Haskett. "You caused this public uproar by going to the press with your accusations. I demand you find my son before he is murdered by these confounded zealots."

"He has an interesting point, Constable," the Magistrate said, having witnessed the heated exchange. "Sherbourne *may* be in danger. Regardless, he needs to be found and taken into custody. Perhaps your time could be better spent out on the streets."

"Yes, sir," Haskett said, growing red in the face. He grudgingly backed away. "On my way, sir." He turned and marched off, glancing back once to give Lucien a scowl meant to be intimidating.

Unimpressed, Lucien turned to the baron. "I suggest we go, sir. There is nothing to be accomplished here. All we can do is wait and hope to hear he is safe."

"You have the right of it," the baron grumbled. "No one in this place is going to listen to reason."

Lucien turned to the Magistrate. "You will let us know if he is taken into custody?"

The Magistrate gave a nod. "I will see to it."

Lucien and the baron had nearly reached the station's front door when the Magistrate called, "Ware, I would speak with you a moment."

"Certainly." Lucien turned to the baron. "I shall find my own way home, sir, and will send word as soon as I hear anything."

"I'll be at Sherbourne House."

"Try not to worry, sir. Sherry can take care of himself."

The baron gave Lucien a searching look, reached inside his coat, and brought out a letter. "In the event, you see him before I do, give him Miss Emily's letter, and tell him his mother is staying strong."

With a single nod, Lucien tucked the letter away. As Lord Sherbourne stepped out the station's front door, Lucien turned back to the Magistrate with a measure of foreboding. "Yes, sir, what can I do for you?"

The Magistrate gave him a stern look. "You can tell me where Sherbourne is."

"I am not aware of his present location." Which was true, although he could have told him where Sherry should be within the next few hours, whenever it was safe to move him into Cade's Club, but that was not what the Magistrate had asked.

"If you should hear from him, you would do well to advise him to surrender to authorities."

"Would I? When the evidence gathered by those authorities is only that which would convict him? Would it not be better to find the murderer first?"

The Magistrate frowned. "Do not get yourself in trouble, my lord."

"Not my intention, sir. I shall most assuredly be looking for Sherbourne, as I fear for his life in the hands of others."

The Magistrate's frown deepened. "I say, Ware, are you suggesting he is in danger from these alleged kidnappers or from the constabulary?"

"Who can say?" Lucien shrugged. "If that is all, sir, I really must do what I can to safeguard my friend."

The Magistrate eyes sharpened. "Haskett is a hard man, overzealous at times, but he will do his duty. See that you do the same."

"I will do what is necessary."

"Those two are not always the same."

Lucien left without making a response. He wasn't sure what to think of the conversation. From the expression on the Magistrate's face, he had the consolation of knowing the man was equally perplexed.

Chapter Twenty-One

"Here now, ye bloody cull." One of the four kidnappers let out a loud oof as Sherry caught him in the ribs with a sharp elbow. "Stop it, ye hear? Mr. Cade set up the snatch."

Sherry stopped struggling. "Cade is behind this?"

"Aye, ain't that what I jest said?"

Sherry grabbed the seat as the coach lurched around another corner, turned into an alley and came to an abrupt stop. The door flew open, two of the four men in the coach hustled him into the back door of a townhouse, and the coach pulled away.

"Come on," the same man urged. "Hurry. This way." They nearly ran through the house, out the front door, and into a yellow phaeton with the bonnet up. Sherry was shoved behind the seat, his presence quickly hidden by the two burly men who took their seats in front of him. The phaeton pulled away at a sedate pace.

"What the hell is going on?" Sherry hissed.

The man who hadn't spoken before chuckled. "Why, matey, youse been rescued."

Bloody hell. Cade wouldn't have done this on his own. His father? No, he would not go to Cade. Egad. Had Lucien actually arranged a gaol break? At first the thought left him speechless, then grim, knowing if Haskett caught up with him, the runner would likely demand a hanging. But finally, he began to grin. *Good lord, Lucien, what an audacious move*…and what a relief to be out of Newgate. That hellhole was not fit for man nor the lowliest of beasts.

Sherry sucked in a deep breath. He was alive and free, and he would not be taken back there—no matter what. If they failed to find Maria's killer, he would go to America and start a new life. Anything would be better than Newgate…or the hangman's noose.

"This is it, sir. Time to switch again."

They had been riding around town so long that Sherry was stiff getting up. They moved him into a delivery wagon and gave him a stack of clothing. By the time the wagon stopped in another alley it was twilight, and Sherry was wearing a long tradesman coat and a worn cap. As instructed, he carried a bag of flour on his shoulder into the servants' entrance of Cade's Club, where the bag was handed off to another brawny man, and Sherry was hurried up the back stairs to a well-appointed set of rooms. He glanced around. They were furnished for the most prominent of visitors, and clean clothes—Egad, his own clothes—were laid out on the bed.

A connecting door opened, and Archibald entered with a broad smile. "Your bath awaits, my lord."

"Archie! It is good to see you."

"I am most gratified, sir, and delighted to have you back with us."

Sherry spread his hands looking around the room. "How did you come to be here? And my clothes?"

"Lord Ware arranged it with Mr. Cade."

"I knew Lucien was behind this. But how? Where is he?"

"I do not know the details, sir. I was told to pack for an indefinite stay and to be here by two o'clock. I believe Lord Ware will be visiting you late tonight."

"No doubt sensible," Sherry said thoughtfully. "Haskett will be mad as hops I got away, and he'll suspect Ware immediately. Lucien needs to stay far away until the initial hue and cry dies down. Now, my good man," he said with an eager grin, "you said something about a bath."

• • •

After leaving Bow Street Station, Lucien collected Finn and his curricle from the street outside White's and went home. He was relieved to find the agreed message that Sherry was safe had been received—in the form of a jar of snuff delivered from Fribourg and Treyer. Cade was, indeed, a careful man.

Instructing Hughes to deny the Bow Street runners entrance to his home unless they produced a warrant, Lucien set out to spend the rest of the day searching for Gaston Breguet. Armed with the name, he was much more hopeful of success...provided the Frenchman was still in London. Any sensible murderer would have fled the country within hours of Maria's death, but perhaps Breguet had other business that would delay his departure. In any event, Lucien intended to find out.

Knowing Sherry had been taken into custody at the Red Fox Inn, Lucien started his search there. At first, Mick, the bald-headed publican behind the bar, was reluctant to talk to him. During Sherry's arrest and the commotion surrounding it, Mick had learned of the murder charge, and he shook his head at Lucien's questions. "I won't be helping no killer."

"The accusations against Sherbourne are false."

Mick took some convincing, but eventually he owned that Lucien's friend might not be guilty. "I guess it won't do any harm to tell you about Breguet. He left here three months ago looking for more permanent housing. I sent him to a boarding house on Briar Road, and I think that is where your friend was going when the runners took him."

"Anything odd about Breguet?"

The publican gave him a jaundiced eye. "Nothing that said he was a murderer, if that's what you mean, although he *was* looking for a woman named Maria."

"Maria Pembroke, the woman who was murdered," Lucien said.

Mick sighed. "Eh, I got the connection. He said she was his brother's widow and had a child with her. He hadn't found them when he left here." Mick narrowed his eyes into a hard look. "Don't get me wrong, I hope the murderer gets what's coming to him, regardless of who he is."

"I could not agree more." Lucien laid a coin on the counter, but Mick pushed it back.

"I don't want your money. I wish you good fortune in finding the Frenchman and getting the matter settled, one way or the other."

Lucien gave a nod and pocketed the coin.

Over the next two hours, he followed Breguet's path. The owner of the boarding house on Briar Road remembered him because of the heavy accent, but all her rooms were taken at the time. She referred him to Miss Stedman on King Street but the prim and proper spinster lady had recently changed her policy and was only taking ladies.

"He had the names of two other places to try when he left here," Miss Stedman said. "I don't know who suggested those places, but I doubt he got a room at Collingwood. The old gentleman who owns it lost his grandson to the war in France just last spring."

"I see what you mean. And the other establishment?"

"I wasn't familiar with it. As I recall, it was on Lark Lane."

Despite her warning, Lucien tried the Collingwood boarding house first as it was the closest, but Mr. Collingwood met his query with indignation. "'Course I remember him, but I don't rent to Frenchies. This is a respectable, *English* boarding house."

"Did he say where he was going next?"

Collingwood gave a dismissive harrumph. "We didn't chat. Now, good day, sir." He closed the door rather firmly.

As the boarding house on Lark Lane didn't have a sign in the window, it took Lucien three tries to locate the right address, however, Breguet wasn't there either.

"I had no objections to him. He was polite enough," the elderly landlady said. "But I have two British soldiers living here. I was worried there'd be trouble, and I don't need that. I referred him to Mrs. Rowe on Bower Street. Her cousin is married to a Frenchman."

Lucien was beginning to wonder if Breguet ever found lodgings, but Mrs. Rowe, a motherly woman with brown hair just starting to grey, nodded. "Yes, Mr. Breguet lives in number three at the back of the house, but I doubt if he is home. Are you a friend of his?"

"Not precisely. I have a personal matter to discuss with him."

"Well, then, I'd try him in the morning if I was you. He rarely leaves before noon."

"Do you know where he goes all day? Is he employed?"

She shook her head. "No, he is looking for a missing relation."

"A child, perhaps?"

She looked startled. "A mother and child, but how would you know?"

"I came to see him about them." When Mrs. Rowe looked wary again, Lucien added, "I know where they are."

"Oh, my." The woman's face lit up. "He will be delighted to see you. He has been searching the better part of the three months he's been with me. Yes, indeed, he *will* be pleased."

Perhaps, not, Lucien thought, not if he is Maria's killer. But he smiled and thanked her, promising he'd return.

The conversation puzzled him. How did Mrs. Rowe not know the woman Breguet was looking for was dead? It was all over the news. Had he not mentioned Maria's name? Of course, a man who has committed murder might well be reluctant to talk about it.

Driving away from Mrs. Rowe's lodgings, Lucien turned the corner, drew the team to a halt, and handed the reins to Finn. "Take the horses back to the stables. I'm going to wait for Breguet and have a bit of a chat. I'll find my way home when our business is finished."

"But sir, I could wait or come back in a bit."

Lucien jumped down to the cobblestones. "Not this time. I can't risk anything tipping him off."

Finn gave a loud sigh. "Aye, gov. Got it." He flicked the reins and set out for home.

Lucien looked at the houses around him. The day had grown late, and candles had appeared in most of the windows while he'd been talking with Mrs. Rowe. Breguet should be home soon. Anyone making inquiries to locate missing persons would likely make them during the day when people were not so wary of strangers.

Grateful the gathering darkness would help conceal his presence, Lucien stepped behind a hedgerow where he could see the rear of Mrs. Rowe's lodgings and the window that belonged to room No. 3.

As night deepened and grew chill with still no lights appearing in Breguet's window, Lucien decided to wait inside where he would at least be warm. He slipped across the street into the alley behind Mrs. Rowe's house and located the appropriate gate. It was latched on the inside too far down to just reach over. He jumped up, balancing his body on the top of the fence, and leaned down to free the latch. Dropping back to the ground, he took another look around to be certain no one had seen him, then opened the gate, and entered the shadowed back yard, fastening the latch behind him.

Once again, Lucien crouched in the dark for several moments until he was confident his movements had not attracted attention. Then he worked his way toward the house, keeping in the darkest shadows near the bushes and along the side fencing. As expected, Mrs. Rowe had not yet secured the back door for the night. Entering the hall, he made quick work of opening Breguet's door with his picklocks and moved inside, locking the door behind him.

Lucien stood still until his eyes adjusted to the dark room. It was an ordinary lodging—single bed, one chair, wardrobe, wash stand, and a small fireplace. Lucien was tempted to light a fire, but that would alert Breguet too soon. He sat in the chair to wait.

Two hours passed. Lucien got up several times to stretch his legs and pace the room. He'd heard footsteps climb the stairs to lodgings on the next floor, but no one had approached Breguet's door. Lucien was losing patience. He stopped to stare out the window, wondering if the Frenchman was coming home that night. Had he taken up with a woman? Was he gambling or drinking?

Then Lucien heard someone in the main hall. Moving swiftly across the room, he stood behind the door and waited to see if the footsteps came all the way to the back this time.

When they stopped at Breguet's door, Lucien took his pistol from his pocket.

The key rattled in the lock, and a male figure stepped inside. Lucien moved forward, closing the door and pushing the pistol barrel against the man ribs. The figure stiffened, and Lucien spoke quickly in French, "Do not do anything foolish, *mon ami*. Go ahead and strike the light. I only want to chat."

Breguet did as he was bid. "Who are you?" he asked in the same language.

"A friend of Maria Pembroke, Monsieur Breguet."

The man grunted in surprise, lit a candle, and then a second one. Lucien moved slowly around him until they were facing each other.

"Why the pistol?" Breguet asked.

"I'm not in the mood for trifling. I heard you were looking for Miss Pembroke. I know she was afraid of you, and now she is dead. Did you kill her?"

"*Mon Dieu. Non.* Why would I? I bear her no ill will."

"I have a difficult time believing that." Lucien gestured toward the chair with his pistol. "Have a seat, and explain how you bear no ill will toward the woman who killed your brother Francois."

Breguet sat and peered up at Lucien. "I saw you in court today. Are you a friend of Andrew Sherbourne?"

"I am. He is not guilty of these charges, and I will not have him hang for the deed of another. Now explain yourself. I know you were searching for Maria."

"I was, yes, but not to harm her. I wanted to offer my help, my support."

"Rather surprising, given the circumstances. Why?"

"For the child. I believe my brother Francois was the father. Maria stabbed him while defending herself." He gave Lucien a heavy look. "You doubt me. Perhaps I need to tell you a bit more."

"A capital thought," Lucien said dryly.

"Maria and Francois had been seeing each now and then…for weeks, maybe months. I'm not certain how they met or why, but Francois imagined himself in love. Maria had made it plain her feelings were not the same. Yet they remained friends—why I'm not sure."

Lucien had a pretty good idea. But he saw no need to mention Maria's spying.

"Perhaps it was a mutual need for companionship," Breguet continued. "Then one night I heard a gunshot from Francois' room, and I found him dead, a knife in his chest, his pistol near his hand. Maria huddled in a corner near the door, bruised and bloody, her clothes ripped and disheveled."

"Did she say what happened?"

Breguet nodded. "Yes. She was shaking and crying, and it took a while, but she said she came to him for help and confessed she was fleeing from French soldiers, that she was leaving France for good. He tried to stop her, begging her to stay and threatening to betray her if she didn't. When he kissed her, she pushed him away, they struggled. In what I can only hope was a moment of terrible rage, he threw her to the floor and...well, he raped her." Breguet stopped and swallowed. "Afterward, she tried to flee, found the door locked, and he fired at her. He missed, so maybe it was only a warning, but when he lunged at her again, Maria defended herself with a knife from the table." The Frenchman's sigh was more like a groan. "I believed her story...and let her go." He paused and seemed to search for his words. "I loved my brother, sir, but he had his faults, and I'd heard rumors. He may have done this before."

Lucien suspected the rumors were true, but it made no difference now, and he did not embarrass Gaston further. "How did you know Maria had a child?"

"I made inquiries of those I knew were in England, just to see how she was. I never imagined there was a child, but considering the date of birth, I felt the infant was a gift to my family—although I have told no one."

"What do you mean, a gift?"

"Francois and I are the last of the Breguet family. Two days after Francois passed, I was gravely wounded in battle with injuries that will not allow me to father a child. I had hoped to acknowledge Maria's infant as a Breguet, claiming she and Francois had married...if Maria would allow it. It would have meant the Breguet family would continue and what is ours would pass to her child."

He spread his hands in a helpless gesture. "Now, the opportunity to set things right may be gone."

For Sherry's sake, Lucien wanted to deny Breguet's assumption that Fanny was his brother's child, but the family resemblance was remarkable—the same widely spaced dark eyes and thin nose that looked so ordinary on Breguet made Fanny's face quite fetching. Still, he had to tell this man what Maria had said.

"She told Sherbourne that Fanny was his child."

"Is that her name? Fanny?" He smiled, but it quickly faded as he realized what Lucien had said. "Has Sherbourne publicly declared the child as his? I could not understand what was said in court today."

"Not yet, but he is willing to do so. Having seen Fanny and now you, I do see a similarity. Maria may have lied to Sherbourne to gain his protection for Fanny."

"May I see her?" Breguet asked eagerly.

Lucien studied the Frenchman's face, looking for signs of anger or deception. He saw none, and the story he'd told was plausible. Then why was Maria running from him?

"Whether you see her or not is not up to me. She has her mother's family in Oxfordshire, and Sherbourne feels responsible for her. Maria left Fanny in his care, and your story is far from proven. If what you say is true, why was Maria running from you? Why did she believe you wished to harm her and Fanny?"

The Frenchman raised his hands to point to his chest. "Running from me? *Mon Dieu.* Yes, I was angry when last I saw her—but not with her, with Francois and *his useless death.* Despite what I knew of him, he was my brother, and I mourned his passing. I placed no blame on Maria, and I'm saddened she thought so. But why did she leave her family home?"

"Did you by chance write to her? She received a letter from France two days before she disappeared."

"A brief note only...to say I was coming to see her. I did not want to arrive unannounced."

"She may have read it as a threat," Lucien said, finally slipping the gun into his pocket. "Her guilt over killing Francois may have caused her to believe you wanted revenge, but I suspect it was the fear you would take Fanny from her that drove Maria from Oxfordshire."

Breguet dropped his head in his hands. "Then I am to blame— my clumsy letter. If I had explained, Maria would not have been in London to meet her death."

"Her murderer is to blame," Lucien said, staring down at the Frenchman's bowed head. "I don't believe that is you, and I must continue my hunt for her killer elsewhere. Good-night, sir. I am sorry your journey ended with such sad news."

Breguet shot to his feet. "Wait, *monsieur*. Fanny...I still wish to see her."

Lucien took his card from his waistcoat and offered it to the Frenchman. "I am Viscount Ware. Contact me in a few days, and I shall see what I can do."

• • •

"So, you believe this Gaston Breguet?" Sherry drummed his fingers on the armchair in his rooms at Cade's Club. "You are convinced Francois was Fanny's father?" Sherry had not raised his voice, but Lucien heard the tension in it.

"There is a definite likeness in their features," Lucien said. "I am sorry, Sherry. I know that isn't what you want to hear." He set down the glass of Cade's very fine brandy and eyed his partner. He had arrived at the club nearly an hour ago, was escorted to a secret wing of rooms by two very large guards, and had been talking with Sherry ever since.

Lucien had first explained how Cade had arranged the escape by bribing guards, described the confrontation with Haskett at Bow Street station, and then heard Sherry's side of the story. Only when that was behind them did Lucien admit he had found the Frenchman, and he had just finished relating his conversation with Gaston Breguet. "Gaston clearly believes so, and once he sees Fanny, he—"

"Yes, yes," Sherry interrupted testily. "You've already mentioned the resemblance a couple of times. And you also believe he is not responsible for Maria's death?"

"Yes, I do. I saw his remorse for his brother's actions and his sympathy for Maria. He held her blameless in Francois' death, and had no motive to kill her. He came to England to see Fanny."

Sherry said nothing as long seconds ticked away. Lucien knew his report was a disappointment. Sherry had hoped the Frenchman was guilty, and now to learn not only was he innocent, but he had a claim to the child…was a blow. Sherry was clearly fond of Fanny and had grown used to thinking of her as a Sherbourne.

Lucien left Sherry to work it all out in his head and switched the conversation to finding Maria's killer. "Eliminating Breguet means we have to look elsewhere for a new suspect."

Sherry drew in a breath and gave a reluctant nod. "I got that too. Where do we start? I know you've been looking into the Edingtons, but did they have a reason to want her dead? You said the old lady had been happy with Maria's companionship, and even Mrs. Edington had not wanted her to quit her position."

"That's true—it is what Olivia Edington said," Lucien admitted, running a hand through his hair. "I'm not sure I believe her. Despite finding nothing—so far—to discredit the Edingtons other than his gambling—there is something about them that makes me uneasy."

"Without a motive, we've got nothing," Sherry said bluntly, still disgruntled over what he'd heard. He sank back into his chair and took a long swallow of brandy. "Perhaps it was a random attack after all."

"You don't believe that," Lucien said, unwilling to indulge his partner's mood. "We have been over how unlikely that is, and we've found the barrow used to move the body. The killer obviously knew where to take her. There was nothing random about it."

"Drat it, Lucien, no need to harp on it. I know all this," Sherry snapped. He leapt out of the chair and paced across the room. After two turns, he stopped to glare at his partner. "So, what's next?"

Lucien lifted a brow but otherwise ignored Sherry's outburst. "I'd like to talk with the old lady again—Mother Edith as Mrs. Edington called her. She appeared to know more about Maria's activities than anyone else, and I felt she was holding back in front of her daughter-in-law. Perhaps she can give us another direction of inquiry if I can talk with her alone. I shall try to arrange such a visit tomorrow. As for tonight, we could both use a night's rest."

"To improve my mood, you mean." Sherry huffed out of breath. "Beg pardon, Lucien. I have been snarly. I *am* grateful for all you've done—it's just..."

"I know. Things aren't going your way. It is frustrating...for both of us." Lucien stood to go. "Look at the good side, Sherry. At least Cade's sheets are an improvement over Newgate."

Sherry gave a reluctant chuckle. "I'd say so, considering Newgate has none." He swept a hand around the room. "My host may have a shady reputation, but I cannot fault his taste. I could get use to all this luxury."

"Enjoy it while you can. I shall return late morning, and we can firm up the next steps to be taken." He took a letter from his pocket. "By the by, I have a letter from Miss Emily that should lift your spirits. You father gave it to me...in the event I saw you. Yes," he added at Sherry's swift look, "I believe both our fathers suspect I know more about your escape than I've let on. I may have trouble evading their questions. May I tell your father I have heard from you and you are safe?"

"Absolutely. I have no wish to worry him, but please don't say where I am. He would come right over, and our attempts at secrecy would be for naught."

"I shall handle it. Good-night, my friend. Rest easy."

But Sherry was no longer listening. He was eagerly unfolding Emily's letter and reading it. "She believes in my innocence," he said, murmuring his relief aloud.

Lucien left the room and quietly pulled the door closed behind him.

• • •

When Lucien arrived at Hays Mews, he was met at the door by Hughes with the tidings that Albert Haskett, the baron, and Salcott had all been there over the span of the evening.

"I told Mr. Haskett you were not here, nor was anyone else other than the servants," Hughes said. "When I refused him entrance, he sputtered and threatened to arrest me, however, he finally left, taking his two constables with him. I am certain he had known you were not home, my lord, because I saw him talking with the man across the street before he came to the door."

"He was just harassing us," Lucien said. "Very good, Hughes. Did my father or the baron leave a message?"

"Not specifically, sir. They both expressed concern over whether you and Lord Sherry were safe."

"Yes, I see. I should have realized...Send Robert to both residences with the message that I have heard from Sherry, and we are both safe and well. Tell the baron his son will send further word when he can."

"I am certain they will be delighted to hear it, my lord. As we all are."

"Thank you, Hughes."

Knowing their inquiry into Maria's death would require them to turn London upside down in the coming days, Lucien took himself off to bed.

Chapter Twenty-Two

The following morning dawned bright and sunny, lifting Lucien's mood. He had just finished his meal in the breakfast room and was preparing to leave the house when Hughes brought him a letter.

"I thought you would want this right away, my lord."

Lucien recognized the handwriting immediately—Lady Anne—and he raised a brow at his butler's knowing look. "Thank you, Hughes. That will be all."

In truth, he had nearly lost hope of hearing from her, and he broke the seal swiftly, unfolded the letter, and began to read. "By Jove," he said under his breath. "Artfully done, my lady. Well, well...I had no idea there was a sister."

As he read on about the confrontation with Moe Mullens, his expression furrowed in a scowl. *Bloody hell*, the woman had a penchant for finding trouble. He should have known better than to ask for her help. What if she had been harmed? He shook his head and read on. Setting aside her audacious methods and the risk she'd taken, it was strange that Edington's man had reacted with such hostility when confronting a lady, particularly the daughter of an earl.

Perhaps proper respect was not in his breeding. From Anne's description, Mullens was not a gentleman nor a tradesman—nothing but a rag-mannered scoundrel. Was the brute on Edington's regular payroll? Had he done other work for him—such as disposing of a body or even committing a murder? Lucien felt a sudden chill across the back of his neck. Good lord...Lady Anne had stood up to the fellow. If the steward had not been present... if she had been alone...would Mullens have tried more than intimidation?

Lucien's jaw hardened. Sooner or later, he and Mullens would cross paths or Lucien would find time to hunt him down. In either event, he would be having a few words with Moe Mullens.

Putting the letter in his pocket, he shoved back his chair and strode out the back door toward the stables. He had decided to ride today and take one of the less flashy bays, but his stallion Aziz, a beautiful gray Arabian, whickered so longingly that he could not resist. He had the stallion saddled, arranged for Finn to meet him in a half hour, and set out for Hyde Park as though he had nothing more important on his mind than a fashionable jaunt with other morning riders.

The trails in the park were more crowded than he had expected—all the better for his purposes, although he had to fob off a few questions about Sherry. After circling the park with a group of a dozen or more riders and taking the edge off Aziz's friskiness, he slipped out a side entrance without drawing much notice. He cut over two streets, watching for possible followers; observing none, he turned toward the small inn where Finn should be waiting. He arrived without incident, left Aziz in Finn's care, and made the five-minute walk to Cade's Club on foot. The alley behind the club was empty, except for a deserted delivery wagon. He took one last look around and opened the rear door. Nodding at Cade's men on duty, he bounded up the stairs to Sherry's rooms.

"Zounds, am I glad to see you." His partner bounded off the bed where he had been lounging. "The accommodations are a thousand times better than Newgate…but nearly as boring. I've had long hours of thinking and wishing I was *doing* something."

"Then you'll be happy to know Lady Anne has written and given us much more to discuss. The Edingtons may not be all they seem. They weren't even Edingtons until recently."

"Your instincts may be right about them, but do we have anything approaching a motive for murder?"

"Possibly. They are a rather shifty pair." Lucien handed him the letter. "Read it yourself."

Sherry took it eagerly and after perusing the first few lines, he exclaimed, "Sister? You haven't mentioned a sister. Did you know about her?"

"Not until I read Anne's letter. She is not staying at the Edington house. It's possible she went back to York."

"I suppose." Sherry sank down to sit on the edge of the bed and continued reading. "So that was the delay in settling the estate—they couldn't find the heir."

"What do you think of the letter they belatedly produced that declared Morville dead?"

"Same as you, I'm sure, it's a fake."

Lucien set a hip on the cherrywood desk and frowned. "But if the fellow is alive, why hasn't he presented himself to the lawyers? The Edingtons act very confident he's dead, and if so, why couldn't the lawyers find proof? Odd affair however you look at it, but it all occurred long before Maria entered the household."

"That's true." Sherry's gaze returned to Lady Anne's letter. "Good lord, Lucien, who is this Mullens fellow? It sounds as though he threatened her."

"Yes, devil take him. Once again, she got herself into a risky situation, and this Mullens is an unsavory sort. I cannot help but wonder what other jobs he has done for Edington."

Sherry's face lit with interest. "Like murder, you mean?"

"It occurred to me. We still don't have a motive, but I'm going to inquire into Mullens' background...and he shall hear from me before this is over," Lucien added darkly.

Sherry lifted a brow. "Lady Anne was not harmed, my friend. Not truly, and now is not the time to engage in a duel."

"I would not duel with a thatch-gallows. But never fear, I shall choose an appropriate time."

"See that you do. At least wait until I'm free to watch your back...," his voice faded as he continued to read the letter while they talked. "The missing heir, Lawrence Stephen Morville," he read aloud, sounding perplexed. "Something about his name..."

He grew thoughtful, finally saying slowly. "Lucien…I believe those were the initials—LSM—on the snuffbox."

"What snuffbox?"

• • •

Lucien found Finn at the stables where he'd left Aziz and sent him to retrieve the snuffbox from Sherry's servants, then he returned to Cade's club. Forty minutes later, Finn dropped off a package.

Sherry unwrapped the engraved silver snuffbox and turned it over. "By Jove, I was right. LSM. Why would Maria have the snuffbox of a dead man in her possession, a man who supposedly died in India several years ago?"

"It would be a bloody unbelievable coincidence if the initials belonged to someone else. I think we have to assume it belonged to Morville." Lucien opened the box and sniffed at the few particles inside. "It's clearly been used and fairly recently. It still has a strong scent, so this isn't something laying around the house for years."

"Maria must have found it at the Edingtons—which means Morville came to London."

"And within the year, I'd say."

"Lord-a-mercy." Sherry stared at Lucien. "So where is he? Are we jumping to conclusions?"

"I believe Maria had a good reason for hiding the snuffbox among Fanny's belongings—where she knew you would find it."

"If you are right, this proves they obtained the inheritance by fraud. Sounds like motive to me." Sherry pointed at the snuffbox Lucien had set on the table. "Is *that* what got her killed?" He looked up in disbelief.

Lucien met his partner's gaze. "I don't know, but I intend to find out."

Sherry picked up the paper wrapping. "As I recall, there was a date on this paper. Yes, here it is—5 October 1812. Is this the date Morville visited? Is he here in London somewhere? Imagine what a shock his sudden appearance would have been…taking away everything they'd lied and schemed to claim. And then what happened to him? *Devil it*, Lucien. Did they murder him too?"

"Hold on, Sherry. We need more information before rushing to judgment. To start with, we need proof Morville came to London—and when. An examination of passengers' logs of ships from India may answer that. If we find him listed, then we can delve into where he is now and how Maria came to have possession of his snuffbox."

"And if he is dead?"

"The Edingtons have some serious explaining to do."

Sherbourne frowned. "I would like nothing better than to have someone else hang for Maria's murder, but it is quite a leap from a snuffbox to two murders."

"But not impossible. It is the best theory we've had. I'll go to the docks today and review the passenger logs. I don't think we should rely on the date on that paper—it is more likely the date she found the snuffbox. I'll look into that date first, of course, but if nothing turns up there, then I'll start with the logs from a year ago, just after the estate closed and move forward. If he'd come earlier than that, the lawyers would have found him. Once we find his name on the rolls—if we do—we'll trace where he went from there. I'm sure Captain Wycliff will help. If Morville came to London, we're going to find him or discover what happened to him. And I think that will give us answers about Maria too."

"While you're doing that, I just sit here, I suppose."

"Can't be helped unless you are missing your mates at Newgate," Lucien said. "You have been out of gaol less than twenty-four hours. Don't get restless so soon."

"Easy for you to say," Sherry grumbled. "I can't help being fidgety—I have been inactive way too long. Those days in gaol felt like weeks."

"I can imagine, but take heart. Thanks to Lady Anne and the snuffbox we are making progress and may be getting close to a solution. I have a feeling about today." Lucien smiled to lighten the mood. "What you need is a hobby."

Sherry grimaced and moved to a chair beside the fireplace. He picked up a book from the table. "How does this look? Maybe I'll catch up on my reading." He showed Lucien the title: *The Castle of Otranto* by Horace Walpole. "They say it was based on a nightmare. From what I've read so far, I can believe it."

Lucien chuckled as he straightened from the desk top. "Where did you get the book?"

"Cade's library. He has a small but varied collection in his office."

"Well, enjoy. I'm off. I cannot predict when I'll return, not if I get caught up in a promising line of inquiry."

Sherry merely grunted as Lucien headed for the door, then added, "Good hunting, I'd rather not take up farming in America."

Lucien paused with one hand on the door, a smile touching his lips. "I shall, of course, do my best, but you might see if Cade's library has a book on crop rotation in the Colonies."

• • •

After hours of tracking down ships' captains, reviewing passenger lists, and convincing port authorities to allow him to access their records, Lucien was ready to concede Morville had never made his way to London.

If that was the truth of the matter, then they needed to reassess what the snuffbox meant. Did it belong to someone significant in Maria's life? Why had she hidden the box among Fanny's belongings? And, did it have any part in her death?

He was puzzling over these questions as he walked down the gangplank of the Seabird and stepped onto the dock. He had been so sure they were on the right track. Everything they thought they knew or surmised about the snuffbox was apparently wrong, and Lucien didn't know where to go from here. He had to figure something out soon. He could not go back to Sherry with nothing but bad news.

Lucien was so intent on his musings that the shouting barely penetrated at first, but finally he heard his name being called and looked up. A small cabin boy was hailing him and running across the docks.

Lucien turned to intercept him. "Over here, lad. I am Viscount Ware."

"Captain Bailey said you was to come back. He found somethin.'"

Lucien's heartbeat raced with renewed hope, and he hurried after the boy who was scurrying back to the *Flying Mist*. When they arrived at the captain's quarters, Bailey, a rough-looking man in his late thirties with a bushy red beard, was sitting at his desk with a log book open in front of him. He stood when the boy knocked on his door.

"Lord Ware, I believe I have found the name you sought. Morville, was it not?"

"Yes. That's it." Lucien joined the captain and inspected the sheet of paper beneath Bailey's pointing finger—Lawrence S. Morville. "How did we miss it before?"

"This is an amended page, indicating late passengers. He— and these other two names—must have come on board at the last minute. It happens from time to time. I found this page and a couple of others placed in the back of the book. They should have been added to the regular pages. Good thing I found it before authorities wanted to inspect the log."

"It appears to be dated and signed," Lucien said.

"Oh, it's genuine all right. Morville arrived in England the fourteenth of March this year."

"Seven months ago," Lucien murmured. So, where was he now? Why had he not attempted to claim his inheritance?

Lucien wrote down the names of the ship and captain, the date of Morville's arrival, and the page number of the log entry. Lucien clapped the captain on the back. "Bailey, I owe you a beer. In fact, I owe you a keg of beer, and I'm going to send one over."

Elated with finally getting somewhere, Lucien returned to Finn and the curricle with a grin on his face. He was eager to follow up on the information. The simple proof of Morville's arrival implied the Edingtons had swindled their way into the inheritance—and if Morville proved to be dead—which Lucien feared was true—his death might be the motive for Maria's murder.

Lucien set out on an immediate search of the inns and temporary lodgings near the docks, hoping to find where Moville had stayed his first night and pick up the trail from there. But by nightfall, he had drawn a blank. Visiting inns and boarding houses, questioning publicans and innkeepers was time-consuming, and he needed help.

He went home to change clothes, and after sending a quick message to Sherry on the discovery he'd made, he took himself off to the Barringtons' dinner party. Based on past experience, he was in for a rather humdrum evening with dinner prepared by an inferior cook, but the hosts were well-liked and no one wanted to offend them by staying away.

It was not social duty that motivated Lucien, however; upon arrival he quickly swept the room for the sight of Miss Barnett and Captain Wycliff. Spotting them with pre-dinner drinks in their hands, he grabbed a glass of champagne and joined them, quickly relating the day's events—Lady Anne's letter, the snuffbox, and ending with Captain Bailey's ship's log.

"Oh, my goodness," Miss Barnett whispered. "Are you about to expose another murder? He surely would have claimed his fortune if he could."

"That is what we need to discover," Lucien said, turning to Wycliff. "If you have time, I sure could use your help in tracing Morville's movements."

"I shall make time," Wycliff assured him. "I am sure Rothe will agree that my current assignment is not pressing."

He had only been with Whitehall's secret spy unit a few months and was still getting the easier assignments. Lucien knew that wouldn't last because Wycliff was a good inquiry agent.

They discussed where to meet and when and had just reached an agreement when Miss Barnett interrupted, curiosity filling her eyes. She kept her voice to a whisper. "I can wait no longer. Tell me about Sherbourne's escape. Who were those men? Where is he now?"

Lucien had expected the question. Her fidgeting during his discussion with Wycliff had made her impatience obvious, but he couldn't risk satisfying her curiosity. He shook his head. "Not a topic to discuss, Miss Barnett. I know him to be safe, but beyond that, I can tell you nothing."

"You mean, you won't. Do you not trust me?" Miss Barnett coaxed.

Before Wycliff could intervene, Lucien gave her an indulgent smile. "If I knew anything, I would not risk being overheard just to satisfy your insatiable curiosity. Tell me about Fanny. Is she still the charmer you thought?"

"Oh, all right, but one day you must tell all. As for Fanny, she is a darling. I have decided I want a dozen just like her."

"A dozen?" The captain gulped. "Would you settle for half that number? Otherwise, I shall have to bow out of this courtship. I could never support a full dozen on a captain's pay."

"Fustian. I come with a substantial dowry," she said, her eyes twinkling.

Lucien laughed. "I think she has you there, sir."

The captain gave an audible sigh, struggling to hide a smile. "Could I at least negotiate for a son or two?"

"Boys would be nice too," she agreed playfully.

Chapter Twenty-Three

Sherry managed to curb his restlessness until after dark, but reading Lucien's note had raised his spirits until he could restrain himself no longer. It had been far too long since he'd been able to stretch his legs and feel the freedom of a world without walls around him. He couldn't claim the air of London was the most desirable, but it was better than the stench of gaol, which he couldn't seem to shake…he smelled it everywhere.

Having decided to slip outside for a few minutes, he sent Archie to bed early and softly opened the hall door, looking out to ensure the corridor was clear. He crept down the backstairs and exited into the alley, savoring his good fortune in avoiding Cade's men. It felt good to be on his own.

He stayed in the shadows until he reached the end of the alley, then walked swiftly down the street. After clearing two more crossroads, he slowed his pace, drawing in a deep breath of the crisp evening breeze and enjoying the simple pleasure of just being by himself. He walked without conscious thought of his direction for a half hour before realizing he was not far from Sherbourne House. Perhaps he could just visit the stables, spend a few moments with his favorite horse, before he had to go back.

Within minutes he spotted the rear entrance to his family's property and stepped behind a tree, waiting and watching to see if any of Haskett's men were around. He failed to see any movement near the back, but he was amazed by the number of lights in the house until it occurred to him that his father must still be in town.

Sherry almost turned and walked away at that point. If his father saw him, their reunion was certain to draw the attention of constables watching the area. From his current position behind the stables, he couldn't even see who was hanging around the front doorstep.

But he was already here…and the path was shadowed all the way to the stables' side door. Putting his doubts aside, he covered the distance in seconds, silently lifted the latch, and slipped inside. One of the stable boys saw him, and Sherry put a finger to his lips.

"Shh, not a word," he whispered. "I'll only be here a minute or two, and you must not tell anyone you've seen me. Go on to bed."

Big-eyed, the lad nodded and disappeared into the overhead loft.

General whickered upon seeing him, and Sherry put a hand lightly over the nose of the big bay. "Miss me, my lad. I shall be home soon—at least I hope so." He ran his hands over the horse's back. The stable smells were so normal. Knowing he couldn't stay longer, he gave General an extra handful of hay and a last pat on the rump.

Returning to the side door, he lifted the latch and the door swung away from him banging against the wall.

"Who's there?" an unfamiliar voice called out. "Show yourself. This is Constable Sims."

Sherry froze. *Bloody hell.* Before he could respond, a figure ran past him, came to an abrupt halt at the corner of the stable, and then stepped out of the shadows in front of the approaching constable.

"Eh wot? Can't a man go about his work without being accosted?" the stranger demanded.

"Who are you?" the constable asked.

"Joe Tulk. Now ifn you don't mind, I'm on me way home, and I'm late."

"Is anyone with you?" the constable asked suspiciously.

"Do you see anyone? You 'bout done with me? The horses are bedded for the night, an' me wife is awaitin'," Joe grumbled.

"Oh, go on." The constable's footsteps could be heard receding over the cobblestone stableyard.

A distance voice called, "Who was it, Sims?"

"Just a stable boy."

Sherry slipped away from the property and was on the next street when the man who'd called himself Joe Tulk caught up with him.

"You about ready to go back to the club?" Tulk asked.

Sherry stopped and looked at him. "I suppose you work for Cade."

"Yes, sir."

"Have you followed me since I left the club?"

"Those were my orders."

Damnation, the fellow must be good. Sherry hadn't caught a hint of him. Of course, he had to admit he hadn't been looking once he was away from the club. "Orders from whom?"

"Mr. Cade, of course. He thought you might seek a little time outside after your stay in Newgate. Although I doubt he expected you'd try to go home where the constables were certain to be watching." Joe gave him a disapproving look.

"I suppose it was foolish. Thank you for the quick thinking."

Tulk shrugged. "It would have cost me my job it I'd let you get caught."

They walked in silence the rest of the way. Outside the club's rear door, Sherry stopped and looked at the man. "Is Joe Tulk really your name?"

"Aye, but everyone calls me Tulk."

"All right, Tulk. I thought I should know the name of the man who came to my rescue. I hope you won't find it necessary to mention this to Lord Ware."

"Well, as I see it, I don't report to his lordship, and I doubt if Mr. Cade will find it worthy of mention."

Sherry nodded and Tulk opened the door. "If you're through strolling about in the dark, how about a game of hazard? I have some mates that would love to take a few quid off you."

Chapter Twenty-Four

Lucien had barely finished breaking his morning fast when the Earl of Salcott was announced. "I never really thought you'd go this far," Salcott said without preamble. "If Albert Haskett can prove you set up Sherbourne's escape, he'll have you both behind bars. Do not think you have done your friend a good turn either. They will use this incident against him in court."

"Good morning, father."

Salcott drew up short and frowned. "Do not take this lightly, my boy."

"I assure you, I do not, sir. I would offer you tea or coffee, but frankly I am on my way out. I have a full schedule today."

Salcott sighed heavily as though in resignation. "I hope you know what you are doing."

"The only thing I can do—investigate a murder that Bow Street considers solved. If I don't do it, no one will."

"I am not objecting to your inquiry, but this latest foolish start...where is he?"

Lucien raised a silent brow.

Salcott threw up a hand. "No, you are correct. It is best I do not know. He is not here, I pray."

"No, not here."

The earl hesitated, appearing to be somewhat reassured by Lucien's respond. "I trust you will take care. I do not want my son and heir to end up in Newgate."

"A sentiment I share, sir." Lucien casually straightened his cuffs. "I fear their accommodations are not up to my standards."

Salcott sighed. "Sometimes I do not understand you, Lucien.

Haskett is not to be disregarded. He will dog you until he gets what he wants."

"I am aware he will try. All the more reason I should be on my way if I am to prove Sherry's innocence and get us both out of trouble." He picked up his hat. "Shall I walk you out, sir?"

"Since I am late for a meeting, yes. This damnable legislation is taking much too long." Salcott cleared his throat. "This inquiry of yours…do you need my help?"

"I appreciate the offer, sir, but I think Captain Wycliff and I can handle it—although it would be helpful if you could keep the baron calm."

"Rather impossible under the circumstances, but I will do what I can."

"Please assure him Sherry is safe and he must not go looking for him, or he will stir up Bow Street even more than they are. I have an idea of what happened to Maria, but I need more time to prove it."

Salcott's brows shot up. "That is good to hear. I shall attempt to keep Lord Sherbourne busy with the details of this pending legislation, but it may not be possible for long. As any father would be, he is very anxious for his son."

"I understand. I believe we're getting closer to the answers. He must be patient just a few more days." They parted at the front entrance, the earl climbing into his coach, Lucien into the curricle that Finn had just brought around. The coach headed south toward Parliament; the curricle turned east toward the docklands.

• • •

Lucien met Captain Wycliff outside the Pelican on Rosemary Lane, where he had left off the search last night. He arrived shortly after the appointed hour of ten and found Wycliff waiting.

"Pardon my tardiness. Father showed up unexpectedly."

"I have not been here long."

"Since we're both here, shall we take this one together? Maybe fortune will smile on us."

Of course, it didn't. The Pelican's proprietor had not heard of Lawrence Morville. At Lucien's insistence, he looked back through his records but still found no mention of the name.

"A lot of recent arrivals stop here for the first night," the publican admitted, "and I'm not likely to remember one man unless he caused problems. But I assure you, if he's not in the book, he wasn't here."

As they returned to the street, Wycliff took up his horse's reins and swung into the saddle. "It would have been too easy."

Lucien shrugged as he settled into his light carriage. "I'll stick close to the Thames, including the Strand, if you want to head toward Cheapside and a street or two north of there."

Wycliff nodded in assent. "I have two likely establishments in mind, and I'll ask about nearby boarding houses."

"Then we meet outside Whitehall in two hours?"

"I shall be there."

Lucien worked steadily, and despite the shaking heads and negative responses, he kept doggedly moving from one inn to another and stopped at two boarding houses in between. As he walked out of the fifth establishment, he heard the sound of a horse galloping up the street. Wycliff reined in his mount, leapt to the ground, and covered the remaining distance with his long stride.

"Morville's dead," Wycliff said grimly. "Murdered in his sleep at the Rearing Horse Inn."

"*Bloody hell*," Lucien swore under his breath. "Do they know who did it?"

He shook his head. "I didn't ask many questions because I thought you'd want to hear the answers for yourself, but it appears the constables are baffled. They have suggested it was a random robbery, but according to the publican, Morville had a full coin purse and a fancy watch in a drawer next to the bed. Neither was taken."

"I knew this was a possible outcome, but hell..." Lucien drew in a deep breath. "Let us see what more we can learn. Finn, tie his horse on the back." Lucien took up the reins, waited until Wycliff and Finn were on board, then set out for the Rearing Horse Inn.

"Morville's violent end surprised the publican," Wycliff said on the way. "He found him to be a pleasant, well-spoken gentleman. He kept to his own business and had not flashed his money around."

"Traveling alone would have made him an easy mark," Lucien said. "And he probably wasn't expecting an attack." Lucien halted the curricle under the inn's large sign of a rearing black horse.

Situated on the corner of Cheapside and Milk Streets, the lodging had a modest but respectable reputation. The interior was dark, and only a few patrons sat at the heavy wood tables this early in the day.

The innkeeper, a man in his mid-thirties with fair hair that needed cutting, looked up from writing in his ledgers and registered surprise. "Ah, captain. I did not expect you back so soon."

"My friend Viscount Ware has further questions regarding Mr. Morville." Wycliff turned to Lucien. "This is Jake Folsom."

Lucien nodded to the publican. "Good day, sir. The captain tells me Lawrence Morville was murdered."

"Aye, several months ago. He journeyed all the way from India, then gets murdered his second night in London." Folsom shook his head. "A sorry end, and bad for business, I might add. Was he a friend of yours?"

"I did not have that pleasure. He was coming to town to claim an inheritance, but he was overdue by six or seven months, and we have been trying to locate him." Lucien's explanation did not really say why he and Wycliff were involved, but the innkeeper nodded. "A dreadful end to our search," Lucien added. "Can you tell us how it happened?"

Folsom shrugged. "He arrived late one night and went out early the next morning. He was back for supper, even quieter than the night before. I thought he had something weighty on his mind. After his meal, he came into the pub, had a pint or two, and eventually joined a lone woman at another table."

"Can you describe her?" Wycliff asked. "Lady or tart?"

"Neither. Modestly dressed, a spinster maybe. Rather tall, but mostly unremarkable. I honestly didn't give her much of a look."

"Tall and thin?" Lucien persisted, thinking of Olivia Edington.

"No. Stocky for a woman, I'd say."

"Did he seem to know her?" Lucien asked.

Folsom frowned and shook his head doubtfully. "I really can't say. She came in, sat by herself at the table next to him, and ordered a meal. Half-way through eating, I noticed she leaned over, said something to him, and he took his pint to her table. They stayed there talking quite a while."

"Could you hear what they were saying?"

'Nah, we were busy. You know how it is, loud voices, laughter."

"Did they leave together?"

Folsom gave his characteristic shrug again. "Maybe. I was filling one pint right after another. When I looked up, they were both gone."

"What time was this?" Lucien asked.

Folsom rubbed his chin. "Don't hold me to it, but half ten sounds about right."

"Did you see either of them again?" Wycliff prodded.

"I didn't. Well, not alive. The next morning this screeching started. Could have woken the dead." Apparently realizing what he'd said, Folsom stumbled over correcting himself. "Well, uh, maybe not—didn't wake Morville."

"Who discovered the body?"

"The maid, Mary. Around here, most guests are gone by midday, so she started her rounds about that time. She told me she knocked on his door, and when he didn't answer she went in, thinking he was out. Poor mite. Screamed her head off, she did." Folsom's lips twisted in a grimace. "Guess I can't blame her. Blood was everywhere, the wall, the floor, even the ceiling." He shook his head. "Throat slashed like it was—were a frightful sight."

Lucien could imagine the scene. While in France, he'd witnessed blood spurt like that from a throat cut—enough to terrify a grown man, much less a young maid.

"You never saw the woman leave?"

"No, as I said, the last time I saw her, the two of them were still sitting at the table. But I heard someone told the constables Morville and her had gone up the stairs together, if you get my meaning."

Lucien's brows shot up. "Perhaps not a lady after all."

Folsom shrugged yet again. "I see all kinds."

"Did he pay special attention to anyone else while he was here?" Wycliff asked. "Any visitors?"

"Not that I saw."

"What about strangers hanging around the inn? Anyone who struck you as suspicious?" Wycliff persisted.

"No, no one. The constables asked me all this too. As usual, people were coming and going all day, but no one stood out as anything other than ordinary."

Lucien asked to see Morville's room, but it was currently occupied.

"The constables finished with it right away," the landlord said with a frown. "We cleaned it—which wasn't easy, I must say—and we've been using it regularly. I don't guess there would be anything to see after all these months, and I'd rather the couple in there didn't know what happened in that room."

"Is there a rear stairs and entrance?" Lucien asked.

"'Course. It leads to the stableyard."

Lucien handed the innkeeper his card. "If you recall something the woman said or did that might help identify her or anything unusual that evening, please let me know." He laid a couple of coins on the counter as added inducement.

"For sure, my lord. I'll ask my wife, and see if she recalls more than I do."

"Appreciate your help, Mr. Folsom."

The innkeeper nodded and moved down the bar to pour a pint for a man who was waiting impatiently, drumming his fingers on the counter.

"A woman," Lucien mused, as he and Wycliff walked outside. "That is a surprise." She wasn't a patron of the inn or Folsom would have recognized her. Had Morville met her on the ship? Or had this been a casual meeting at the pub? The fact that the woman spoke first was highly unusual and hardly fit with the modest spinster Folsom had described.

"I thought so too," Wycliff said. "Do you suppose they had met previously? He didn't sound the type to take up with a strange woman."

"It's obvious that she approached him, almost as if she came in specifically to meet him."

Old friends reuniting? Unlikely. As far as they knew, Morville had lived his entire life in India. A set-up then...for what? Not robbery, because his valuables were not taken. What kind of trouble could he get into in less than twenty-four hours? He would have gone to see the Edingtons—nothing else made sense—and the most likely mystery woman was Olivia Edington, except—

"You spoke with Mrs. Edington," Captain Wycliff said, breaking into Lucien's thoughts as they reached the horses. "Could it be her? Perhaps she was trying to persuade him to give up the inheritance, even offered him money to do so, and when that didn't work..."

"I doubt it was her. Description is all wrong. She's fragile looking, and by all accounts, they have no funds to offer—nearly penniless. Nor can I imagine the Edingtons welcomed his appearance. Wouldn't any man be wary enough of her change of attitude to refuse her if she offered to come to his bed?"

"Any sane man," Wycliff agreed.

"Precisely. Nonetheless, this mystery woman has to be the killer. She most likely waited until he fell asleep, then slit his throat or let someone else into the room to do it."

"Good lord, that is cold-blooded," Wycliff said.

"Yes, I think it was. I'm nearly convinced he was killed so the Edingtons could keep the inheritance. Not only would they lose status, but they would owe the estate a lot of money that they don't have. That gives them a compelling motive."

Wycliff agreed. "We know Morville was at the Edington house at some point for him to lose the snuffbox Maria Pembroke found.

So, all you're saying seems plausible…but who the devil was this woman—unless…could she have been Maria? Could the Edingtons have sent her to get rid of him?"

Lucien shook his head. "The timing is off. Maria did not arrive in London until a month later, and she was young, petite, and very pretty. Folsom would have remembered her well."

"Then we're left with an unknown woman, possibly acting on behalf of the Edingtons."

"It's progress," Lucien said. "All we have to do is get someone to admit Morville was in the Edington home and then find the woman." Where would they find a woman willing to kill for hire? Lucien stopped in his tacks. "I almost forgot—Olivia has a sister. If she is in London, we might have another suspect."

"Seems promising, if we can find her. We should also inquire into the Edingtons' alibis for the times of the two killings. It would at least tell us if they had a direct hand in the murders."

"Their servants would know where they were." Lucien looked at Finn who'd been listening while holding the horses ready. "Could you talk with their coachman?"

Finn grinned. "Aye, milord. I kin do that."

"Good man." Lucien turned back to the captain. "A trip to the solicitors might be worthwhile. I'd like to know if anyone informed them that Morville was in London."

"You would be the better choice to question lawyers," Wycliff said.

Lucien chuckled. "You mean my title would. I dare say that is the truth of it. I shall see to it. I expect they will be shocked to learn of Morville's death, and that may make them more cooperative."

"I think I might hunt down the constables and see what progress they've made investigating Morville's death." The captain tipped his hat as he mounted his horse. "It could be they have learned something we have not."

"An excellent division of tasks. Barring an urgent development, I shall see you at White's this evening. Say eight?"

"Just so." The captain nudged his mount into a trot. Lucien stepped up into the curricle, flicked the reins, and turned the team toward London's business district where the estate's solicitors had their office.

• • •

Wylie & Osborne's office was only one street away from Lincoln's Inn, the massive structure where future solicitors and barristers studied and prepared themselves for lives dedicated to the law. Lincoln's Inn was very Oxfordesque with high ceilings, a large hall and marble floors. The law office building Lucien entered had attempted to emulate its neighbor's distinguished atmosphere with tall windows, dark, heavy furniture, marble floors, and a family crest on the wall.

The secretary informed him that Mr. Wylie, the barrister, was meeting with a client, and Mr. Osborne, the solicitor, was in his office, preparing for court. "I shall ask if Mr. Osborne has a few minutes to speak with you, Lord Ware."

Lucien gave a nod to the man and sat to wait, placing his hat on his knee. He was barely settled when the secretary returned, accompanied by a short, stocky man with silver hair and round spectacles perched on his nose.

"Lord Ware," the older man said. "I am Ronald Osborne. How may I be of assistance?"

"A private word if I may, sir."

"Of course. Please step this way, my lord."

Osborne's office was spacious and furnished in highly polished mahogany and rugs from the Orient, confirming the partnership was well-established and profitable. Once they were seated, the solicitor gave Lucien an expectant look.

"I believe you handled the Edington estate," Lucien began.

"That is correct, sir, but it has been closed nearly a year now." The solicitor frowned. "I hope you do not have another unpaid debt."

"No, I am following a line of inquiry that may involve the present estate holders, Olivia and Nigel Edington, formerly Smythe. I understand you were unable to find the original heir, Lawrence

Stephen Morville, and thus the Smythes-Edingtons inherited by default, so to speak."

"Yes, all that is a matter of public record."

"Were you aware Lawrence Morville had arrived in London seven months ago?"

Osborne gave a visible start. "My heavens, no. Where is he? Why has he not come to us? This is a serious complication." His deepening frown allowed the spectacles to slide down his nose, and he pushed them back.

"Well, not complicated in the way you assume," Lucien said slowly. "He will not be making a claim for the estate. He was murdered twenty-four hours after his ship docked."

"I say." Osborne sat back in his chair, his mouth agape for a moment before he recalled himself. "My lord, to say I am shocked is not nearly sufficient."

"None of this has been reported to you?"

"Oh, no, I assure you, it was not." The solicitor appeared too astonished to continue for a moment, and he struggled to compose himself. "By your expression, I gather there is more you have not yet told me."

"At present it is speculation only, but I believe Morville went to see Nigel and Olivia Edington before he died."

"They should have notified us," Osborne said indignantly. "Immediately."

Lucien leaned forward in interest. "What would have happened if they had?"

"We would have informed the court, and the estate may have been reopened. At the very least, Mr. Morville would have had an opportunity to explain his delay in coming forward."

"If his reason was good enough, might the court have reversed its decision and given the estate to him or have ordered reparation?"

"It is possible." Osborne pursed his lips in thought and nodded to himself. "The letter reporting his death…we always thought…I assume it was fraudulent. The court would certainly be interested in that." His gaze came up to meet Lucien's. "Who murdered him?"

"No one has been charged."

"I see," Osborne said slowly.

"Yes, I think you do. It is apparent who had a motive." Lucien paused, giving the solicitor time to reach the same conclusion. "Did you have other concerns about the Edingtons' claim to the estate?"

"As I said, my partner and I were never satisfied with the letter, and it was very odd the authorities in India could not locate a record of his death. It did not sit right with us, but when Morville did not come forward…well, we had no alternative."

"I'm sure you did an inquiry into the Smythes' past. Did you find anything that caused you concern?" When Osborne fiddled with adjusting his spectacles as though delaying while he considered what to say, Lucien added, "I appreciate your reluctance to talk about clients, but this is a matter of fraud and possibly murder."

"I realize what is at stake." Osborne tapped his fingers on the desk, then seemed to make up his mind. "Our client was the estate, not the Smythe-Edingtons, so I feel I can reveal our findings. They have a regrettable history of questionable business dealings, unpaid debts, and they lied to us on several matters, but as for past acts of violence…nothing of the sort. They were rather desperate to get their hands on the estate's funds and wrote frequently, even stopping by the office on two occasions as I recall, to demand an early settlement."

"Which one was putting on the pressure, him or her?"

"In truth, it was both. And the sister too. Fortunately, she only came with them the one time."

"Ah, the sister did come to London. What was her name?"

"I do not recall. She may have been introduced, but I did not pay much mind, and since she didn't need to sign anything, I won't have her name or direction in the file. A rather blunt, out-spoken woman."

They talked a bit longer, but Osborne said nothing to suggest the Edingtons would commit murder. His tone implied he found them rather vulgar, but that was a long way from a willingness to kill.

Lucien continued to mull over the conversation as he drove home. Maybe he didn't have the evidence against the Edingtons yet, but greed was a strong motive, and the couple had certainly coveted the estate funds. They lied about the letter, probably forged it themselves, and had failed to inform Wylie & Osborne of Morville's appearance—all of it self-serving and dishonest. The estate lawyers would have had no trouble in convincing the courts of the Smythe-Edingtons' lack of good moral character. The chances Morville might have reclaimed the estate were high.

He turned onto Hays Mews, brought the bays to a stop at his front door, and tossed the reins to Finn. Still musing, he climbed down and entered the house. He would put good money on the Edingtons having a hand in Morville's murder...and Maria's too. But he still had to prove it.

Chapter Twenty-Five

"Sorry, gov, but that be what he said." Finn twisted his cap in his hands and shuffled his feet. He'd just returned from chatting with the Edingtons' coachman regarding the couple's alibis for the times of the two murders. "Half ten to three in the mornin' when Miss Pembroke was kilt, and he took 'em straight home."

Lucien heard Finn's apologetic tone, realized he was scowling at him, and sighed. "Pardon my cross crabs, Finn. It is not with you. I am just disappointed the Edingtons appear to have an alibi for Maria's murder."

Finn frowned at Lucien's use of the word *appear*. "The coachman, he was very certain they was at the Torringtons' ball, milord."

"I'm not doubting what he said, Finn, but they still might have slipped out during the ball and taken a hackney."

"I s'pose." Finn peeked up at him. "He couldna say nothin' about the other night though, the one when that cove was kilt. Mr. Edington give him and the stableboy the night off. Told him they wasn't goin' nowhere and wouldna need 'em."

Lucien cocked his head. "Did the coachman say it was common for staff to get a night off like that?"

Finn grinned. "No, gov. He were ver-ry surprised. Never happen before."

"Well, well. I must dig a bit deeper into their activities that night. Fine work, Finn. How did you get him to tell you this?"

"It were easy, gov. He dint like the master or mistress. They don't pay regular like and dock his wages fer anything lost or broken. He been lookin' fer another post."

Ah, yes, an excellent reason to keep your servants happy, Lucien thought, otherwise, they talk too much. "Regardless, you're quite adept at getting people to talk to you, and I appreciate the help."

The small man nodded and walked away with a swagger, a grin on his ruddy face.

• • •

When Lucien met Wycliff at White's that evening, they ordered brandy before getting into serious talk and exchanging information. It had been a long, frustrating day of ups and downs for Lucien, and Wycliff's report was about the same. The constables looking into Morville's murder knew nothing about the inheritance or the dead man's connection to the Edingtons.

"I gave them the details," Wycliff said, "but they didn't show much enthusiasm. Still, they listened politely—no Albert Haskett types this time—and I believe they will make a few inquiries. I'll talk with them again tomorrow to see if they've learned anything new and urge them not to close the matter."

"Appreciate it, captain. Without your help I would never have gotten this far."

"Perhaps not so swiftly," Wycliff conceded. "We still have a long way to go, but you can count on me for whatever you need."

Lucien finished his drink and checked his pocket watch. "I think I'll take what we have learned and discuss it with Sherry. If I keep him informed, I'm hoping he will stay in hiding and leave the investigating to us."

"It must chafe him, but he should know by now that Bow Street is watching, just itching to drag him back to gaol."

"Absolutely, he knows, but patience is not his best quality."

"I can sympathize." Wycliff gave him a speculative glance as the two men rose to leave. "Someday, when this is behind us, I should like to hear the story of his escape and where he has been all this time."

Lucien shot him a raised brow.

Wycliff held up a hand. "No need to look concerned. I was not hinting for you to tell me now. I'd rather not have to lie if Margret or anyone else asks me."

"You are a good man, captain."

Wycliff tipped his hat. "It is easy to remain so when you know nothing."

• • •

Sherry was clearly shocked by Morville's brutal death but displayed a surprising lack of concern over the Edingtons' alibis for Maria's murder.

"They needn't have done the deed themselves—they hired someone. Or as you suggested, they might have sneaked out of the Torrington Ball. We both know how easy it is to slip away in a crush."

"I have done it myself, but I didn't try to return unnoticed, and they would have to be gone quite a while. Someone should have noted such a lengthy absence."

Sherry itched his ear while he thought about it. "Maybe one of them killed her, and the other got rid of the body. With just one absent at a time, the other could cover—'my wife is in the powder room,' or 'my husband has gone to fetch me a glass of lemonade.'"

"It would take careful planning and timing. And that reminds me, if the coach on King Street was part of the plan, who was driving it? A third person?" Lucien shook his head, frustrated by all the things they didn't know. "I'll ask around to see if anyone noted their absence from the ball. In the meantime, they'll be getting another visit from the constables. Wycliff set the authorities on them for Morville's murder and the fake letter that was part of an obvious swindle. They are at least guilty of fraud."

"Very true," Sherry said absently. "What about the house servants? The night of Morville's murder, when they gave the stable hands the time off, did they dismiss the household staff too?"

"I hope the constables think to ask. I'd prefer to have as much information as possible before we consider approaching the Edingtons, including a clear link to Maria's death. After all, that is our priority."

"Good point," Sherry said. "Haskett has yet to accuse me of Morville's murder."

Lucien's head shot up. Why the devil would they accuse him of that? Then he saw the twisted smile on Sherry's face. Well, sarcasm was better than giving in to despair.

"I wish I had brought good news, my friend, instead of more unanswered questions. I know the waiting is tedious."

Sherry sighed. "Ah, confound it, Lucien. My peevish temper must be showing again. But," he said, straightening with a smile, "my time here has not been wasted. I'm getting rather good at hazard with the bodyguards. If things don't work out for me, perhaps I have a future ahead of me as a professional gambler wherever I go."

"Good to know you have not been idle. Seen anything of Cade?"

"Not at bit. He is your friend, not mine." Sherry grinned at him.

Lucien snorted on his way out the door—*friend*, indeed—but he was pleased to leave Sherry in better spirits.

• • •

With much work ahead tomorrow, Lucien skipped his evening invitations and made an early night of it. He woke from a sound sleep with a start at the sound of loud pounding on the front door. Groping for his night robe in the dark, he stubbed his toe on the chair before finally making it to the window. The sliver of moon provided little light, and he couldn't see who might be creating such an infernal racket. He found a pair of breeches on the back of the chair and slipped them on. A few moments later, Hughes, in his nightshirt and robe, entered the room carrying a candle. Lucien immediately spotted his elusive robe.

"It is Albert Haskett from Bow Street once again, my lord," Hughes reported, his lips curling with distaste. "He brought four constables with him and says he has a warrant to search the house."

"At this time of night?" Lucien grumbled, slipping on his robe. "Did he show you the warrant?"

"No, but I did not ask. I told him I would speak with you, then I shut and locked the door."

"If they have a warrant, we shall have to comply."

"I understand, my lord. Shall I wake the other servants?"

"I doubt they have slept through the noise, but yes, warn them we are about to be invaded." Lucien glanced at his pocket watch on the stand. Two o'clock. "I shall lodge a complaint with the Magistrate tomorrow. There is no reason for them to rouse us from bed at this ungodly hour."

He stomped down the stairs in his slippers and yanked open the front door. "What the devil is the meaning of this impertinence? Oh, it *is* you, Haskett," he said the name with obvious annoyance. "I should have known. What do you want?"

"Andrew Sherbourne. I have a warrant right here to search your townhouse for said escaped prisoner," Haskett sneered, waving a legal paper at him.

"Does it say you can do so at this unconscionable hour?" Lucien asked, his tone deliberately cold and haughty. "Of course, it does not, and I shall bring that to the Magistrate's attention."

For just an instant, Haskett looked uncertain before he recovered. "You, *my lord*, are suspected of concealing a fugitive. If I had waited for morning, you would have spirited him away. As it is, constables are also at your back gate. He won't escape this time."

"Except he is not here," Lucien said. "Whatever made you think he would be?" He held out his hand. "Let me see this warrant." When Haskett gave it to him, Lucien took his time, reading it twice. It accused him of concealing a fugitive. He looked up. "Even if your accusation were true, I would hardly be foolish enough to hide him in my own home. But see for yourself." Lucien stepped aside. "Be sure you leave the property as you found it. No mess, no breakage, no going through drawers or desks. A man could hardly hide inside those."

"We'll see what we can do," Haskett said with a triumphant smile. "You heard him, lads, get in there and find our man."

The constables poured into the residence, but as Lucien's servants appeared, he tasked each one with witnessing a constable's search and seeing there was no unnecessary disorder left behind.

Haskett and his men covered every level, opening each door, wardrobe, or large cabinet, and even scrambled through the attic. Lucien stood in the main hallway and glowered his displeasure at any of the constabulary who appeared.

Haskett finally had to admit that Sherbourne wasn't there. "Don't think you've fooled us," he said as he followed his men out the door. "We'll be back."

"I sincerely hope not." Lucien firmly shut the door. He turned to his waiting servants. "Thank you. Go back to bed. I believe they are done for the night. Good lord, I shall be glad when this is over."

Chapter Twenty-Six

Lucien secretly enjoyed himself the next morning when he made his complaint to the Bow Street Magistrate. The justice's frown at Haskett implied he was dismayed by the runner's tactics, although he did not say so while Lucien and Haskett were arguing in front of him. As soon as Lucien had lodged his complaint, he walked away before the Magistrate could ask troublesome questions about Sherry that Lucien was not willing to answer.

As he reached the station door, however, he paused and suppressed a smile when he heard the Magistrate tell Haskett to stay a moment longer. If Lucien had interpreted the Magistrate's voice and expression correctly, the runner would be receiving a verbal flogging for his ill-timed, middle-of-the-night raid on the home of the Earl of Salcott's heir.

. . .

Lucien sat at his desk late that afternoon, his grey eyes staring unseeing at the trees outside the window, a frown wrinkling his forehead. The cup of coffee he'd hoped would clear his thoughts was empty, and yet he was no closer to sorting out Maria's murderer than he had been an hour ago. He'd even re-examined Breguet as a possible suspect but rejected him again.

Hughes' footsteps echoed in the hall, and Lucien's gaze shot to the door, hoping his butler was bringing good news, but Hughes passed the study without stopping. Lucien exhaled heavily.

He dropped his gaze to the desk where it landed on Lady Anne's letter. He picked it up, wondering if he'd missed something in it, then put it down again. Her information pertained to the Edingtons, and it looked as though they had alibis for Maria's murder. Even if they were involved in Morville's death, it didn't necessarily follow they had murdered Maria, not without some kind of proof. Had he been concentrating too much on the wrong murder?

Lucien stood and went over to stir the fire, kicking a hot coal back into the fire. He should still confirm their alibis. Perhaps he could complete that task tonight at the Dawsons' soiree. The Torringtons and many of the guests from their ball should be there, but honestly, who among them was likely to recall the presence or departure of such an inconsequential couple?

A reluctant smile twitched his lips. Sophy, of course...if she had been in attendance. He couldn't count on her being at tonight's soiree—she had been spending most of her time with the Castlebridge family since her engagement had been announced—so he grabbed a blank sheet of paper from his desk, dashed off a brief note, and rang for Hughes.

"Have the footman carry this to Mrs. Stine with all haste. And tell Robert to wait for a reply."

"Certainly, sir. I shall see to it. Can I get you anything else? Tea perhaps?"

"Not now. Thank you, Hughes."

Lucien felt better having *done* something, and he picked up Lady Anne's letter again, reading it through once more from beginning to end—just to be thorough.

He frowned as one sentence stood out, a loose end that he had not yet followed—the missing sister of Olivia Edington. When he first read Anne's letter he had assumed the sister had returned to York, but the London solicitor had also mentioned her. If she was still in town, he needed to talk with her. By all accounts, she was a rather disagreeable woman. She might refuse to talk with him, but he would like to try—a difficult task without a name.

He'd noticed a couple of other things in her letter—one was a reminder of this Mullens fellow. He'd neither seen nor heard anything of him in London. Had Anne mistaken what she thought was a London accent for something else? Well, time to run him down when Sherry's future was safe again.

There was something else that bothered him...he glanced through the letter again and stopped at her description of the first visit to Edington manor. Who was this neighbor who had accompanied her? She referred to "he," yet never mentioned his name. Was this a friend of her father's, a childhood friend of her own, or possibly a suitor? Lucien frowned at the thought and put the letter down. Did it really matter who *he* was? But Lucien remained lost in thought until Hughes tapped on the door.

"Yes. What is it?"

"Robert has returned, my lord."

Sophy—that was quick. Lucien rose and met Hughes half-way across the room. He took the lavender note and opened it quickly.

"Will that be all, sir?"

"Yes, Hughes, for now." Lucien's attention was already centered on what Sophy had written, and his eagerness faded as he read the confirmation that the Edingtons had indeed attended the ball. Sophy wrote that Mrs. Edington had been dressed in a low-cut gown of emerald green that caught the eye, and she was frequently on the dance floor with her husband. Sometime after midnight, Olivia Edington had caused a brief commotion by fainting. Solid alibis.

Then he drew in his breath, his interest piqued by her next words.

"*I had not observed the Edingtons to attract so much attention prior to that night. I cannot but speculate whether it was intended.*"

Oh, Sophy, how clever you are. She was suggesting they might have been establishing an alibi. Perhaps the idea of a hired assassin was not so outrageous. Yet, how would one go about finding a murderer for hire...unless you approached someone like a crime lord?

Lucien's lips tightened, his eyes narrowing. Had Cade lied to him to conceal his own complicity in one or more of the two deaths? Instead of collecting gambling debts, Reginald could just as easily have been at the Edingtons' house to collect for deadly jobs successfully done.

He placed Sophy's note on the desk and paced the room, his expression hard. That Cade had the ability to make such arrangements was not in doubt. Look how quickly he'd put together Sherry's escape. How would any of this square with Cade's assistance in setting Sherry free? Assistance...*Devil it*, he'd arranged it all. Had Cade accepted such a risky undertaking just to fool Lucien and distract him from Reginald's true activities? Or was arranging an escape—or a murder—just another business deal to Cade?

He stopped in front of the study's window and watched the tree branches whip around in the stiff wind. It had clouded over and would rain soon. He'd have to take the closed carriage tonight.

Lucien resumed pacing and finally stopped with a grim laugh. He was crediting Cade with too much social feeling, was he not? The man would not go to such lengths to conceal his activities. To do so, he would have to care what Lucien or anyone else thought—which he did not. Cade would never bother to lie about it.

Where does that leave the hunt for Maria's killer, Lucien pondered. Was he looking for a hired assassin—such as the mystery woman who likely killed Morville—or for an entirely unknown killer with an unknown motive? Was he no further along than when he started?

• • •

The soiree that evening was just as expected, overcrowded and quite loud as each person had to raise his voice to be heard over nearby conversations. Since he already had Sophy's verification of the Edingtons' alibis, Lucien had no inquiries to pursue among this crowd, and he decided not to stay long. He found Miss Barnett and Captain Wycliff, told them of Haskett middle of the night raid, and on a light note, he gathered stories of Fanny's stay with the Barnetts to take back to Sherry.

"My only problem with having Fanny is Mother's frequent hints about grandbabies," Miss Barnett confessed, throwing the captain a teasing look. "Maybe that pressure is why we have set the date for a spring wedding."

"We expect you to attend," Wycliff said.

"Of course, I shall be there." Lucien clapped the captain on the back. "I would not miss seeing you get leg shackled."

"Really," Miss Barnett said, turning to confront her fiancé with pretended outrage, "is that how you view our coming nuptials?"

"He said it. I didn't," Wycliff protested. "I would not dare."

She playfully tapped him on the arm with her fan. "I see I shall have to work hard to keep you in line."

Although Lucien enjoyed their banter, he was not to be distracted from Sherry's situation for long. After a few minutes, he excused himself and moved on to join a group discussing the latest offerings at Tattersall's Horse Auction. He had just left them and gotten a fresh glass of champagne when his father came up behind him.

"How are things?" Salcott asked.

Lucien turned, shaking his head. "Not going as well as I hoped. I thought I knew what had happened, but so far it isn't falling into place. The people I thought responsible have alibis for one of the murders."

Salcott frowned. "Murders? Is there more than one?"

Lucien glanced around. "I should not have said that. I cannot explain here, sir, without naming names. You know how gossip flies, and I need to keep my suspicions quiet from those involved until I know more. I would, however, appreciate discussing it with you when you have time."

Salcott looked pleasantly taken aback, and he smiled. "Of course. I have time now. I see one person with whom I require a brief word, but after that I could meet you at your place—presuming you are ready to leave."

"More than ready. Shall we say half an hour? If your conversation runs longer, I shall await your convenience."

Salcott nodded. "I shall expect a glass of your very best brandy."

Lucien finished his champagne, bid good-night to his hostess, and left the soiree. As he had predicted, it had begun to rain during the evening, and the dirt roads were turning sloppy. His coachman Gregory took a longer route home than he normally would, choosing streets paved with cobblestones whenever he could. Lucien was concerned his father might arrive before him, and he signaled to be set down at the front entrance to his townhouse.

Lucien jumped out, headed for the front stoop, and the coach pulled away. Hunched over against the pelting rain, he almost missed seeing the large figure that sprang from behind the bushes growing along the wrought-iron railing. He turned just in time to avoid the knife plunging into his back, but it caught his shoulder, ripping his coat. His assailant recovered his balance and came at him again. Lucien snaked out a foot, tripping the big man, who threw himself upon Lucien, and they both went down hard.

Attempting to twist free, Lucien was pinned by his assailant's greater weight. They grappled for what seemed like minutes with Lucien clutching the arm holding the knife and beating it against the iron fence. The weapon finally fell, but his attacker swiftly wrapped both hands around Lucien's throat, attempting to throttle him. Desperate for air, Lucien punched him sharply in the kidneys two or three times, and hearing a groan, he put as much force as he could into a final sharp punch. The big man reared back, and Lucien squirmed out from under him, sucked in a ragged breath, and scrambled to his feet.

A gunshot startled both men, and the attacker took to his heels, disappearing into the rain and mist. Lucien bent over with both hands on his knees breathing hard.

"Are you all right, my boy?" Salcott was suddenly beside him, one hand on his shoulder.

"Yes, I believe so." Lucien straightened, pulling at his cravat. "Was that you with the pistol?"

"I fired in the air, and the cutthroat ran—as I had hoped. I am getting too old to trade blows with his kind. Who was he?"

"The devil if I know, but he was a strong brute. Shall we get inside out of the rain?"

Hughes already had the door open, peering out anxiously. "Is something wrong, my lord? I thought I heard a shot."

"You did, but it is over now. What we need are a dry towels," Lucien said, running a hand through his wet hair.

"My lord, your coat, your arm. You are bleeding, sir."

"Damme, Lucien, he's right," Salcott said, staring at his shoulder.

"He came at me with a knife." Lucien craned his head to see where Hughes was pointing. "Drat the man. He has ruined my favorite blue coat. I just replaced it. Talbot will not be pleased."

"I am sure he will be more concerned about your injury, my lord," Hughes said calmly. "I will send for him and the medical supplies."

This was not the first injury Lucien's staff had tended. In fact, they had become quite efficient at it. Instead of bringing bandages and medicine, Talbot insisted upon adjourning to Lucien's bedchambers where Talbot bemoaned both the coat and injury, although the latter was hardly more than a deep scratch. Nevertheless, it was cleaned and bandaged accompanied by admonitions that Lucien really needed to be more careful of his person.

"I have to agree with him," Salcott said as the two men descended the stairs and entered the study. "That cutthroat was intent upon killing you."

"It certainly appeared that way."

Salcott gestured toward the brandy decanter on the sideboard. "May I do the honors?"

"By all means."

Once the men were settled before the fire, the earl gave his son an appraising look. "What has happened to bring an assassin to your door?"

"I cannot say for certain," Lucien mused. At Salcott's prodding he related everything that had occurred over the past days. "I was ready to abandoned my present course of inquiry—namely the Edingtons—but this attack is rather heartening. It seems I have rattled someone."

Salcott sighed. "Only you would be encouraged by such an attack. However, it does appear likely you have struck a nerve somewhere. If you are content it is not this Frenchman Breguet, then alibis or not, the Edingtons must still be considered suspects in at least one death. Is it possible the two murders are not related? Might his death be a random killing? It would not preclude the Edingtons from having killed Maria for some reason yet unknown."

"Yes, it is possible, of course, although it would be a rather huge coincidence. Even so, I shall endeavor to learn more of Edington's activities and those of his wife. Perhaps I should try again to talk with his friend Barnaby Thrup...if I can find him when he isn't in his cups."

"Might I suggest you concentrate on the sister first," Salcott said. "If she is in town, I suspect she could answer all of your questions...if you can charm her into talking to you."

Chapter Twenty-Seven

Chadley Hall, Warwickshire

When the butler announced she had a caller, Lady Anne was reading to her mother. Miriam Chadley, looking frail and wan, was propped up in bed by extra feather pillows and listening with her eyes closed.

"Mr. Harcort," Anne repeated, puzzled at the unfamiliar name. "Did he say what he wanted? I don't know who he is."

"Yes, you do, my dear," her mother said, opening her eyes, a smile adding life to her pallid complexion. "It is Henry, the steward from Edington manor."

"Oh, yes, of course," Anne said, popping to her feet. "Please show him into the drawing room, and I will be with him directly. And order a tea tray."

"Yes, my lady." The butler bowed and left.

"I have not seen Henry in years. What could he want?" her mother asked.

"I have a suspicion he may be needing a reference. Why don't you rest now, and we can continue reading when I get back?"

"The book will wait until after you explain what Henry wanted," her mother corrected.

"Yes, mother. After that." Anne smiled, adjusted her mother's shawl, and kissed her cheek before leaving the bedroom. It was no secret she'd inherited her intense curiosity from her mother's side of the family.

Anne hurried her steps toward the drawing room. Had that Mullens brute turned the staff out? She bit her lip, hoping she had not been the cause.

Henry came toward her the moment Anne appeared. "My lady, I am sorry to bother you."

"You are not bothering me, Henry." She clasped his hand briefly with both of hers and gave him a warm smile. "I am delighted to see you. Tea is on the way, and we shall have a nice chat. Please sit, and tell me what has transpired to bring you here."

"In a word, Mr. Edington. That oaf Mullens sent him word of your visit. Edington arrived in a rage yesterday morning, throwing around wild accusations which I shall not bother to repeat, and he fired everyone—even the gardener."

She raised one hand to cover her lips. "Oh, Henry, I am so sorry." She leaned toward him in dismay. "What can I do to help?"

"Well, my lady, that reference you mentioned…"

"Yes, of course. But do you have a place to stay? Were you allowed to collect your belongings?"

"All of us are still at the house," Henry said, "packing and making arrangements. Surprisingly, he gave us a week. After ranting at us, Mr. Edington went into his study for a few minutes and then stormed out to his carriage taking Mullens with him and saying he would be sending Mullens back to make sure we cleared out."

"What a horrid man."

"There is more that I think will interest you. As soon as he left, I smelled smoke and went into his study looking for the source. I found burned remnants of the letter regarding Morville's death in the brass cigar ashtray."

"Well… Getting rid of the evidence, I suppose," Anne said with a nod. "I would say that proves it was a fraud. I wonder if Lord Ware has acted upon the information I sent him, and it frightened the Edingtons." She smiled with satisfaction, then remembered the consequences her actions had brought to Henry and the rest of the servant staff. "I am so sorry it backfired on you and the others."

"Not to worry, my lady. Your visit may have hastened our dismissal by a few days, but we all knew it was coming. The maid and cook had already found new positions. I too had made inquiries and only need to provide a suitable reference."

"Well, that you shall have, and a glowing one it will be."

"Thank you, my lady. I cannot express how grateful—"

Thankfully, the maid arrived at that moment with the tea tray, ending what might have become an overly effusive expression of gratitude. Over tea, Anne listened to his future plans and his concern that the Edington estate would be allowed to deteriorate from neglect.

"If it does, that will be to his discredit, not yours," Anne said. "I am sure you will do your next employer proud."

"Yes, my lady. I sincerely hope to do so." A few minutes later, Henry left with a calmer look on his face and an excellent letter of reference in his pocket.

Anne was just ringing to have the tea tray removed when Daniel Allerton was announced. Their friendship had been sorely tested when he had learned of Anne's second visit to the Edington manor, but they'd been friends too long for it to cause a permanent breech. After staying away two days, he had resumed his daily visits, although there was an underlying coolness that had not been there before.

"Was that the Edingtons' steward I just passed?" he asked.

"Yes." She explained what had happened and folded her hands in her lap. "You may say it now."

"Say what?"

"You are just itching to say I told you so."

"I did warn you against meddling," he said matter-of-factly.

"Yes, but how uncharitable of you to mention it."

Daniel spread his hands. "You were the one who brought it up."

Anne snorted softly. So she had. Perhaps it was her own feelings of guilt that prodded her. "I shall write to Lord Ware and apprise him of this development. Whatever he did with the information I sent, it must have frightened Mr. Edington."

"Would this be the same Lord Ware who assisted a fugitive to flee from a murder charge?" Daniel asked, holding out a news sheet from London.

"Whatever do you mean?" Startled, Anne looked up at him, but she had an ominous feeling she knew the answer.

"Read it."

She took the paper, read the article regarding Sherbourne's escape from custody, or his possible abduction, and speculating rather wildly on what and who was behind it. And yes, one of those theories hinted that Sherbourne might have been aided by friends, and in the very next sentence mentioned the constables had spoken with Viscount Ware. The implication was hardly subtle.

"Such audacity," she said, "to bandy about his name in the news sheets. I must say the London press is getting bolder by the day. This is nothing more than gossip." But Anne wondered if it was true. She could well imagine Lord Ware taking such a daring step if he felt it was necessary.

"Printing rumors may be in poor taste, but they would not have done so without reason. What kind of friends are these, Anne?"

"Good ones," she snapped, then softened her voice. "I do not for a moment believe Sherbourne murdered anyone."

"That's another bone I have to pick," Daniel said, giving her an indignant look. "When you asked for my help, you did not mention your friend was charged with murder. For heaven's sake, my dear, how could you not tell me?"

"I knew how you would react. Honestly, Daniel, when did you change so much? I thought you were more… more…open-minded than this."

"*I've* changed? It is you who has changed…ever since you went to London and mingled with all the aristocratic snobs."

"They were not snobs, leastwise, not the ones I knew. And you went to war, Daniel," she added quietly. "We are no longer children, and we both have changed."

He studied her silently with a baffled frown. "Too much, Anne?" He took her hand, his eyes meeting hers. "I always thought…well, I assumed we'd marry one day. I wanted to ask you when you first came home this summer, but your mother has been so ill and now we appear to be at loggerheads. I…"

"You are not so sure we are suited?" she finished. "I too have done much thinking over the past week or two. I am sorry to say it, but we make better friends than we would husband and wife. As friends we are on equal footing and able to disagree upon occasion without upsetting our entire lives. That would all change if we were to marry. I hope we shall continue to be good friends, Daniel. I *am* fond of you, and I doubtless shall remain so."

Daniel's face had gone from disappointment to blank, his emotions quickly tucked away. "Fondness is not the issue, is it? I cannot quite take this in, Anne. It has happened so fast. How did we go from a discussion of…of impropriety to this?"

Anne shook her head regretfully. "Because you see impropriety where I see practicality. Some circumstances require setting aside traditional rules in order to do the right thing."

After Daniel had gone, Anne sat for a long time, thinking over what had been said and blinking rapidly to keep the tears at bay. Of course, she was sad. Daniel wasn't the only one who had dreamed from time to time of a rosy future together. Now the dream was over, and regardless of what she had said, their relationship would never be quite the same.

She was not worried about her future. It was secure. Besides, had she not had three proposals in her first London season? Not that she'd considered accepting any of them—the *very* young man suffering through his first calf love, the sweet older gentleman looking for a wife to see him through his aging years, and the charming rake who was mostly interested in her fortune. Given her position and dowry, there would be others who wanted to wed an earl's daughter, and maybe one of them would be the right one for her. She had wondered if her friendship with Viscount Ware might one day evolve to something—but she wouldn't go there.

Instead, she got up, went to her desk, and picked up a quill to share the latest interesting development with the viscount. If he wrote back, maybe he would tell her how Sherbourne had escaped. She smiled as she began to write. What harm could there be in asking? In fact, he would probably be surprised if she didn't inquire.

Chapter Twenty-Eight

London, October 1812

Lucien entered Hyde Park astride his stallion Aziz. He felt the gray Arabian quiver with excitement as they turned into a broad open stretch of Rotten Row, and Lucien nudged him into a gallop. For the next few moments, he let the Arabian have his head, and they flew over the ground, the swift pace easing Aziz's pent-up energy and Lucien's frustration.

Although he had thought to start the day by searching for Olivia Edington's sister, he quickly realized he did not have the vaguest idea where to look. He had no name, no address, and a description that could fit half the women in London—hence, the frustration.

He reined his horse in to a more proper pace as they approached a section of the park where ladies and well-appointed gentlemen were taking a morning stroll. He tipped his hat to acquaintances, then smiled and bowed his head to four elderly ladies proceeding sedately along the path.

The sight of them gave him sudden inspiration. There *was* one person who might tell him about Olivia's sister and fill in other missing information…if she were so inclined. Edith Edington. His intention to talk with her again but been put off several times with one delay and another. It was long past time. Despite her physical infirmities, the old lady had a sharp mind. She saw things, and she'd been very well-pleased with Maria, while her tone and sly glances indicated she was not so enamored with her daughter-in-law. Yes, Mother Edith might talk freely…provided he could catch her alone.

He took another turn around the park to stretch Aziz's legs, then headed home to change clothes. Sending Robert off ahead of him to fulfill his instructions, Lucien stopped to look around the neighborhood for Haskett or other constables before setting out in his closed carriage. In truth, he had not seen anyone hanging about since he lodged the complaint at Bow Street, but he still told Gregory to keep watch for followers. They drove aimlessly around for ten minutes. Lucien finally tapped on the roof, satisfied he wouldn't be dodging the law all day, and gave Gregory the signal to head for Brewer Street.

The neighborhood surrounding the Edington house was quiet, and Lucien's coach stopped several houses away to avoid drawing the notice of someone in their household. He had originally thought to watch the house on foot, but any person who lingered out front for long would be the object of curiosity, and he'd likely be recognized. While a strange coach might be noticed too, this carriage was unmarked, no coat of arms or other designation on the doors, and he'd had his coachman leave his livery behind, dressing as any hired jarvey might. As long as Lucien kept himself out of sight, observers were free to speculate all they wanted. He settled in to wait, keeping watch on the Edingtons' front entrance.

Only a few minutes passed before his footman Robert arrived at the residence as expected. He knocked on the door and held a brief conversation with someone inside. When Robert left, he turned in the opposite direction from where the coach waited, and Gregory started the horses, turning the corner and intercepting Robert two streets over.

The footman climbed inside with a grin. "Just as you said, I made certain he saw I was carrying a note, and I asked if his master or mistress was home. He said his master was out for the day, but he could deliver the message to Mrs. Edington. I acted surprised at the name, and told him I had the wrong address."

"Excellent. You've done well, Robert. At least one of them is already out of the house. I shall continue to wait in hopes Mrs.

Edington has morning calls to make or other errands, shopping would be good. That usually keeps ladies busy for hours."

After Robert took off for home, Lucien again took up a position where the front door was visible. Time passed slowly, and it was near to an hour before his persistence was rewarded. A liveried footman left the house, then a few minutes later a hackney arrived and Mrs. Edington emerged from the residence. She wore a stylish gown of cream and violet that suggested she was attending an afternoon soiree. If he was fortunate, she should be away from home an hour or two.

When the hackney disappeared around the corner, Lucien waited a bit longer in the event Mrs. Edington had forgotten something, then he instructed Gregory to pull the carriage onto King Street, the next road over, and stop. Lucien swung down from the coach and walked back to the Edington residence. He tapped on the door, asked for Mrs. Edington, and when he was told she wasn't at home, he asked to speak to Edith Edington. He was shown into a sunny parlor, where the elderly woman sat with a basket of knitting beside her.

"Well, Lord Ware," she said, setting his card on the table and squinting her eyes up at him. "I did not expect to see you again. I suppose they told you Olivia is out. Did you wish to see me?"

Lucien smiled. "Of course, Mrs. Edington. How could I stay away from such charming company?"

"Oh, don't call me that. Olivia and Nigel may feel the need to be Edingtons, but I am still Mrs. Smythe."

"I stand corrected, and I very respectable name it is, Mrs. Smythe. I shall not take up much of your time. I had a few questions I thought you could answer as well as anyone."

"Very possibly. I am more likely to tell you the truth than Olivia." She gave him a sly glance. "That is what you thought, is it not?"

Lucien chuckled. "Caught me. Let us rather say, I hoped you would be more forthcoming, ma'am"

The old woman nodded, accepting his answer. "No doubt you would be correct. Sit down, young man, and we can talk. You may call me Mother Edith. Everyone does."

"Thank you," he said seating himself. "I hear Olivia has a sister. Is she around?"

Mother Edith pursed her lips, looking confused. "Do you mean today? I certainly hope not. That woman is a nuisance…and she is often unkind."

"I am sorry to hear that, but back up a moment…do you mean she is in London?"

"Course she is. I was certain you had met her."

Now Lucien was confused. "I don't think so. What is her name?"

"Martha. Martha Doud. She was Maria's landlady."

Lucien's brows shot up. "Indeed, I have met her but was not aware of the relationship." He thought rapidly, absorbing this surprising information and all its implications. "Neither she nor your daughter-in-law mentioned it."

Mother Edith snorted. "I am not surprised. Olivia doesn't want anyone to know her sister is in trade, and she would have sworn Martha to secrecy. They bought her that boarding house, you know, so I guess Martha feels she owes them." She slowly shook her head. "My poor Nigel, marrying into such a family. You cannot believe a word that comes from either of the sisters."

"What makes you say that?"

"Experience. Mind what I say, and be careful around them… and that useless son of mine, for that matter. He was ever a dull lad, my Nigel, but he was never bad until he wedded up with her. I would not give two pence for the pair of them—the three of them, I should say. They took everything I had—my home, my money, and there's nothing left. But I reckon this isn't what you came to hear, so what else did you want to know?"

It was precisely the kind of thing he wished to hear, but he didn't know how much time he had, so he moved on to another question. "Do you know a man named Lawrence Morville?"

"The old man's heir? I know the name. Has he turned up?" Her eyes lit with mirth, her lips curling. "Wouldn't that be something. Olivia will be furious."

"I think he was already here," Lucien said carefully.

"In this house?" she demanded, leaning forward, her eyes huge. "Surely you jest, sir."

"Not at all. It would have been around seven months ago, March, in fact."

"I don't understand. If he has come back, why are we still living here? No one—" Edith's brow wrinkled as she abruptly stopped. "Now that I think back, there was a visitor in the early spring, a stranger, very mysterious too. They wouldn't tell me who he was or let me meet him. Are you saying that was Lawrence Morville?"

"I cannot say if *that* stranger was Morville with any degree of certainty, but he arrived in London in March, and it would be reasonable to assume he immediately came to this residence to announce his return. Sometime later, I believe Maria found his snuffbox, proving he had been here."

"Oh, my goodness. She *did* find it…just a week or so before she died. We were in the family parlor, and she found it behind the sideboard. It had initials on it, I believe."

"Yes, SLM—Stephen Lawrence Morville."

"Oh, my."

Lucien could not believe what he was hearing. They'd gone so long without a solid break. "Does the 5th of October sound about the right date of her discovery?" he asked, thinking of the date on the paper wrapped around the snuffbox.

Her brow puckered, but she finally shrugged. "Could have been. I just can't recall."

"That is fine. How did Maria find it?"

"I'd laid my yarn on the sideboard, and it fell behind. Maria used my cane to pull it out. She felt something else behind there and kept working at it until she had that pretty engraved box. Those are his initials, you say?"

"Yes."

"Why hasn't he claimed his birthright?"

"He is dead," Lucien said bluntly. "Murdered the second night he was in London, shortly after I believe he was here."

Mother Edith's eyes widened, and she covered her mouth with both wrinkled hands. For a moment, she looked frightened, then sad as though she might cry. "Oh, Nigel, what have you done?" she murmured. She looked up at Lucien. "You think he murdered him, don't you?"

"He may be involved."

He could see the wheels spinning, and she turned an ashen shade, deepening the lines on her face. "Oh, Maria," she said sadly. "If they killed Morville, then that snuffbox gave them a reason to kill her too."

Her mind was still very keen, he thought. She'd quickly figured it out. "Yes, it is possible," he agreed.

"Good heavens." She looked stricken, her voice catching, "I told Olivia about the snuffbox. She said it must have been there for years, but I knew that wasn't true." Her eyes suddenly turned wary at sight of something over his shoulder.

"Lord Ware, might I ask what you are doing here?" Nigel Edington's voice boomed from the doorway.

Mother Edith flinched, drawing into herself. Lucien doubted if she feared physical retribution, more likely she shrank from seeing the truth of Lucien's accusations on her son's face.

From Edington's attitude, Lucien worried he had overheard at least part of the conversation, but he improvised an excuse in hopes he was wrong. "I came to tell your mother that Maria Pembroke's child will be in the care of kinsmen who very much want her. Your mother had expressed concern for the child's well-being, and I thought she would be pleased to know a grandparent and uncle have come forward."

After a moment of silence, Edington spoke slowly, his gaze going from his mother to Lucien and back again, as though he was uncertain what to think. "That is excellent news, is it not, Mother?"

"Yes, Nigel, I was delighted."

Perhaps he had not overheard as much as feared, Lucien thought. If he left now, maybe Mother Edith would be all right.

"I hope Mother has not been going on about nothing," Edington said. "She has a tendency to do so. Do you not, my dear?" He took her hand and patted it.

"If you say so, Nigel." At this meek reply, her son turned back to Lucien, and she gave the viscount a knowing smile from behind her son's back.

Reassured by her smile, Lucien took his leave. "As I have delivered my message, I should not keep you further. Good day, sir, ma'am."

Once back on the street, Lucien strode swiftly around the corner, found Gregory with the coach, and went straight to Gerrard St. to speak with Mrs. Doud. Why had she hidden her relationship to Olivia Edington? Where was *she* the night Maria died?

Lucien knocked on her door twice but no one answered. He stepped over to look into the front windows. As far as he could see, there was no movement inside. He stood for a moment, thinking over what to do next, then he returned to his carriage. It was time to consult with Sherry.

• • •

Cade's guards hardly gave him a glance this time as Lucien entered the back door to the club and climbed the stairs to Sherry's suite. Lucien shook his head. He was grateful for Cade's assistance in the escape and for sheltering his partner so long, but he continued to be uneasy with his indebtedness to the crime lord, gentleman or not—and such familiarity with his staff of ruffians was worse than just bad form.

Lucien knocked on the door, a guard answered, and Lucien stepped inside to discover he had interrupted a hazard game.

"Lucien." Sherry rose in eagerness. "Have you good news this time?"

"I certainly have news. We need to talk—in private."

Sherry nodded to the other two guards who had stood the moment Lucien entered. "Leave everything as it is, lads. We shall finish the game later."

"That'll be good, sir."

Lucien heard the respect in the guard's voice. Sherry's easy-going nature had made him new friends—no matter how questionable the acquaintance might be.

"So, tell me. What is it?" Sherry asked as the door closed behind the three men.

"I had a chance to speak alone with Edington's mother, and she had quite a bit to say." Lucien pulled up one of the chairs abandoned by the guards and related a large part of his conversation with Mother Edith. Half-way through he got up again and paced the room with Sherry's eyes following him as he crossed and re-crossed the oriental rug.

Lucien thought better on his feet, and even as he talked, he was attempting to fit the new information with what they already knew. "I should have realized the relationship between the sisters, even though, other than both being tall, there is little resemblance." He pictured Olivia and Martha, and realized how much stronger and muscular Martha Doud was. He had been thinking all along that the murderer had to be a man—the brutality, the strength required to move the body—but perhaps he was wrong. "Martha Doud is a very robust woman and might well be described as stocky."

"Robust? Stocky? Why describ— Oh, you think she might be the killer." Sherry said.

"Possibly."

"Strong enough to move the body on her own?"

"If she had help getting it into the barrow."

"Good lord, Lucien, would you kill anybody—possibly two people—for a sister? Oh, don't give me that look—of course, you would, as would I, under the right circumstances, but not for money or social standing." Sherry was clearly disgusted by the prospect. "I grant you the Edingtons are a mercenary family, driven by greed, but Martha Doud didn't benefit much from two deaths. She is running a boarding house while Olivia and Nigel are living as the privileged class, rubbing shoulders with the aristocracy. Why would she have killed for so little gain?"

"Your account is true enough on the surface, but Edington

squandered the estate funds at the gambling tables even before he was the legal heir. He failed to discover his debts would swallow up most of the estate until advised by the lawyers at the time the inheritance was transferred. They had already perpetrated the fraud for nothing, and they still owed money all over town—the dress shops, the gambling dens. Martha Doud may have been promised a fortune, but there was little to share. I'm thinking they didn't tell her the true state of affairs until after they'd involved her in Morville's death."

"Bloody hell." Sherry scooted forward in his chair. "No matter which of them did the killing, if what we think is true, they've murdered twice for little or nothing. The first murder was to get their greedy hands on an estate they'd already made worthless, and the second was to conceal the first." He clenched his jaw in anger. "Maria died for nothing."

"Both did. As a theory, it all makes sense, but it will fall apart in a hurry if Martha Doud has an alibi for one or both nights," Lucien cautioned. "We cannot declare this solved yet. We need proof."

"Then why are we standing around? Let's go after it." Sherry came to his feet with a determined glint in his eyes.

Lucien frowned. "You are staying here."

"Not this time. I am thoroughly repulsed by sitting around, and I will be going with you or following right behind you. Either way, I will be there."

"You cannot be—" Lucien stopped at the militant look on his partner's face. "Oh, devil it." Lucien had to admit he would not have been patient this long. How could he demand more of Sherry? "You are a stubborn fellow, my friend, but I cannot stop you. Come on, then. Fortunately, I brought the closed coach, so Haskett shouldn't see you as long as you remain inside."

"Well, I have no intention of doing that either. I mean it, Lucien. I've had it with hiding and playing it safe. If there is a chance of catching the real killer and clearing my name, I want to be there when it happens."

"Bloody hell," Lucien muttered under his breath. "I said come on, did I not?" He strode out the door, explained to the guards that Sherbourne was coming with him, and they hurried down the back stairs.

"Where are we going first?" Sherry asked when they were in the coach.

"The Rearing Horse Inn."

"If you wanted a drink, why didn't you say so—"

"Don't be caper-witted, my friend. There is one man who can shed some light on Morville's killer, and he is tending bar at the inn."

"What do you mean?"

"The publican, Jake Folsom, said he could identify the woman with Morville the night he died. I want him to take a look at Martha Doud."

"By Jove, Lucien, I can't wait to see her face."

They found Folsom talking with one of only two patrons having a pint that early in the afternoon. The conversation broke off as Lucien and Sherry approached, the patron sidling away to take his pint to a far table.

"Lord Ware, are you here for a drink this time?"

"'Fraid not, but I'm willing to pay well for your time. I want you to take a look at a woman and tell me if she was the one with Morville the night he died. If you're willing, I'll pick you up as soon as I locate where she is today."

Folsom gave a doubtful frown. "I can't leave the inn unattended, and I'm not sure I want to get involved, going to court and all."

"You must have someone who occasionally steps in for you." Lucien took a fat pouch from his pocket and set it on the bar. "I said I would pay well."

Folsom unfastened the leather ties, looked at the coins inside, and his eyes widened. "I'm sure I can make arrangements, my lord. How soon?"

"With any luck, within the next hour or two."

As they left the inn, Lucien glanced at Sherry, "Next stop is Gerrard Street. If Doud has returned, this should not take long."

No longer concerned about tipping the landlady off to their suspicions, Lucien instructed Gregory to pull up in front of the boarding house. He and Sherry knocked on the door of Doud's rooms, but as before, no one responded. While Sherry stood next to him to block prying eyes, Lucien used the picklocks he'd acquired during his years in France to open the door, and they slipped inside.

"This looks bad," Sherry said, gesturing toward the open drawers and cabinets.

Lucien went straight to the bedroom and opened the wardrobe. It was empty, likewise the dressing table drawers. He returned to the main parlor. "It appears she has fled. Finding me with Mother Edith must have caused a bit of panic." He gazed around the room. She'd taken everything—personal items, pictures from the walls. His eyes fell on a spot over the fireplace where a dusty imprint resembling an x remained from something that had once hung there. He drew in a sharp breath.

"Sherry, look." Lucien gestured toward the wall.

"At what? Nothing's there."

"Not anymore, but what did Pettigrew say was the likely murder weapon?"

Sherry eyed the imprint, then his mouth dropped open. "A sword—and it appears that crossed swords once hung there. Could it be…?"

"It fits, does it not?"

"She *was* the murderer. And now, she has slipped away from us. If she gets out of town, she'll disappear and never face punishment—nor will we convince Bow Street I'm not guilty."

"This is not the time to lose heart. We may still catch her. Perhaps the lodgers know where she went."

No one answered at the first door, but their knock on the next one brought an elderly gentleman. "Good day, sirs. Them fine looking horses out front belong to you?"

"They do," Lucien said with a smile. "I am Viscount Ware, and this is my friend Mr. Rayburn." For obvious reasons, he couldn't use Sherry's true name, so he gave the one his partner had used in France. "We need to speak with Mrs. Doud. Have you seen her today?"

"I have. Would you care to come in?" the gentleman offered, stepping aside to encourage their entrance.

"Thank you, but we are pressed for time," Lucien said. "When did you last see her?"

"No more than a half hour ago. As I was returning from my walk, she was getting into a hackney with several bags and a large trunk. I thought she must be going on a long journey, and I called out to ask who would be looking after the boarding house in her absence. But she must not have heard me."

"Any idea where she was going?"

"You're in luck there, sir. She said something to the driver, and I heard him repeat 'Brewer Street.' I believe that's where her sister lives."

"Thank you very much." Lucien turned, urging Sherry toward the coach. "Let's go."

"They may all be fleeing London," Sherry said, springing into the carriage. "In the event we can still catch them, shouldn't we pick up Folsom on the way?"

"Absolutely," Lucien agreed and ordered Gregory to spring the horses.

Chapter Twenty-Nine

Lucien, Sherry, and Jake Folsom arrived at the Edingtons' house in less than thirty minutes. The innkeeper was a bit fidgety, but he was sticking to the agreement, and he straightened as though preparing for a fight as they knocked on the door. When no one responded, Lucien exchanged a worried look with Sherry before knocking again. This time they heard footsteps inside, and the door swung open.

The footman recognized Lucien immediately. "Sorry, my lord, Mr. and Mrs. Edington are not receiving."

Lucien's heart raced. They were still there.

"They will receive *us*," he said, stepping forward, forcing the footman to move back. "Do you wish to show us in, or shall we search the house?"

"My lord," the man protested, shaking his head and dropping his voice to a near whisper. "I dare not. I have my orders."

"Then tell us where they are, and we'll announce ourselves," Sherry said, pushing forward and staring down the hallway.

"Parlor, second room on the right." The footman gestured behind him. "They are busy, sir. We are preparing to leave London."

"I see that," Lucien said, looking around him at the hasty preparations. Sheets already covered the furniture he could see in the drawing room, and several half-full trunks stood open in the hall. "All the more reason we speak to them immediately."

The footman stepped back, giving up any effort to dissuade. "Very well. They're your problem now." He spun on his heels and disappeared into the back of the house.

"I say, sir," Folsom whispered from behind them, "should we be doing this? I mean, barging in like this?"

"Come along, my good man," Sherry urged, following Lucien. "We're here to catch a murderer, no need to mind the niceties."

Lucien pushed open the parlor door, his sudden appearance startling the occupants. For a moment, Olivia and Nigel Edington, Mother Edith, and Mrs. Doud stared at them without speaking. A large, rough-looking man scowled and took an aggressive step forward. Mullens, Lucien assumed, based on Anne's description of a low-class ruffian attired as a respectable man of trade. Something about the fellow was familiar.

Olivia Edington put a hand on the big man's arm to restrained him and swept forward with a smile. "I am sorry, my lord, but we are not receiving today. We have been called way on urgent family business. Another day upon our return perhaps?"

"Pardon for the intrusion, ma'am, but this could not wait, particularly as it appears you are preparing to flee." Lucien turned to Folsom. "Well, sir, is the woman you saw in this room?"

The publican's gaze immediately settled on Martha Doud. "Aye, that's her, the one by the window. She was in my pub all right."

"In the company of Lawrence Morville on the night he died?" Lucien clarified.

"Aye, milord. That's true." The publican shifted uncomfortably, but his voice was firm. "They sat at a table together for quite some time. She had kidney pie."

"Well, Mrs. Doud, have you anything to say?" When she just stared at him apparently dumbfounded, Lucien turned to the Edingtons. "Were you there when she murdered Lawrence Morville, the heir to the property you have falsely claimed?"

Edington puffed out his chest. "See here—how dare you force your way into my home? Who are these other men?" He glared at Sherry and Folsom. "I am appalled by what you are implying."

"I was not *implying* anything," Lucien said. "I do apologize for not introducing the Honorable Andrew Sherbourne and Mr. Folsom, the owner of the Rearing Horse Inn. However, I thought I stated quite plainly that you, your wife, Martha Doud, and possibly Mullens here are all responsible for the death of Lawrence Morville."

"And Maria Pembroke," Sherry said.

Mr. Edington threw his wife a desperate look. "I...we did not kill anyone and I know nothing about it."

"You should leave...now," Olivia Edington said sharply, pointing toward the door. "Mullens, see them out."

As the big man started forward, Lucien stepped in front of him. "We won't be leaving just yet." Mullens was big, but Lucien reckoned he had learned to fight on the streets, using mostly his size and weight. He had never trained at Jackson's boxing club.

"Oh, eh?" Mullens took a swing with his ham-like fists, but Lucien ducked, moving forward to land a punishing blow to his opponent's nose. It spurted blood and Mullens stumbled back, sitting down hard. He swore lustily and grabbed his injured nose, blood streaming through his fingers.

Lucien stood over him with a black look. "Lady Anne sends her regards." He might have let it go at that, but he had recognized the way Mullens moved and knew why the big man seemed familiar—the last time they met, it had been outside Lucien's townhouse, and Mullens had a knife in his hand.

The big man looked up, realized Lucien wasn't done with him, and attempted to get up, but Lucien was quicker, grabbing him by his jacket and yanking him half-way to his feet. He hit him again, let go, and Mullens tumbled back to the floor.

"That was for ambushing me and cutting my favorite coat." Lucien turned aside, shaking his stinging hand. Mullens had a very hard nose.

"For heavens' sake, stop this. And get out," Olivia Edington snarled, dropping all pretense at civility.

"Not until we are finished." Sherry stepped over the fallen man and confronted Mrs. Doud. "You're the one who murdered Maria and then tried to blame it on me."

Martha Doud recovered her voice. "You're Sherbourne, are you? No wonder you're keen to accuse me or *anyone* else of Maria's death, but I was her friend. You're the one with a reason to kill her—and rid yourself of any obligation to your by-blow child."

"You're full of lies, aren't you?" Sherry snarled.

"Let's talk about Morville first," Lucien interrupted, keeping a wary eye on Mullens, who was slowly getting to his feet. The big man appeared undecided if he should have another go at Lucien or take off. "Mr. Folsom has identified you Mrs. Doud as the last person seen with Morville before he was found brutally murdered."

"He is mistaken," she said.

"Oh, no. She's wrong about that." Folsom spoke up from the back of the room. He had moved toward the back wall, away from the confrontation, but he stopped and defended what he'd seen. "It was you, wearing that same bonnet with yellow flowers. If I have to, I'll swear it in court."

Her's eyes flickered before her angular jaw set in defiant lines. "Oh, all right, I was there. So what? We talked, and I left."

Lucien lifted a brow. "How'd you know he was in London? Did he come to this house to claim his inheritance? Before you deny it, we have his snuffbox that Maria Pembroke found behind the sideboard."

"That dratted girl, I knew she was trouble," Mrs. Doud muttered.

"Martha, whatever are you saying?" Olivia Edington stifled a look of alarm and put on an air of injured innocence. "You knew Lawrence Morville was in London, and you never told us?"

Mother Edith, who'd watched in silence as events unfolded, gave a loud, derisive snort. She appeared to be enthralled by the scene.

Mrs. Doud jerked her head toward her sister, her face flushing with anger. "Oh, is that how it's going to be? Just like when we were children—you are putting the blame on me?"

"My dear sister." Olivia's voice projected sisterly concern, and she put a hand on Martha's arm. "Why are you saying this? Morville was never in our home, and I was not aware you had seen him. What have you done, Martha?"

"What have I done? Well, honestly!" Mrs. Doud shrugged off her sister's hand and turned a furious gaze on her brother-in-law. "And why are you being so high and mighty quiet? You said you'd protect me."

His expression became pinched, and he glanced helplessly at his wife. "I, um, Martha, what do you expected me to do? If...if you saw this man, you should have said so."

"Bollocks!" Mrs. Doud let out a small shriek of fury and lunged at Nigel.

Lucien grabbed her arm although he certainly could not fault her. The Edingtons were doing everything they could to distance themselves from her admission, which only made Martha Doud angrier, and yes, frightened. There was growing fright in her eyes as though she could picture the bleak future ahead of her.

Her mouth tightened, and she shrugged off Lucien's hand. "I won't hit him. But I was not in this alone. They knew it all and helped plan every bit of it," she blurted with a twist of her mouth that was almost feral.

"Both murders?" he asked quickly.

Mrs. Doud hesitated, as though realizing she had said more than intended. She might have closed down completely at that point if her sister had not fed the fire.

"Shut up, you stupid, stupid ninny," Olivia Edington ordered, grabbing her sister's shoulder. Her nails must have hurt, because Mrs. Doud flinched. "He cannot prove—"

Martha Doud twisted free and shoved her away. "Shut up? Stupid ninny? You say that now, but that wasn't how you talked when you asked for my help...when you were too cowardly to do what had to be done. I even had to find Mullens for you. Not that he's worth much," she added, glaring at the big man who'd been edging toward the door. "And don't think you are getting away unscathed, Moe. You're as deeply into this as anyone."

"I never done the deed," he growled.

"Will you both stop talking?" Olivia Edington shouted. "Sottish, foolish prats. Listen to me before you get us all hung. They have no proof or they would have brought the constables." She whirled to face Lucien and Sherbourne. "Is that not true?"

Lucien nearly laughed. It was much too late to put the genii back in that particular bottle. The unbridled squabbling between the siblings was giving them all they needed.

Edington must have thought so too. He belatedly attempted to halt the damage and take control. "I say, sir, my wife told you to leave. Unless you do so immediately, I shall call a constable."

"Good idea," Sherry said. "We could use one about now."

As though on cue, the front door banged open, and Albert Haskett's voice boomed, "Andrew Sherbourne, I know you're here 'cause you were seen. You're under arrest."

Mullens bolted for the door, knocking over two constables as Haskett and six men from Bow Street poured into the room. The four constables left standing grabbed Sherry, and he offered no resistance.

Lucien stepped forward. "Just a moment, officer."

Haskett came to an abrupt halt. "Fancy seeing you here, Viscount. Now don't you give me no trouble. I'd have to lock you up for interfering with me duties. I might do it anyway."

"You just let one of the murderers get away," Ware said. "Do you want to arrest just anybody or the right person? And also get credit for solving a second murder?"

"Eh, wot? 'Course I would," Haskett said, his interest caught. To Lucien's satisfaction, the runner reacted swiftly, sending the two constables in the hallway after Mullens. "And take him to the station when you get him. We won't be here long," he added before turning to Lucien, "Kin you prove what you said about another murder?"

"Would a confession suit you?"

Haskett's eyes narrowed. "I'm listenin', milord."

Lucien tried to state his theory with the details to prove each accusation, but the Edingtons and Martha Doud weren't giving up so easily. They protested nearly every word, and Mrs. Doud shouted recriminations at her sister and brother-in-law as she felt the noose settling around her neck.

The three of them were so loudly disruptive that Haskett threw up his hands long before Lucien finished. "I've heard enough to

know there's somethin' havey-cavey goin' on. We're gonna take it
to the station. Take them all," he told his constables.

• • •

Despite Lucien's repeated protests, Haskett insisted on
transporting Sherry in shackles. Silently fuming, Lucien rode in his
own coach with Jake Folsom and Mother Edith. The elderly woman
had asserted her right to accompany them to "say her piece," and
Lucien was glad for it. She was the only one who could directly
connect the two murders through the discovery of the snuffbox.

His coach arrived at Bow Street just as the constables were
marching their prisoners into the station, and he followed in time
to see the Edingtons, Mrs. Doud, and Sherry taken somewhere
in the back. Lucien helped Mother Edith Smythe to a seat in the
visitors' area. She wrinkled her nose at the odor of unwashed
bodies but was too polite to say anything. Lucien seated her as far
from the riff-raff as he could.

Asking Folsom to wait for him inside, Lucien stepped back
into the street, found a willing lad, and sent him to Cade's Club for
the snuffbox. Sending a constable to retrieve it was simply not an
option. Any association with the crime lord would only increase
Bow Street's suspicions and undermine their credibility.

When Lucien entered the station again, Haskett was waiting—
impatient and irritated. The runner wanted to finish getting the
story from him before interviewing the others. Folsom pleaded to
join them so he could give his evidence and leave.

"I am a working man, sir, and the inn needs tending."

"The law comes first," Haskett said with a scowl, "but I s'pose
that will work." He gestured for Folsom to follow them into his
cramped office. "Keep quiet, mind you, until we get to your part in
this sordid business."

The runner's small work space held a desk and three worn
wooden chairs. The walls were covered with yellowed sheets of
sketches of wanted criminals, letters of departmental rules, various
newspaper clippings, and scribbled notes that must have meant

something to Haskett. The men had to step around each another to be seated, but once they were settled, Haskett tipped back in his chair and crossed his arms over his chest.

"All right, Ware. Convince me that Sherbourne is not guilty."

"The easiest way to do that is by telling you how and why someone else committed two murders," Lucien said levelly. "This entire affair began with an old man dying up north in Worcester and a missing heir…"

Chapter Thirty

Forty-five minutes later, Lucien finished giving his statement to Haskett and answering a multitude of questions. The runner wasn't easy to convince, but he eventually gave a reluctant nod, which Lucien took to mean he'd made progress. Folsom then spoke briefly to identify Mrs. Doud as the woman he had seen with Morville at the Rearing Horse Inn and to confirm he'd heard her damning admissions at Edington house.

"Can I go now?" Folsom asked.

"For now," Haskett said gruffly, as though resenting the need to allow it. "But mind you, you'll be needed at trial."

"I'll be there." Folsom glanced at Lucien. "In spite of the trouble, I'm glad I could help. That woman is a nasty piece of work."

Lucien assumed he meant Martha Doud, but his remark fit either sister. "Thank you for coming, sir. I'll have my coachman take you home." Lucien rose to his feet.

"Now don't you be goin' nowhere, your lordship," Haskett said hastily. "I still need to hear what the others have to say, and I want you there."

"No need to bother with me," Folsom broke in, forestalling an argument. "I can just as easily grab a hackney. Good fortune, my lord."

He left the room quickly as though worried Haskett might change his mind. Most of London's citizenry were loath to spent time at Bow Street, and Folsom was clearly of that mind.

"Now that's settled," Haskett said nodding toward the office door with obvious satisfaction, "let's talk with the Edingtons." He stood, looking around his office. "We can't all crowd in here, but I'm sure the Magistrate will give approval to use the courtroom."

Since court wasn't in session, the proper consent was obtained. Haskett was just leaving to collect the Edingtons and Mrs. Doud from the back of the station when Moe Mullens was brought in by the two constables who'd given chase. All three men looked disheveled, suggesting Mullens had not given up easily.

Haskett diverted to meet the new arrivals. "Well, Moe, this ain't the first time Bow Street has seen you. I think you can sit in the back cells until I'm done with the others. I know you ain't the brains behind this."

Disappearing into the back, Haskett returned with Edington, his wife, and his sister-in-law. As the constable steered them toward the Magistrate's hearing room, Edith Smythe waved frantically from her seat in the lobby.

"Have you forgotten me, young man?" She got up and hobbled toward him, her cane tapping loudly.

Perhaps it was the "young man" that caught Haskett's attention, for that he was not. In forty-odd years his frame had broadened and his hairline had moved so far back it looked more like a neck warmer. He responded to her with unusual tolerance. "Come along then, my lady. I may as well hear from the whole family at once."

Throughout the interviews so far, the Magistrate had remained working in a nearby room. Lucien had taken a peek earlier and noted the justice didn't have a much larger working space than Haskett—it's size greatly reduced by the bookcases and shelves of heavy law books. Now, the Magistrate came to stand in the courtroom doorway as the noisy procession got settled. Lucien assumed his interest had been drawn by the unusual involvement of so many members of the upper classes.

Lucien watched him for a moment, wondering if the justice was curious if these activities might change the testimony in the case that had bound Sherry over for trial. As Lucien still had little trust in Haskett, he welcomed the Magistrate's presence and hoped he would stay to listen for a while.

When Mother Edith insisted on sitting next to Haskett, he sighed and began by questioning her about the mysterious male visitor from last spring and gradually pinned down the date to early or mid-March. She admitted she had only heard his voice in the next room and that no one had told her the stranger's name.

"I now believe it was Lawrence Morville," she volunteered before being asked. "And they tried to hide it from me." She turned and frowned at Nigel. "I told you that wife of yours was no good."

"Now, Mrs. Smythe," Haskett cleared his throat, bringing her attention back to him. "Tell me what you can about the snuffbox."

While she was explaining how the engraved box had been found, a constable slipped into the room and handed Lucien a small package. "This was just delivered for you," he whispered.

Lucien nodded his thanks and handed it to Haskett. "I think it might be helpful, constable, if you could see the snuffbox for yourself."

When the constable pulled the wrapping away, Edith Smythe leaned forward. "Yes, that is it, the very one Maria found."

"And you told your daughter-in-law Olivia about finding it?"

She nodded. "I wish I had not. It was just idle conversation. I never imagined Olivia would have the poor girl murdered over it."

"Nonsense, Mother Edith," Olivia Edington snapped. "Your mind is addled and playing tricks on you. None of that happened. My mother-in-law has never approved of me," she said, appealing to Haskett. "Nobody was good enough for her precious Nigel."

"Certainly not you," Mother Edith interjected. "Look what you've done, gotten him into this dreadful muddle. He'll be lucky if he doesn't hang."

"Now ladies," Haskett said sternly. "You will both get your turn. For the moment, I'm talking with Mrs. Smythe. Now, ma'am, have you anything further to say that would bear on either murder?"

"Only that you cannot believe anything Martha says. She is even worse than her sister."

"You are batty in the head," Martha Doud said scornfully. "Someone should have put you in an asylum long ago."

"Ladies, enough!" Haskett was starting to look a little desperate. "Mrs. Smythe, as we appear to be finished, I will have a constable escort you home."

"There's plenty more I could say about her...and her," she pointed at Olivia and Martha, "but I guess you don't want to hear it."

"I have heard enough," Haskett said. "Thank you for giving information."

Edith Smythe got up a little unsteadily, and Lucien quickly offered his arm. "I will see her out."

This time Haskett raised no objection. He merely nodded, clearly relieved, before turning back to his three prisoners. "Now, Mr. Edington, I understand you recently inherited the Edington estate..."

When Lucien returned after putting Mrs. Smythe in his own coach and watching her depart, Nigel Edington was summing up the lawyers' failed search for Lawrence Morville and how the court had awarded the estate to him. "That was the end of it as far as I was concerned. The courts had made their decision. I had no knowledge of Morville's return to England or that he was murdered until Lord Ware said so today."

"You deny he visited your house?" Haskett asked watching him closely.

"I thought he died years ago. So no, to my knowledge, he had not been in our home. If he was, no one told me."

Edington was a poor liar. His left eye twitched when he strayed from the truth, and it had twitched a lot during his statement. Lucien was certain Haskett had noticed too. In fact, the runner wasn't such a bad investigator when he hadn't already made up his mind or was blinded by his disdain for the upper classes.

Olivia Edington cocked her head at her husband. "Are you implying I was the one who received him? And then what? Kept it a secret from you?"

"No, not at all, my dear. I'm certain he was never there."

"Then how do you explain the snuffbox?" Haskett asked. "Your own mother says it was found there."

"I cannot. Perhaps he came while my wife and I were out."

"'Pon rep, sir." Haskett looked at him in disbelief. "Are your servants in the habit of inviting strangers into your private parlors for a pinch of snuff when the family is away? And then forget to mention it?"

"Uh, well, there is no accounting for servants," Edington quibbled, belatedly realizing he had carried his story too far. By not thinking it through, he had unwittingly drifted into the absurd. "Why are you asking *me* about Morville?" he asked sounding trapped. He pointed a finger at Mrs. Doud. "Ask her. She is the one who was last seen with him."

Martha Doud gaped. "You sniveling, little… I should have known better than to trust you."

"Oh, Martha, leave him alone." Olivia Edington sniffed. "It's all your fault. I you hadn't met with Lawrence Morville behind our backs… Were you plotting to take the estate away from us and get a portion of it for yourself?"

"What? You are a nasty piece, for sure." Martha Doud stared at her sister as though she was seeing a stranger.

The magistrate spoke from the doorway. "Constable Haskett, you may have reached the point where it would be better if you spoke privately with Mrs. Doud to take her statement."

The runner jerked his gaze toward the door as through he'd forgotten the Magistrate was standing there. "Yes, sir, I believe you have the right of it." He turned to the two constables present. "Take the Edingtons back to a holding cell until they're needed."

"You cannot do that," Olivia Edington protested. "Nigel and I had no part in whatever my sister has done." She and her husband continued to argue with Haskett, Nigel going so far as to push the officers away.

In the general disturbance, Lucien saw Martha Doud edge toward the doorway, and he put a hand out to stop her. "I don't believe he is finished with you, Mrs. Doud."

Her lips curls, but before she could say anything, Haskett spun toward them.

"Eh, wot! Trying to sneak away was she?" He gave Lucien a nod. "If we can clear the room, Mrs. Doud and me, we're gonna have that private chat."

Lucien stifled an impulse to argue his exclusion. Haskett was pushing for a full confession, and Lucien very much wanted to hear it. Nonetheless, this was Bow Street's investigation, and he had no legitimate reason for being present during official questioning. As he walked out of the courtroom, the Magistrate joined him. "Nice work, Viscount Ware."

"Thank you, but it is not over yet."

The Magistrate shrugged. "The legalities of court remain, but the end result is nearly decided. I anticipate Constable Haskett's report will recommend Andrew Sherbourne's release."

"I take nothing for granted," Lucien said. "I will not leave here without him."

"Then you are in for a long evening…as am I. Haskett won't give up your friend until he has a confession from everyone involved."

"I suppose, but Martha Doud is almost there. Nigel Edington will be easy, and Mullens no challenge at all. Olivia Edington will be the holdout, but I have every hope your constable will get there now he is headed down the right path. I know from experience how persistent he can be."

The magistrate smiled. "It is his finest quality."

The station's front door flew open, and Baron Sherbourne strode in. "Where is my son? A reporter told me you have him. Ah, Ware, there you are. What have they done with Andrew?"

The Magistrate disappeared into his office rather than face an irate parent, and Lucien attempted to reassure Sherry's father.

"It is not as bad as you may think, sir. Come, sit down," Lucien said, urging him toward the lobby, which had mostly cleared out by now. "I will explain."

Although the baron appeared much relieved when Lucien finished, it was still a long anxious wait. Five hours passed and dark had fallen long before Lucien and the baron walked out of Bow Street station with Sherry between them.

Haskett had done a thorough job; the Edingtons, Martha Doud, and Moe Mullens were all under arrest for murder, although Haskett was uncertain the charges against Nigel Edington would stand.

"He's a milksop, sir, if you'll pardon my language," Haskett had said at the end of the interviews. "Although he knew what they'd done, none of it was his idea. Now, them women—brassy they are, schemed it all. Olivia Edington hired Moe to be right there with Martha Doud…both times, and he admits to moving Maria's body. I'm still thinking he helped murder Morville, and I'll get him to tell me before the trial."

Haskett had expressed no remorse or even admitted he'd been mistaken about Sherry, although he had said he hoped there were no hard feelings—and he had taken the time to tell them the results of his interviews, including the details of how Morville and Maria had died. Lucien reckoned that was as close as the runner would come to an apology.

Hearing the ugly story had been sobering, and the three men were quiet as they stood in the street in front of Bow Street Station. The baron's and Lucien's carriages were both waiting.

"Lucien, I don't know what to say—" Sherry began.

"Say anything. Go home, get some sleep. I'll have Cade send Archibald along with your things." Lucien grinned. "Cheer up, my friend. It's over."

"I can barely take it in," Sherry admitted. "There were times when I thought…well, never mind that now."

"You must know how grateful I am too," the baron said, resting a hand on Lucien's shoulder. "No matter how bleak it looked, you kept believing the answers were out there. And, if I said anything I should not—"

"You didn't," Lucien interrupted. "I'm just relieved we were able to win Haskett to our side. He is a rather formidable opponent."

"Do I hear a hint of admiration?" Sherry asked, cocking his head at Lucien. "I'm not feeling at all happy with him. He was out to hang me."

"If it is any consolation, my friend, I believe he will be just as dogged in bringing the wicked sisters to justice."

Chapter Thirty-One

As usual for this time of night, Cade's Club was lit from top to bottom and bustled with activity when Lucien strolled in the front entrance. Voices drifted from the game rooms, some already a bit loud from too much whiskey, and a piano-forte provided background music from the direction of the bar and dining room. A whiff of cooked food drifted from the same direction, reminding Lucien he hadn't eaten since morning.

Reginald spotted him quickly. "Good evening, Lord Ware. I hear you were at Bow Street this evening."

"Is there anything you do not know within minutes of it happening?" Lucien asked.

"Very little, sir. However, we are still waiting to hear the outcome." The house manager gave him a questioning look.

"Sherbourne is a free man."

Despite his habitually impassive face, Reginald's lips twitched in what Lucien was sure was the beginning of a smile. Sherry had acquired some interesting friends during his stay at the club. "I am sure you are pleased, sir."

"I am, Reginald. I surely am. Can you arrange for his manservant and belongings to be sent to Sherbourne House?"

"I will see to it." He glanced toward a footman who had just come down the staircase. The man gave a nod, and Reginald turned back to Lucien. "Mr. Cade would like to see you, sir."

"I assumed he would want a firsthand account."

"Just so, sir," Reginald said, reverting to his customary stoic mien. "Shall I have someone take you up?"

Lucien gave him a wry look. "I believe I can find the way, but I would take a finger of brandy first. It's been a long day and evening." And Cade could not always be depended upon to share his special stock.

Reginald flashed a smile, snapped his fingers to a footman, and a brandy glass was soon presented on a small tray. Lucien downed the drink in one swallow. Returning the glass to the tray, he headed for the stairs. No one intercepted him or demanded to know his business as he climbed the steps and made his way to Cade's office. Lucien sighed. He missed the days when they challenged him at every step.

Lucien tapped on the open door and Cade gestured for him to enter. The Gentleman Thief was seated behind his desk as was his manner, and he closed a ledger when Lucien stepped inside.

"Sherbourne has been cleared of the charges," Lucien said without waiting to be asked. "He has returned to Sherbourne House, and we both wanted to express our gratitude for your considerable assistance."

"I am pleased. My staff has grown to like your partner, although I understand he is only a middling hazard player. My guards may have taken advantage."

Lucien laughed. "I have told him for years that he shouldn't play, but he insists. In truth, I am indebted to your guards for keeping him occupied so that he stayed here as long as he did."

"Have a seat." Cade stood and went to the sideboard, pouring himself a glass of brandy and waiting until Lucien was seated before gesturing with the bottle to offer him a glass. Lucien smiled but nodded, and Cade poured a second drink. He handed it to Lucien. "I confess I am curious—who was the murderer?"

"Murderers," Lucien amended. He went over the story again—the missing heir showing up in London, the murder of Morville by Mrs. Doud. "She bedded him, then stabbed him in his sleep, poor fellow."

"A high price to pay for pleasure," Cade murmured.

"She would have gotten away with it, except for the snuffbox. It proved he'd been in the Edington house."

"And that discovery led to the second murder, did it not?"

"Yes, when Miss Pembroke found the snuffbox, she realized its significance from talking with Nigel Edington's elderly mother and took it with her. She may have intended to tell Sherbourne of her suspicions, but I wonder if she thought to blackmail Edington to obtain funds to flee the country, perhaps to America."

"Running from the Frenchman? I thought her fears of him were groundless."

Lucien shrugged. "Regardless what she told Sherbourne, I believe Maria's real fear of Breguet was that he would take Fanny. His deceased brother is most likely the father, and the Breguet family wants her very much."

Cade raised his brows. "Hadn't Sherbourne already claimed the chit?"

"He was willing, but having met Breguet and seen the family likeness in Fanny, I cannot doubt her paternity. Sherry won't stand in the way. Fanny's future will have to be worked out between Gaston Breguet and Hugh Pembroke."

"Ah, just as well. Sherbourne is too young to raise a child without a wife. But you have not said who killed Miss Pembroke and why her body was moved to the alley?"

Lucien cleared his throat. "The alley, the barrow, and a coach seen on King Street certainly led us down the wrong path. We had speculated the body was brought home in a coach, that the barrow was stolen because the alley was too narrow for the coach to enter, and that a coach seen on King Street was waiting to pick up the killer. It did not happen that way." Lucien finished his brandy and set it down. "In fact, Miss Pembroke was murdered in her own lodgings when she came home and interrupted Martha Doud searching her room for the snuffbox. Doud had brought a sword from over her fireplace to steady her nerves during the search…or so she said. She denied planning to kill Miss Pembroke, but I think she lied about that. In any event, she needed help moving the body out of her boarding house and appealed to the Edingtons. They sent Moe Mullens. He stole the barrow on the way over, dumped the body in the alley while Mrs. Doud cleaned the room, and got rid of the cart at the nearest backyard that was unlocked. The waiting coach had nothing to do with it."

"A sordid tale." Cade sighed, then he looked up, a hint of amusement in his eyes. "Was anything said about Sherbourne's escape?"

"Oh, yes, Haskett wanted to harp on it, but Sherry denied any part in arranging it and refused to say where he'd been staying. The magistrate gave me a long look, but he owned how witnesses said Sherbourne had fought with the alleged kidnappers, and he let it go with a brief lecture on flouting the law. He knew I could have told him more—the man is no fool—but he did not ask me."

"The Bow Street court has ever been a bit unusual. The Fielding brothers have made it so."

"Very true." Lucien stood. "I must be on my way. If there are outstanding bills, send them to me. Otherwise, I trust I shall hear from you in due course."

Cade lifted a brow. "Bills, no? Everything was covered by the funds you provided. It is true you and I have unfinished business, but I am in no hurry."

Lucien frowned as he left the building. A fine mist was falling, but he paid it no mind, his thoughts still on Cade's last comment. Much as Lucien disliked being in anyone's debt, it appeared Cade was going to savor the moment. He stood in the street outside the club, staring back at the building, then shook the water from his hat and climbed into the carriage. He still had things to do before the night was over.

Minutes later his coach stopped in front of the Salcott town mansion. The house was mostly dark, and Lucien assumed his father was still at Parliament for a late session or already abed in preparation of more negotiations tomorrow. He wrote a brief note informing his father of Sherry's release and inviting the earl to dine at White's tomorrow night to hear the full story, and he left it with the butler. He found himself quite looking forward to sharing the details with Salcott.

With a sense of satisfaction that his part of the world had returned to normal, he arrived at his townhouse and retired to the study with a glass of port. Soon he and Sherry would have to talk about whether they would continue their work for Whitehall, but Lucien's temper had cooled somewhat. As a war spy, he had always known he and Sherry were dispensable, that Rothe must think in the big picture, and maybe the same applied here. He was at least open to a discussion.

He stood and crossed the room. One more task before he sought his bed—a pleasant one, to be sure. He sat at his desk, took a sip of wine, and picked up a quill pen. He wished to thank Lady Anne for the large part she played in uncovering the killer's motive and to satisfy her curiosity over Sherry's escape from custody.

A smile tugged at his lips, and he stifled a chuckle as he began to write:

London, October 1812

My dear Lady Anne,

London had been rather dull this autumn until Sherbourne, as you know, became embroiled in a murder. The affair is now resolved, and I am free to give you an accounting of what happened. I shall come straight to the point—due in part to your timely efforts, Sherbourne is free of all charges and suspicions, and the murderess is in gaol. For yes, it was a woman, or perhaps I should say, a pair of women.

I realize such brevity—while relieving understandable anxiety over Sherbourne's welfare—will not satisfy your avid curiosity. Therefore, I shall pick up where I left off in my earlier letter and relate recent events in such fine detail as to satisfy the most inquisitive mind...

Epilogue

Three days later, Lucien brought Sherry and Gaston Breguet together. Once Sherry had heard the Frenchman's story and saw his striking resemblance to Fanny for himself, he simply could not deny her parentage. Lucien didn't miss the flash of disappointment in Sherry's eyes, but it was swiftly concealed and Breguet was included in the plans to travel to Oxfordshire and deliver Fanny to her grandfather.

"Maria left the child in my protection," Sherry explained, "and I promised Hugh Pembroke I would return Fanny to him if I became convinced I was not her father. Since that appears to be the case, I must put her in his hands. The two of you will need to discuss her future."

"I understand," Breguet said. "Your actions on her behalf do you credit. I shall leave you now and make preparations for our journey."

When they were alone, Lucien studied Sherry's pensive face. "That cannot have been easy."

"No. She is a sweet chit. I have grown fond of her. It will be hard to let her go, and I hope Pembroke will write of her now and then. Perhaps someday I shall have a child of my own."

Lucien hid a smile. Miss Emily Selkirk might be of a similar mind. Determining a change of topic was in order, he leaned one hip on his desk and asked, "What do we do about Rothe?"

"What about him?"

"He did not exactly come to your rescue," Lucien said dryly.

"No," Sherry said slowly, dragging out the word. "But I've done some thinking about it. He did not hinder your inquiry, and he gave you the Bow Street report. I cannot say I felt so charitable toward him while confined to a cold cell in Newgate prison, but I grant that he was in a tough spot."

"You are more forgiving than I."

Sherry shrugged. "Are you suggesting we quit the spy business?"

Lucien let out a breath of frustration. "Part of me wants to say *yes* and be done with it…and him."

"And yet?" Sherry prompted.

Lucien rubbed the back of his neck. "I own he may have been of assistance behind the scenes, particularly in arranging for your hearing." He gave a wry smile. "I doubt he thought I'd take the opportunity to set up your escape."

"But he didn't ask you about it, did he?"

"No, he did not." Lucien took a moment. "I get your point. He could—and probably should have—done more to assist Bow Street."

"Well, I hadn't gone quite that far in my thinking, but yes, Rothe might have found me if he had tried."

Lucien frowned. "Bloody hell, Sherry. I don't understand why we are on opposite sides of this."

"We're not. It only looks that way because you're offended on my behalf. I appreciate the thought, but egad, Lucien, what else could Rothe have done?"

Lucien snorted and paced across the room. "He let you go to gaol. You might have been imprisoned for life or faced the hangman's noose."

Sherry shook his head, a smile touching the corners of his lips. "Rothe knew you would never let that happen."

That brought Lucien to an abrupt halt. "He shouldn't have counted on me. What if I had failed?"

"Is that what is bothering you? Good lord, *I* never doubted you'd find the killer. My only concern was whether it would be in time. And, of course, you saw to that. The matter is closed, my friend," Sherry said gently. "Leave it there."

Lucien took in a deep breath and gave a reluctant nod. "I know you are right. It was just…well, enough said."

• • •

When Sherry returned from Oxfordshire at the end of the week, he washed off the grime of the journey and went to find Lucien at home.

"Welcome home," Lucien rose from his desk, dropping the letter he had been reading. "I trust you had a successful journey."

"Better than I expected. It was good to see the affection developing between Fanny and Breguet. He and Pembroke talked and decided she will remain with her grandfather in England, but when I left, they were discussing visits to France and what might be done about producing a marriage certificate that would entitle Fanny to the Breguet family name."

Lucien raised a brow. "Is that likely to happen?"

"I believe so. The Breguets do not lack money or influence in France. It would certainly be in Fanny's best interests." Sherry waved a hand toward Lucien's desk. "Did I interrupt important correspondence?"

Lucien gave an amused snort. "Recognized Lady Anne's handwriting, did you not? She wrote to thank me for sharing the story of your escape and the capture of Maria's killers."

"Will she return to London soon?"

Lucien frowned. "Unfortunately, not. Her mother remains gravely ill."

"Sorry to hear that. I miss her lively company, don't you?"

Well, yes, of course he did, but Lucien welcomed the knock at the study door that cut off the necessity for him to admit it. His butler stepped into the room. "What is it, Hughes?"

"I message for you, my lord." He held out a silver salver with a letter on it.

Lucien took the note and thanked him. As Hughes left, Lucien turned to Sherry. "You should also recognize this handwriting. Lord Rothe." He unfolded the paper, read swiftly, and lifted a brow. "He would like to see us on an urgent matter."

"What do you say?" Sherry asked, eyeing him.

Lucien sighed with a reluctant grin. "I say…let us find out what kind of trouble his lordship is getting us into this time."

About the Author

After retiring from a legal career with the Juvenile Court System, J.L. Buck published sixteen urban fantasy/paranormal novels under the pen name of Ally Shields. In 2019 she decided to write mysteries set in the Regency period of history she had always enjoyed, and she began work on the Viscount Ware Mystery series.

She lives in the Midwest with Latte, a mischievous Siamese cat, who often attempts to co-author her writing by taking over the keyboard, and an energetic miniature pinscher pup, named Pippin, who keeps everyone on their toes. When not writing or running two blogs, Ms Buck enjoys her eight grandchildren (and a great-grandson), reading (preferably on a sunny deck), travel (USA and abroad from Africa to Europe to the British Isles to Disney World in Florida), and binge-watching any sub-genre of mystery shows.

Ms Buck loves to hear from readers and can be contacted through her website or social media (twitter: @janetlbuck or her fantasy pen name account: @ShieldsAlly)